29

LIKE A HOLE IN THE HEAD

LIKE A HOLE

IN THE HEAD

A Novel

JEN BANBURY

LITTLE, BROWN AND COMPANY

Boston   New York   Toronto   London

FIRST EDITION

The characters and events in this book are fictitious. Any
similarity to real persons, living or dead, is coincidental and
not intended by the author.

The author is grateful for permission to include the follow-
ing previously copyrighted material:
   Lyrics from "Anything Goes" by Cole Porter. Copyright
© 1934 (renewed) by Warner Bros. Inc. Reprinted by per-
mission of Warner Bros. Publications U.S. Inc.
   Lyrics from "Black Superman" by Johnny Wakelin.
Copyright © by Francis, Day & Hunter Ltd. (PRS). All
rights for United States and Canada controlled by Jewel
Music Publishing Co., Inc. Reprinted by permission of
Jewel Music Publishing Co., Inc.

Library of Congress Cataloging-in-Publication Data

Banbury, Jen.
   Like a hole in the head : a novel / Jen Banbury.—
1st ed.
      p.   cm.
   ISBN 0-316-17110-7
   I. Title.
PS3552.A4737L54   1998
813'.54—dc21   97-16935

      10   9   8   7

Book design by Julia Sedykh

MV-NY

*Published simultaneously in Canada
by Little, Brown & Company (Canada) Limited*

Printed in the United States of America

For Andrew,

who is so damn good

Acknowledgments

vi I am also wildly grateful to my agent, Paul Chung, and my editor, Amanda Murray, and to a remarkable and generous woman, Marie-Anne van Aubel (Bonne Maman).

LIKE A HOLE IN THE HEAD

1.

I woke up with a hangover and roof tar on my feet and a vague recollection of pacing around up there half the night. I think I threw a bottle at the building next door and somebody yelled something.

After a shower and two bowls of Cap'n Crunch, I really felt like crap. I thought about getting back into bed but the clock said quarter till. Besides, the lady below me had put on her Chuck Mangione record so I was just as glad to be leaving.

On the way to the bookstore, a guy in a convertible Mercedes almost ran me off my bike. He didn't notice. Later, I caught up to him at a light and watched him pick his nose. He didn't notice that either. Oblivious. I said, "Hey buddy!" He looked over. I said, "Did your mother teach you to pick your nose that way?" He gave me the finger. A different finger than the one he'd been picking with. I said, "Oh yeah? Do you tickle your mother with that finger?" The light went green and he took off.

Eleven o'clock and it was already hot as hell. By the time I got to the bookstore I could feel the sweat rolling down my cleavage. Like a ride at a water park. The Boob Slide. Little kids screaming the whole way down.

The cat had puked all over the bathroom. "Oh cat," I said. "Cat, cat, cat, cat, cat." I spied the cat sitting on top of one of the high bookshelves toward the front of the store, looking at me. As I watched, the cat began to heave again. "No cat," I said. "Down cat." The cat's body convulsed in and out like a furry accordion. "No cat. You're on the rare books, cat," I said. I grabbed a paper grocery bag from behind the desk. Opened it up and held it over my head, under the cat. As his body heaved, he made a noise. "Wirt . . . wirt . . . wirt . . . wirt. . . ." I couldn't see the cat because the bag blocked my view. Finally, the cat said, "Ack," and a small ball of cat vomit passed me on the right and landed on the carpet. The cat jumped down and exited by the front door, which I had propped open in the heat. I used half a roll of paper towels cleaning up the cat vomit. It didn't need all that, but I wanted an absorbent barrier between myself and the vomit. Then I took all the balled-up paper out back and threw it in the Dumpster that belonged to the copy shop next door.

The owner had left about a hundred books for me to shelve but I ignored them and sat down behind the desk. I turned on the register, the computer, the radio. A local jazz station promised to play Bessie Smith all day.

Whenever I worked at the bookstore, I worked alone. The owner was either out trying to buy books or visiting his friends in San Francisco. He went to San Francisco a lot, which meant I worked a lot. That was fine with me. I liked the store better than my apartment. It was quiet. I could sit and read for hours at a time. The whole day, if there was nothing else to do. I recommended titles to people who came in. Sometimes they recommended stuff to me. If things got too dull, I found a way to have some fun. But mostly I sat and read and kept the place neat. And for that I got paid fifty dollars a day, cash under the table. Just enough to keep my apartment and buy food every now and then.

The mailman dropped off the mail. Couple of bills and a notice about the Antiquarian Book Fair happening over the weekend in Las Vegas. The mailman took his job seriously. He reprimanded me for using sloppy penmanship on outgoing letters. And he always said "Okay?" before he released his grip on the mail. Sometimes I couldn't help myself. I'd accept the mail with both hands and nod my head in concentration. Then as he left, I would let a letter or two drop to the floor. Watch his shoulders tighten. Bye, Mr. Mailman. Bye-bye.

No one else came in for the first hour and I read *In the Bush: The True Story of a Canadian Pioneer Woman*. Her cabin burned down. Her husband died in a logjam. She had bad luck. But she loved Canada.

The cat reappeared and licked at the spot where the vomit used to be. "Cat," I said, "boy are you stupid," I said. I opened a can of sliced beef and heart that I had bought at the mini-market down the block and dumped it onto a saucer. Paul, the owner of the bookstore, just gave the cat dry Cat Chow. But I knew that cat. He really went for the muck. I always picked up a can of cat food on the days that I worked. One day I also bought a banana and a soda. The Korean guy behind the counter said, "Good lunch. More balance than usual." His face never cracked.

I locked the register and went to use the bathroom. While I was in back, I made some instant coffee with six table-spoons of instant creamer. I figured I'd either feel better or toss it like the cat. Luckily, the water cooler had a hot tap so I didn't have to fool with the microwave. My sister had me believing they fry your ovaries. She won't use them. If she has to, she wraps a wad of tin foil around her hips.

The door to the back room had been removed by the previous tenant and no one had bothered to replace it. The whole bookstore was only about the size of a suburban living room. But you could always find something worth reading. Paul kept things neat, well alphabetized. And he never overstuffed the shelves. The back room was a different story, though. A total mess. Unmarked books and old postcards, plastic book covers, a mini-refrigerator that always had a couple containers of old crusty shrimp panang from the Thai place next door. The bookstore had been robbed once. The guy hid in back behind the vacuum cleaner and *The Works of Voltaire* — a twenty-two-volume set. After closing time, he broke out the front door with sixty-five bucks and the computer under his arm.

I finished making my coffee. The cat had cleaned its plate so I let it lick my coffee spoon. A nice treat. It was mostly creamer.

Back at the desk, a dwarf was waiting for me. He drummed his fingers on the corner of an adjacent display

6

case. He had to lift his hand above his shoulder to do it. He said, "Paul here?" I sat down and put my coffee on an old paperback so it wouldn't leave a ring on the desk. Paul loves that desk.

"No, I'm afraid he's out of town for a while."

"Ah, right. La la. So." He looked around the store. I opened my book. "You know how busy I've been this morning?" he asked. "How much I've been running around?" He peered at me over the display case. From my angle, he was all head. Hair greased back with some oily pomade.

I smiled politely. "No," I said. I couldn't tell if he had a dark complexion or was filthy as a stray dog.

"When I started out this morning, I was six feet tall." He laughed and I could smell the cheap cigars, a life's worth. Still, he wore a nice suit. The phone rang. I smiled again and turned my back on him.

"Hello, Bitter Muse Bookstore," I said.

"Joe? Blahah Joe?"

I sighed, blowing the hair off my forehead. "Listen, you moron," I said. I spoke in a hushed voice so I wouldn't scare the dwarf. "Listen, once and for all there is no one named Blahah Joe here. No matter how many times you call this number, Blahah Joe will not pick up the phone. Understand? He does not exist at this number."

"Oh, he's no there? Is important."

"No. Blahah Joe is not here. He will never be here. Never. You will probably never speak to Blahah Joe again."

"Okay. Thank you." The line went dead. Within a few minutes, a woman would call and ask for Blahah Joe. I could picture her, her cleaning interrupted, the moron beside her.

7

Her voice would sound timid, far away because he held the receiver between them. Waiting to hear if her fingers had been luckier. Waiting for Blahah.

"Trouble at home?" asked the dwarf. I turned to him.

"Did you want to leave a note for Paul? Or a message? I'll probably talk to him sometime today." I fished some paper and a pen from the drawer of the desk.

"Oh pooh, let me think. Well, it's too bad. It's just too bad he's not around. I need to — I wanted to sell him something. This — la la — this book. Thought it might interest him. I know he's in the book business." The dwarf hoisted a book onto the display case and nudged it in my direction.

"I really don't do any of the book buying," I said. "I just mind the store." He slid the book closer to me.

8   "Take a quick look-see, why don't you. I'm anxious to sell it. Maybe you'd want it just for you. For your own enjoyment." What the hell, I thought. He looked like he might cry if I said no. I lifted it into my lap. *The Cruise of the Snark*. Jack London. I opened to the copyright page. 1911. Macmillan. Looked like a first edition. I started to get excited. London is popular with the collectors, and all his first editions bring a purse. This was completely unexpected. I figured I'd be looking at *The Condensed Works of Erma Bombeck. My First Social Studies Book*. Some crap or other. Not a first-edition London. Christ, it still had a jacket. Firm binding. Less than average yellowing of the pages. Cherry condition. Like it had spent the last eighty or so years in a vault. From what I knew, the book could be worth a couple hundred bucks.

The phone rang. I lifted the receiver and put it right back down again. I stole a look at the dwarf, but he had turned away. Then I flipped a page and saw the inscription. "Dear Francis, This book almost killed me. Hope it does the same for you. Love Captain London." Holy Jesus shit. Was it really "London"? It looked like "London." This was too much.

"Do you mind if I take this in back for a second?" I asked. The dwarf had been staring out the front display window, watching the pedestrians.

"Huh? In back? I'm in a kind of a — ooh — kind of a hurry."

"I just want to make sure we don't already have this book," I said. I was already up and past the History section. "It'll just take a second." I triple-jumped to the back and grabbed the signatures book. The cat was asleep on the *First Editions* and I shoved him over. "Oh cat," I said. "This could be good, cat." I double-checked what I already knew. It was definitely a first. Four hundred bucks just for that. Then I matched the signatures. Same swish on the "L." Tight "o." The "n," the "d" — identical. I wasn't sure what kind of liability the "Captain" would prove to be. Could have signed your whole name, you jerk. Still, a modest jackpot for me. I strolled toward the dwarf.

"I think I might like to buy it," I said. "I like books for young people. And I have a nephew with a birthday coming up."

"How about fifteen dollars?" asked the dwarf. Jesus, I thought. This is pathetic. This is going to kill me.

"You know," I said, "I'm not sure, but it might actually be worth a little more than that. Well, yes . . . maybe a little bit more."

9

"How much more?"

"I really don't know. But some." I didn't know what my problem was. Most of the dealers would tell him the book was junk, offer him two bucks and settle at ten. But I wasn't a dealer. I was no good at that stuff.

"Well, I just want to get rid of it."

"But . . . I just want to make sure — if you find out it *is* worth more you won't come back and go nuts, right?"

"I'll take fifteen bucks. I'm in a hurry."

"Tell you what. I have a twenty. You can just keep the twenty."

"Twenty-five."

"Aw Jesus, you were going to take fifteen a second ago."

"All right, twenty. Twenty is plenty."

10   I dug my wallet out of my backpack and took a wadded twenty from behind my library card. Rainy day money. I had a five in the main part of my wallet and I got that out too.

"Here's twenty-five," I said.

"Oh," he said, "twenty-five! You're some kind of haggler, you are." He held out his hand. The words *eggs, tooth p.,* and *posture* were written in marker across his palm.

I held the money and hesitated. I said, "And . . . it's not stolen is it?"

"Nah. Got a great-aunt, some aunt, who — ooh la — died and just left me that. That and some other stuff." He wiggled his fingers in the direction of the bills. "I'm parked in the loading zone," he said. I handed him the money. "Thank you. Very much." He snapped out the bills, then refolded them and stuffed them into his pocket. He left by the front door.

"Have a nice day," I said. I watched him go down the street. He didn't get into a car.

The next few hours passed uneventfully. I had wrapped the book in a plastic bag and put it on the hold shelf. I was waiting for one of the dealers to show up. Paul keeps his prices pretty low and the dealers and other used-bookstore owners come in and buy his stock with their twenty percent dealer discount, then they reprice the books and put them on their own shelves at a markup. It's a real parasitic business. Sometimes they just leave Paul's price on and make a profit off the extra twenty percent. So far, none had come along. They tended to drop by in the late afternoon.

A customer got chatty with me — a young guy in beat- **11** up overalls and specs. It happened often enough. I guess I'm all right looking for someone who works in a used bookstore. Blond, with my mother's pale face. The guy and I talked literature for a while. We got along pretty well until he started jawing about his acting career. That froze me right up. He said something about playing a villain on a kid's action show, how he got to wear a cape. But they cut out all his best stuff. I said, "Hmm." Then I went back to my book and he browsed a bit more and finally bought a Calvino paperback, but it didn't help. He had lost me. While I rang it up, he said, "Nice ring." He meant a cowrie shell ring I had been given a few years back. I held it up so he could get a better look. Guys always remarked on the ring. I said, "I like it because it looks like a vagina dentata." I gnashed my teeth. "You know, vagina with teeth." He said, "Oh. Right. Neat." He left.

I had a lot of browsers that afternoon — looky-loos Paul calls them — but not many sales. The local homeless guy came in and sat in a chair by the Metaphysics section. He spent an hour ripping a sheet of notepaper into pinhead-size pieces that fell to the floor. Sometimes he dozed off. But he didn't bug anyone and he always cleaned up all the pieces afterward. Hell, what did I care. He smelled okay.

I finally got around to shelving the books. It was mind-less work. When a book didn't fit, I had to shuffle around half a case worth to make a hole. That drove me nuts. My right arm started to ache from hauling all those books and I was sweating again. Vodka sweat. I had on jean shorts and a T-shirt and they both felt wet. Every few armloads, I stopped in front of the fan and flapped my T-shirt up and down until it dried out a little. Once, I had to jockey for po-sition with a lady in a suit, whose makeup was slipping down her face faster than she could catch it.

"It's like a coffin in here," she said. "Whoof."

I said, "Hmm."

"Well why don't you air condition the place? I mean, my God!"

"We're saving the ozone layer for the children," I said. "Don't you care about the children?"

On my last trip to the pile, Timmy Harris came in the store. Timmy owned a place out by Venice Beach that dealt mostly in the rare stuff. He didn't mix with cheap paper-backs like we did. But he loved the old adventure novels. He saw me. "Hey," he said. I said, "Hey yourself." He started right in on the New Arrivals section. I sat down at the desk with some water from the cooler and watched him. I had a good view.

Timmy was tall and lanky with dark hair and sad eyes. They say that over sixty percent of book dealers are either alcoholics or gamblers. Timmy was both. He fit the profile like a fat hand in a kid's mitten. His mother had been Jenny Harris before she choked on her own vomit at the age of forty-six. The papers said it was Quaaludes, scotch, and canned frosting. She had tried to get Timmy into show business, too. You can spot him sometimes — a serious little kid with the trademark circles under his eyes — in movies like *Dog Gone and Jelly* and *Thirsty Pete*. He got out after just a couple years, which was part of the reason I liked him. But there were traces. Once I saw him stamp his foot.

13

I let him look around. He started making a small pile of the stuff he wanted. He said, "Not much new stuff." I said, "Yeah. Paul's been busy. He just left on a buying trip, though." Timmy nodded his head. I watched him pull down books, flip some pages, check the binding, reshelve them. He had careful hands. But big. I liked the idea of selling him the London book. I'd be doing him a favor. He would make a good profit when he turned it over. I wasn't planning on being greedy.

I was about to call out to him when the water delivery guy showed up. He came in a couple of times a week to buy philosophy books. Sometimes, he even delivered water.

"I read some deep shit last night," he said. He leaned against the display case. His shirt said, "Greg," but he had told me once that his real name was Charles. He was a statuesque black guy with glasses and an old burn scar on his neck. Because of the scar, he wore his collar up and held conversations in profile.

"This is some deep shit," he said. He held out a beat-up paperback for my inspection. *Crowd Theory*. "This goes beyond. It gets in there. I am recommending this book to you," he said.

"You know I'm off any philosophy, psychology crap," I said.

"But this guy you'll like. I'm telling you, he really does the job."

"I don't want to know all that stuff — the why and the what for."

He shook his head back and forth in disgust, like someone at a cheap funeral. "You are missing out, my friend. You got to keep things moving up here." He tapped his head with his index finger. "You got to go below the surface. It's a whole other world. That fiction stuff is just a sedative."

"Yeah, well I love being sedated. I'm swell at it."

"You're a gone cause," he said. "Every day I'm wasting my breath. Flapping my gums."

"I read some nonfiction. Lately I'm on an Antarctic exploration kick. *Endurance. The Worst Journey in the World.* Excellent books."

"You say potato," he said, "I say potahto." He walked back toward the Philosophy section and straddled a chair.

I kicked off my clogs and sat cross-legged. Timmy was in front of the Photography shelves. Flies had gotten in the store and I watched him wave his arm around his head to keep them away. Jesus, he was good-looking. Sometimes his hair fell into his eyes.

14

Charles came back and tossed a cheap copy of *I and Thou* onto the desk. I started to ring it up. I said, "Don't you already have this?"

"I lent it to a buddy and he skipped town," he said. "I just never learn." I gave him change on three dollars. "Thanks," he said. "I got to go."

"Everyone's in a hurry."

"I'm trying to quit early. They have me on the weekend shift. Plus it's Myrna Loy night at the museum. First one starts at five."

"Okay. Since you insist, I'll meet you for the second."

"Sorry," he said. "Someone asked me." Before he left he said, "You ought to keep your shoes on. Your feet are offensive." I watched him climb up into the cab of his Aqua Mountain truck. He kept a book propped open on the steering wheel for the red lights.

15

The station playing Bessie Smith had switched to local news and traffic reports, so I put a tape in. Blues and more blues. Timmy walked over with a short stack of books. I slipped my feet back into my clogs.

"Nothing too exciting," he said.

"Hey, I just work here," I said. He bent over to look in the display case where we kept the expensive stuff.

"How much is the Anaïs Nin?" He meant a signed copy of *The House of Incest.*

"Three seventy-five."

"Hmm. That would be a nice book to own. Not to sell."

"I didn't take you for the Nin type," I said. He looked at me funny. I felt like a jerk. He straightened up.

"Well, that's going to be it for now, I guess."

"I have something I think you might be interested in," I

said. "Something I'm selling." I reached up for the London book and carefully removed it from the bag. "I found this at a garage sale in some town halfway to San Francisco." He took the book from me and held it gently in his hands. As he began to peruse it, he let out a low whistle.

"Hiya mucka!" he said.

I said, "I had the signature checked and it's the real thing."

"Wow," he said. He looked at me. "What's your name again?"

"Jill," I said.

"Jill," he said, "you really got a hole in one with this. You, like, hit the clown right on the nose."

"Yeah," I said.

" 'Captain London.' Yup, he liked to mess around with his signature. Sometimes use a different name altogether. A couple people did that. JFK would sign his books 'Louis B. Mayer.' "

"Hmm."

"It's still a great find."

"Yeah, I couldn't believe it when I saw it. Next to some old boots and a jar of marmalade. Just there."

"Hmm? Marmalade?"

"It looked like marmalade."

"Huh. And you say you had the signature checked out?" He spoke in a slow, absent kind of way. The way you speak if you've lived near the beach your whole life.

"Uh huh. But you can compare for yourself if you want."

"Okay." I went and got the signatures book from the back and opened it to the right page and held it toward him. He

16

looked back and forth from one to the other about twenty times. Back and forth. Finally he said, "Well, Jennie —"

"Jill."

"I'm sorry, I'm sorry. I'm so bad with names. My ex-wife tried to get me to take a course. To help remember people's names."

"It's okay."

"I never took it. Anyway. I am totally interested. But what were you thinking price-wise?" He stood close to me. He smelled like he used a fancy moisturizer. Something made from fruits and vegetables.

"Well," I said, "without the signature it's worth at least four hundred. I thought I would take that."

"Oh. Four hundred." He flipped through the pages of the book, checking for marks.

"It's in great condition," I said.

"Yeah, I see." He squinted at me. Then he smiled and shook his head. "You know," he said, "I'm just trying to remember your name. I feel like a real dingbat. Don't help me."

"Roxanne," I said.

"Right," he said. Then, "No, that's not it."

"Jill," I said. "Jill as in 'Hey look at that girl going to fetch a pail of water with her friend Jack.'"

"Jill! Good, now I'll remember it, now that I have that visual thing. Anyway, Jill, here's the deal. I'll pay you the four hundred, Jill. But there's a but. BUT! If the 'Captain London' thing doesn't pan out, if it's a fake, Jill, you got to give me two hundred back." It was a weird deal, but he was a weird guy.

17

"What are you going to do, have your own guy check it?"

"That's right, Jill."

"How do I know you won't say it's a fake no matter what, just to get the extra two hundred?"

"You know how you'll know? Because — what are you doing? Look what you're doing to your arm," he said.

"What?"

"You scratch yourself when you talk."

I had scored a road map across my forearm. "Oh. It's all right," I said. "I have pretty thick skin." I held my hands behind my back.

"So anyway . . . where was I . . . oh right. You know how you'll know? Jill? Because I'm a nice guy." Then, after a moment, he said, "It's true."

"Uh huh."

"C'mon. I have a feeling you're making a decent profit on this no matter what. If I pay you four and that's all I can get back for it . . . well, that sucks for me."

"All right. You give me two hundred cash and a check for two hundred and I won't deposit it until I get the okay."

"How about two checks — both for two hundred —"

I was shaking my head. "Nope. It's got to be cash. I need it today."

"What's the hurry?"

"I have needs," I said. "Needs." Then I looked up at him and smiled. "It's my down payment on astronaut school." I said it with a bit of an accent.

"All right. It's cool. Use it for whatever your secret little heart desires. It's not my business. I'm going to have to go to the bank and come back but it'll just be twenty minutes or so."

"I'll be here," I said.

Actually it took half an hour. He had stopped to buy a smoothie.

He counted ten twenties into my hand and wrote out the check in small block letters. As he wrote, he stuck his tongue out the corner of his mouth. "How come you're not selling it to Paul?" he asked.

"I told you," I said, "I want the money today." Then I added, "But I think it's better if he doesn't know about it. He might get mad."

"Hey, no problem." He gave me the check. "This has worked out pretty well."

I started ringing up the other stuff he was buying. "You better still want these," I said.

"Huh?" He had been looking through the London book. "Sure, I'll take 'em." He paid me for the other books and I bagged them.

"Jill," he said. "See? I've really got it now. And you know, my name is Tim."

"Yeah, I know."

"Oh. Okay. Well. Great. I'll call you here and let you know about the signature. A day or two. And then, I guess I'll see you around."

"Yeah," I said. "I guess I'll see you." He left and I sat down. The twenties and the check in my back pocket made a bulge like an old man's handkerchief. I cupped my hands in front of my mouth and tried to smell my breath. Stale coffee but not too bad. Before my mother died, she lost her sense of smell completely. Whenever I saw her, she asked me to smell her breath, her armpits. "Do I smell?" she would ask. She never did.

2.

I called my friend Scott. I said, "Don't sell the Honda. I'm coming over after work."

He said, "Shit, Jill, I got a guy riding it around right now. He seems interested. And he doesn't know squat. He'd probably give me three fifty."

"C'mon, don't give me that crap. You've got to tell him you changed your mind."

"Aw, damn. Tell him I changed my mind. The guy drove all the way from Alhambra."

"So — that means you'll never see him again."

"How'd you get the money, anyway?"

"I turned a couple tricks. Va voom."

"Yeah, right."

"Scott, you said it was mine for two hundred."

"Yeah, but I was all fucked up when I said that."

"Scott —"

"Aw, shit. Hang on, I think the guy just dumped it." I could hear Scott put the phone down. I heard his girlfriend's kids. One of the kids began yelling. "I want pancakes! I WANT PANCAKES!" I looked at the clock. Six-fifteen. After a couple minutes, Scott got back on.

"Yeah, he dumped it, but it's okay. His wife's having a friggin' fit, though, yelling and shit—" Scott pitched his voice high and whining "'—I told you motorcycles are dangerous, my brother's best friend's brother was killed on a motorcycle, you're gonna die.' Anyway, I don't think he'll take it. I'm gonna try to get some damage money off him. Come over before ten."

One other dealer came in that evening. Guy named Sonny. **21**
A real scumbag. He always cut on Paul behind his back. Talked about how he had no taste, how he mispriced everything. But he fed off Paul's stock more than anyone. I buried my nose in a book to discourage him from griping at me. I was itching for seven o'clock to roll around so I could close up and head for Scott's place. I had been trying to buy his piece of junk Honda 250 for months but every time I raised the dough, something else came up. Who would have thought that a dwarf would turn my luck around. I had very good feelings toward that dwarf.

When I looked up to check the time, I saw Sonny snooping around the back room. Trying to get a jump on the other dealers by looking at the unmarked stuff. He wasn't playing fair and that bugged me. I stood and walked toward him.

"None of that is for sale yet," I said. He jerked at the sound of my voice, like a dog caught drinking from the toilet bowl.

"Just taking a peek," he said. "And I was going to borrow your little boy's room."

"I prefer if you ask," I said.

"Oh I'm so sorry."

"Well," I said, "go on." I waved him into the bathroom and closed the door behind him. Then I stood listening. Silence. I said, "You can run the sink if you can't go with me standing here." He came out.

"I'm all done, thanks." His eyes darted all over the place, trying to get a last look. "Can I go out the back door?" he asked.

22   "All right." I unlocked the back and he started to leave. Then he remembered a package he had up front by the display case. I waited for him to get it. He called to me. "Excuse me, but I can't seem to find my package." I sighed and went to help him look. No package. "I may have left it at the place I went to before this," he said. "If you find it, just put it aside." He went out the back again and I watched to make sure he went straight for the door. I was going to have to go back there to close up in a few minutes anyway, so I didn't follow him.

Ten till seven. Not enough time to read, too early to start locking up. Paul sometimes called at a minute of the hour to make sure I was still there. I couldn't really blame him. The guy who worked for him before me was a real boozer. He'd go through eight cans of rummed-up soda in a day. By three o'clock, anytime someone asked about a book, he'd howl with laughter. The name Studs Terkel sent him off his chair.

I heard the back door open. Fucking Sonny. I made my way to the rear. Before I got there, I saw the dwarf standing in the door frame in his underwear. Old saggy undies, socks, shoes, nothing else. "What the hell?" I said. "What's wrong with you? Were you mugged?"

"Excuse me, please," he said. He had his arms crossed in front of his chest and he toed the carpet with his patent leather lifts. "There was a mistake. I need — la la — to get that book back from you." His voice shook like he had his finger in a wall socket, and he wouldn't look me in the face. He kept one arm over his chest and reached out with the other. When he uncurled his fist, I saw my wadded-up twenty-dollar bill. I guess he had spent the five.

"Aw c'mon, man." I couldn't believe it. "You told me you wouldn't do this. You specifically said." **23**

"I know, but these are unusual circumstances. Bad. Please." The hand holding the money shook along with his voice.

"Listen, I don't know what's going on with you. But we had a deal. Here. Tell you what. I'm going to give you twenty more bucks, you can buy some clothes, and then that's it." I made a move for my back pocket.

"No! No. I need the book back. That book. The book!"

"Listen, fella. I don't have the book and you're not going to get it back. So face up to it. I've got forty more bucks for you and then we call it a day." I dug around in my pocket, trying to separate two bills from the rest of the wad. Suddenly, another guy appeared behind him. A guy about three times his size. A very big guy.

"Hello," he said. "I couldn't help noticing this difficulty in negotiations here." He spoke through his nose like he'd had it broken for him a few times. And when I heard his voice, the guy seemed familiar.

"Who are you?" I asked. I turned to the dwarf. "This guy with you?" The dwarf nodded very slowly. "Oh, great," I said. "Listen," I said. "It's the same answer whether I tell it to a little guy or an enormous guy. I. Don't. Have. The. Book."

"Well, I'm sure it can't have gone too far." The guy wore an old baseball cap and a suit. He pushed by the dwarf and, as he entered the store, he removed his cap and wrung it bashfully in his hands. Like he was a high school kid and I was his girlfriend's dad. The meager amount of hair he had stuck up every which way. He said, "I'm sure it must be in the vicinities somewhere." He craned his neck and shuffled forward. "If I was a book, where would I hide?"

"Hey," I said. "I mean it! The store is closed." I blocked the archway between the back room and the front of the store.

He said, "Pretty please?"

"Oh rats," I said. I stepped aside with the idea that I would bolt out the back and get a little help from the family at the Thai joint next door. They usually left their rear entrance unlocked. And the daughter had once shown me the pepper spray she kept on her key chain.

The big guy made a slight bow as I ushered him toward the front of the store. But he stopped short at the sound of the dwarf's patent leather shoes tap-tap-tapping across the parking lot.

"Excuse me," the big guy said. He quickly put his cap back on, turned, and loped out the back door in pursuit of the dwarf. It took him about two seconds. He caught him by the hair. Wrapped some of it around his fingers so his grip wouldn't slip with all that oil. I stood in the doorway watching. Too fascinated to close it, lock it, and get the hell away. I stood there like an idiot.

The big guy lifted the dwarf off the ground by his hair. By now the late-day sun was casting some strange light. The sky was going pink and orange and on the concrete the scene played out in twenty-foot shadows. The dwarf howled. He windmilled his arms, trying to land a punch. The big guy lifted him high and whispered something in his ear. I don't know what it was, but the dwarf stopped moving, stopped screaming, just hung down. A piñata waiting for the next kid at bat. The guy set him on the pavement but still held him. Held him tight by the shoulder now. In that light, they looked like a father/son portrait. *Evening Idyll.* Or maybe *Junior's Bath Day.* Then the big guy put his free hand into his pocket for a second, removed something, and flicked his arm. I actually heard a small "pop" or a "whoosh" before the top of the dwarf's head burst into flames. It was all that oil. Jesus. The big guy shoved the dwarf, hard, back into the store. Toward me. Kicked him in the ass so he went stumbling. I said, "Fuck!" jumped back, tripped, and landed on a pile of books. The dwarf fell right inside the door and he was screaming. Flailing on his belly and just screaming. I scrambled, crabwise, away from him. The big guy came in and grabbed the old blanket that the cat sleeps on and smothered the fire on the dwarf's head with it. The dwarf lay on his belly, sobbing. The big guy squatted next to him and wrapped the blanket around his head like a turban.

I had my back up against some boxes of books. My knees in my chest, my hands pressing the floor. I was breath-

25

ing hard. And too scared to move. The big guy looked up at me.

"I can't believe I just did that," he said. I guess I nodded. "I feel bad." I could smell burnt hair and burnt skin. And there was smoke. "He's okay, though. It was just a few seconds."

"Jesus Christ," I said.

The dwarf began to whimper. "I'm sorry I'm sorry I'm sorry I'm sorry I'm sorry," he said. "I'm sorry I'm sorry I'm sorry." The big guy patted him on the back.

"Shhh," he said. "Hush up. It's all over."

"Jesus," I said. The big guy smiled at me. He adjusted his cap and sat carefully on a small stack of books in between me and the dwarf.

26

"Boy," he said, "I sure do wish you would give me that book."

"Oh, Jesus," I said. My feet were pushing me harder against the boxes. I felt the cardboard buckle slightly behind me. "I don't have it. I sold it to someone."

"Well that was fast. My friend said that you were going to keep it for yourself? Or give it to your nephew? Was that not correct?" His voice retained an eager-to-please tone that terrified me.

"That's what she told me," whispered the dwarf. "That's what she said."

"I sold it to someone who really likes Jack London." I was trying to hold steady but I knew I couldn't even stand.

"Who's Jack London?"

"The — the author. The guy who wrote it."

"I see. And now you wouldn't be lying, knowing that you

would be holding up the processes of medical attendance for my friend?"

"No, I swear to God, he wrote it. You can look it up."

"I was referring to your selling of the book, miss."

"No. I sold it."

"You sold it to . . . ?"

"A guy. A guy who buys books."

His voice changed. He dropped the courtesy act. "Oh, a guy who buys books. Now we know. All we gotta to do is go see Johnny Buys Books who lives on Buys Books lane and we can get it back."

"I don't know his name. He's never been to the store before. He saw the book and offered me fifty dollars and I took it because I need the money." I knew I was dumb to play dumb. But I couldn't roll over on Timmy. I felt one of my hands climb up my head to touch my hair but I forced it down to my neck, then back to the floor.

"Do you have a check from this guy?"

I shook my head. "He paid cash." I looked over at the dwarf. He seemed to have passed out from the pain. His face was mealy white and covered in sweat. I looked the big guy straight in the eye. He nodded slowly.

"I'm formulating an idea," he said. He slid off the books and crawled a little closer to me. I made myself as small as possible. "I have an idea that you can get this book back for me and save me some effort and driving time." Now he spoke quietly, earnestly. "You see, this book has extreme sentimental value and my friend made a grievous error when he sold it to you. It is not his book. He has what they call a psychological problem with taking things. He took that book.

27

He took that *nice suit.*" The big guy removed his hat and reached around to thwack the dwarf on the head with it for emphasis. The dwarf said, "Awooo oh oh."

"The suit we got. But the book's more important." He replaced the hat and leaned toward me with his hands on the floor for balance. Like a chimp examining a dangled banana. "So the thing that must be understood is that you will return this book so that I may forward it to its rightful owner. And that any attempt to do otherwise veez a veez police involvement or flight from duty will be met by a situation similar to that which you have recently witnessed here." He leaned even closer. The brim of the hat just touched my forehead. And he said, "In other words, no matter how safe you think you are, you won't be safe. You will be wide open. I find everyone, you understand? Your friends, your family, your freaking refrigerator repairman. All wide open. Ya got it? S'aright? S'aright." He leaned back and withdrew a business card from his breast pocket and held it up for me to see.

Joke Man
869-9930

"See it?" he asked. I nodded. He replaced the card. "That's my telephone number. The name, not the number. Ignore the number, remember the name. The name is the number. Understand?" I nodded again. "It's a code. You call me tomorrow evening and that is more than ample. If I don't hear from you, that means I got to pursue you. Don't make me do that. I hate to drive." He stood up and stretched, shook himself out. He said, "Oof! Squatting like that is bad

28

for my back. I gotta not do that." He nudged the dwarf with his foot. "C'mon, kiddo, we're going to go put some Solar-caine on your noggin." The dwarf didn't move. But I could see him breathing. The big guy nudged him again, then stooped over and picked him up in his arms. He looked at his face and smiled. "Someone's sleepy," he said. He started for the door and pushed it open with the dwarf. "Before nine-thirty P.M. because I go to bed early." I stood and followed him on jellied legs.

I cleared my throat. "What area code?" It was so quiet.

"Same as you," he said. "Almost neighbors." He tucked the dwarf under one arm and opened the door to a big black Caddie. The interior was red. He dumped the dwarf in the back seat and then got in the front. When he saw me watching, he waved with his fingers. A too-de-loo wave. He drove away slowly, with care. He used his turn signal when he left the parking lot.

29

3

I dialed information and got the number for Timmy's store. Listened to that robot voice say the number twice with the receiver jiggling against my ear. That shake the dwarf had was catching. I had to pull myself together a little before talking to Timmy. I had to have a drink.

I locked the store and sprinted across the street to the mini-market. Rounded up an airplane bottle of vodka and a tall can of light beer. That way I wouldn't get too drunk. While the guy was getting my change, I turned away from the counter and sucked down the vodka.

"No! No drink in the store! *You can do that!*"

"Sorry. I'll take another of the same, please." I pointed at the empty bottle. The guy put the beer and a second bottle of vodka in a paper bag and stapled it shut. He looked as if I had really let him down. A look I'm used to. "I know," I said, "no nutritional value." I pocketed my new change and jogged back to the bookstore, where I locked myself in.

After the second vodka, things started to seem okay. I hadn't eaten anything besides that cereal early on, so the liquor went right to me. The beer sprayed everywhere when I popped it. Shouldn't jog with beer. I drank what was left and called the number of Timmy's store. No answer. Shit. He had closed up already. I yelled into the dead phone. "You cock!" I yelled. "You motherfucking bookbuying child-acting sucktoast!" The beach was an hour and a half by bicycle. Two hours by bus. Somebody knocked on the front window of the store and I jumped. A well-dressed woman peered through the glass. I could hear her muffled yell. "Are you open?" "Closed!" I yelled, shaking my head. She made a pleading face. Put her hands together like she was praying. The kind of person that's used to getting special favors. I gave her the finger. "Closed!" I yelled again. Her face changed fast. She gave me the finger back and walked away from the window.

In the Westside phone book, I found Timmy's home phone number and address. I dialed the number and the machine picked up. "Hello this is Timothy Harris yadda yadda yadda . . ." I didn't leave a message.

I tore the address out of the phone book. 138 East Canal St. Come to think of it, Paul had told me once that Timmy lived in a house on the Venice Beach canals. They were a big tourist attraction once upon a time — a place to get smoochy and let your fella pole you around Italian style. But now not that many people knew about them. Totally residential. Most of the houses were sandwich jobs — two acres of house on a half acre of land. Expensive. People paid a lot to live around all that duck crap. Paul made a point of saying how it wasn't book money that bought the house — it

31

was residuals from Timmy's movie days. That and family money. No one made that kind of dough selling books.

I rubbed my hands over my hair. Then I stood and jumped up and down pogo style. The cracks in the ceiling getting bigger then smaller, bigger then smaller. I stopped suddenly and sat hard on my ass, on the floor. I couldn't stop touching my goddamned hair. My hands were clammy and I wiped them on the carpet. Filled with that keyed-up dread a kid feels at the top of a long dark driveway on Halloween. I was a princess four years running. A princess, for Christ's sake. A Goody Two-shoes. And scared of everything. My mother used to wait in the street and make me go the rest of the way alone. She'd call out to me so I would know she was there. Her voice nudging me through the night. Half the time, I turned back before I got to the front door. It was the one thing we fought about, my mother and I. Right up until she died. For my own good she wanted me to be stronger.

32

Scott lived up around Laurel Canyon, which was a hell of a lot closer than the beach. I locked up the store and got on my bike. It weaved a bit, but I've ridden drunker. I had decided to go get the Honda on loan. I needed something with an engine to get me to the beach fast. The Honda was my best option.

I kept to the sidewalks mostly — it was safer to risk colliding with pedestrians than with cars. Riding calmed me down and I started to think that twenty-four hours was plenty of time to get a lousy book back to its rightful owner. The book would be at Timmy's house, maybe the store. I could get it that night and have the whole thing fixed before I had to open Bitter Muse in the morning.

I cut through a residential area. Looked at all the crazy Candyland houses with bars on the windows and Jeeps parked on the front lawns. Half the neighborhood was out walking dogs. People saying, "Look, Bourbon, it's Rascal! Say hi to Rascal! Say Hi! Yeezzzz! Bourbon loves Rascal!"

I felt sick from exercising so quickly after drinking, so I slowed up a little. Plants and trees were blooming all over, but then every season is blooming season in this town. Purple trees, orange bushes, flowers that look like birds. I'd see a bush half the size of a house and recognize it as the same kind of plant that struggled to fill a teacup on the kitchen windowsill when I was a kid. Sometimes it was just too much. My only blind date in L.A. . . . the guy had just moved out here and we walked to the movies from my apartment. He kept saying, "What a riot of color! It's a riot of color." I have no idea what that guy is doing now.

After fifteen minutes or so I got to the base of the hill. Scott lived near the top. On the other side was the San Fernando Valley. It wasn't a small hill. I got off the bike and began walking it up but there was no sidewalk and almost no shoulder so I was practically pushing it through the bushes. I would have to find a faster way.

I stopped at a small grocery store and locked my bike to a handicapped parking sign. Loitered near the entrance to the store. A lot of aging hippie types live around Laurel Canyon. There's a real neighborly feel to the place. A forty-ish guy with a bushy beard, potbelly, and "Washington Grew Hemp" T-shirt came out of the store. Pushed the door open with his butt. In his left hand he carried a reusable canvas

33

shopping bag full of eggplant. In his right, the latest issue of *Mother Jones*. He was tailor-made.

"I really hate to bother you," I said. I wrung my hands together. "You see I got a call at work that my kid is sick and the baby-sitter's freaking and my husband's out with the car somewhere and someone gave me a ride to here but they were in too much of a hurry to take me the whole way. . . ."

"Oh man!" he said.

"My house is only a mile or so from here."

"Sure. I'll take you. Okay. Yeah. My car's right over here."

I walked as if I was in pain over to his car. A new white Saturn. I said, "Nice car," so I would seem nice.

"Just got it," he said. "I really like their politics."

"Yeah, I know what you mean."

"They're just folks." He smiled and aimed his gadget at the car and beeped the alarm off.

He kept one hand in his beard the whole time he drove. Like he had a pet mouse in there and he was playing with it. Every time I gave him a direction, he said, "Well whattaya know," or, "That's my way, too," and I started to worry that I had seen him before, like maybe he was one of Scott's neighbors. And then we got to Scott's place and I told him to stop and he said, "I know who lives in this house. You don't live in this house." I shrugged my shoulders. "Why does everyone feel they have to lie all the time?" he said. And I said, "Please don't let my own selfish behavior prevent you from doing good works in the future, Daddy-o," and it sounded even worse than I had meant it.

As I walked away from the car, he said, "People like you ruin everything for everyone." He was probably right.

Scott was in the driveway, duct-taping the side mirror back onto the motorcycle. He lived in a dumpy little house with his girlfriend, Debi, and her two kids, Cox and Nellie. Debi grew up rich in New Jersey and came to California and got into drugs. She tried to be an actress but she was bad at it so she married a club owner and had the two kids. When he went bust and moved back to Iceland, she went into rehab and then got her beautician's license. She worked at an eight-dollar-haircut place until one of her regulars got a record deal and became semi-famous with the mall rat crowd. Now she spends most of the time on tour with this pop singer and Scott's saddled with the kids. Scott's a guy I know from college.

"You get any money off him?" I asked. Apart from the side mirror, the bike looked the same. Which wasn't saying much.

"Yeah, he gave me twenty bucks." While Scott was talking, I kept moving toward the front door of the house. "His wife's idea was to sue me. She kept saying, 'Punitive damages, what about punitive damages!' I sold him a couple joints, too."

"I've gotta use the phone," I said. I hopped over some kid toys on the front steps and went inside. Walked straight through the living room where Cox and Nellie and some friend of Cox's were eating bowls of cereal in front of the TV. I've never seen those kids eat anything but breakfast foods.

The kitchen was at the back of the house, separated from the living room by a small dining area. The phone was on a wall next to a message board. Someone had written the

35

word *fuck* in tiny letters at the bottom of the board. I tried Timmy's place again, hoping. But there was still no answer. I thought I should leave a message. Something about not doing anything with the book. Not moving it, not showing it to anyone, and definitely — oh shit — definitely not selling it. After the beep, I said, "Hi Tim, uh this . . ." and then I hung up. I slowly dragged my hands down my face. "It's all right," I said. "You have twenty-four hours."

On the way back out to Scott, I paused to talk to the kids. "Hey, you brats," I said. Acting normal made me feel normal. Nellie put down her bowl and ran over and hugged me around the knees. Not that she liked me that much. She greeted everyone that way. Like a golden retriever — always sticking her wet nose in your crotch.

36

"Hey, Cox," his friend said. "Watch!" The friend put a huge milky spoonful of cereal into his mouth, then let it drool out the sides as he saucer-eyed my chest and said, "Mmmmmm! Titties!" The kid was about eight years old. Cox doubled over and pounded the couch and the other kid was so hysterical he spat the rest of the milk against the TV screen and then they cracked up about that. I started bawling and ran to the bathroom holding my boobs and slammed the door. Inside the bathroom with the door locked, I had to sit down on the edge of the tub because I had started crying for real. No sound. I pressed the palms of my hands against my eyes and tried to ride it out. "You stupid bitch," I said. "Stop, you stupid bitch." I was shaking and not breathing so well. But I couldn't blame it on Cox's friend or on having my life threatened — this was a feeling that affected me often. For four years and counting. I undressed and stepped into the tub and turned on the shower. It felt good and I stayed there until I felt all right again. When I turned it off, I heard that someone had been tapping on the door. Cox's friend.

"I'm sorry," he said. When I heard his voice, I knew he would be playing out this apology scene the rest of his life. Different women, same script. "Look, I was just foolin' around. I didn't mean anything."

I said, "You made me feel so bad I tried to scrub them off."

"But I was just foolin'."

I got dressed and looked in the medicine chest for aspirin. All they had was kids' chewable stuff. I chewed eight.

"Please come out," said the kid. I figured he had learned his lesson for the day.

37

I called Timmy's place again with no luck. I wasn't really hungry but I made myself a fast peanut butter and banana sandwich. Took it outside with a couple of cold beers.

"What was going on in there before?" Scott asked.

"Usual stuff."

Scott opened a beer and drank down half. "You know," said Scott, "this may sound weird and don't tell Debi, but it's like, I really don't like those kids. I mean, I try to like them. But I don't like them. I just can't communicate with them." Scott lit a joint and began to smoke it. He offered me a hit but I shook my head. He talked around the smoke in his mouth, keeping his lips tiny. "Cox kicked me in the nuts yesterday. Hard. What do you do? You don't hit him. Nellie's okay but she's dumb. Not a smart girl. And Debi always takes their side. And now she's gone half the time and *I* have to look after them? I don't know. I don't know."

"How's the band?" I had heard the "I don't really like the kids" speech a hundred times. Unless you cut him off it was a double feature.

"Dave's definitely going to law school in the fall so we have to find a new bassist."

I knew I should get going but all I really wanted to do was stay and drink beer with Scott. Pretend it was just another night, empty as a sneaker on the side of a highway. I liked them that way. "You're better off without him. You guys are really great, you know?"

"Thanks, Jill."

"You'll be famous."

"Yeah."

I sighed. "So listen, I've gotta take the bike for a day or two, but I can't really give you any money."

"Oh man, you are so like . . . if I could just think of a thing you are it would be unbelievable."

"I'm just going to borrow it."

"So that's what all that 'the band is so great' stuff is all about? Getting me to lend you the bike?"

"I need it."

"So you don't think we're any good."

"No, you are good. I meant that."

"Well, I can't believe you now. How am I supposed to believe you now? You've gotten cold, Jill. Really cold. You're some sort of . . . ambulatory permafrost."

"I've always been cold. I just have an easier time expressing it now."

"Nah, nah. You're meaner." He straddled the bike and

pretended he was throttling it. He said, "Vrooom vroom. I'm not going to lend it to you unless you tell me why you need it."

I put my elbows on the handlebars. "Scott, I've had a very bad —*very* bad— day. If I could tell you what it was for, I would."

"An abortion?"

"Jesus! If it was for an abortion, I'd tell you. An abortion. I don't even *have* sex anymore."

"Really? Me neither. You know, speaking of sex —Jim Perry called me a couple days ago. He's moving out here for film school. Wanted to know what happened to you. What you were up to." Jim Perry was one of my closest friends in college. We had started sleeping together senior year. Basically dating. But I'd lost touch with everyone I knew then. Except Scott. "And you know what I told him?"

39

"What?"

"I told him you'd gotten really cold."

"Thanks. That's great. Scott, I need the bike. And I need to leave now."

"What — it's a matter of life and death, right?"

"Sure," I said. "Yes."

"You're full of shit as always."

I held his face in my hands. Looked right at him. His eyes weaved around my face. I said, "If I say it's important, you've got to believe me that it's important. Now I am asking you nicely, please, *please* don't make me kill you just so I can take the stupid goddamn bike."

"Fuck, fine, take it," said Scott. "What do I care." He got off the bike. I held my hand out for the keys.

"Thank you," I said.

"Yeah, whatever." He felt around his pockets.

"You're a good person."

"Fuck you."

Nellie came running out of the house then, crying and waving her finger, which was bloody. Cox ambled out behind her, wearing a wet suit. He often wore his wet suit around the house the way kids used to like wearing cowboy outfits.

"Aw shit, what happened?" asked Scott. Nellie was crying too hard to speak and wrapped her arms tightly around him, leaving a small bloody cipher on the seat of his jeans.

"She sliced open her finger cutting a bagel," said Cox. His friend was nowhere around.

"Didn't Debi tell you to always use the bagel slicer? Huh?" Scott held Nellie at arm's length. Nellie nodded. It looked as if she had been finger painting a deep red sun, red fields, a blood-red room, a dead woman.

"Uh, Scott . . ." I said. I wasn't too crazy about the sight of blood.

"Then why didn't you?"

"I fwagot."

"Maybe you should give her a Band-Aid," I said.

"What were you doing?" he asked Cox.

"What! Don't blame me for everything. I was watching TV." Nellie began to flick her hand. Flick away the hurt like it was a piece of scotch tape stuck to her finger. Blood flew.

"Scott . . ." I said.

"You're supposed to watch her," said Scott.

"Fuck you, *you're* supposed to watch her."

40

"I told you not to — ah! — not to *swear* at me."

"Hey!" I said. "She needs a Band-Aid!" And as I said that, Nellie pitched forward into the dirt and we all stood silent and looked at her lying on her stomach, her face turned to the side, as white as a doll.

4.

The problem was, I had only ridden a motorcycle four times before. I had it down pretty well, but not that well. I think Scott had forgotten this. He had tossed me the keys after dribbling some water from the hose on Nellie's face and carrying her inside to the couch and wrapping her finger with gauze until it was the shape of an inverted pear. I inched down the hill in low gear. Scraped my clogs along the pavement. It's harder to ride a motorcycle slow than to ride one fast. Still, I took my time. Cars passed me honking. One guy waved his fist at me. People don't seem to do that as much anymore. I said, "Eat me."

Once I got to the bottom, things improved. Starting and stopping gave me the biggest trouble. At a light, I rear-ended a convertible beetle. Just nudged it. When the driver turned around, I said, "Sorry, I thought you were someone else." After that, I made a point of keeping about thirty feet between me and the car in front of me. I stuck to major roads, skipped the freeway. Scott had lent me a helmet and somehow I got him to let me wear Debi's leather jacket. Or he might not have realized that I took it. I would bring it back when I returned the bike. She had too many clothes.

I couldn't get a song out of my head. A jingle from an old kid's toy ad. I sang it out loud because it kept my mind off things. I liked to hear the wind eat it up.

> Digga the dog
> Digga he goes with you, when you explore
> Just pull his leash and he'll go for a walk
> He's your dog, you whore.

I guess in the original version, that last line is different.

43

I parked the bike just before I got to the canals and walked around until I found Timmy's place. The house had been built in the "King Arthur meets Goldilocks" style that you can only find in L.A. Turrets and an imitation thatched roof. A couple of stained-glass windows. It was dark inside and no one answered the bell. I went around to the front of the house, the side facing the canal. A couple dozen ducks were sleeping on a small brick patio. There was duck crap everywhere. When I stepped toward some French doors leading up to the house, the ducks started quacking like crazy. I backed off slowly. Timmy clearly wasn't home. I decided to head for the nearest bar and look for him.

A few blocks away, I saw a couple stumble out of a smoked glass door, laughing. A likely spot. I crossed the street and tried to peer through the door and at that moment, someone else decided to come out and I got clocked on the nose. She said, "Oh, I'm sorry!"

"Oh my nose! Oh, Jesus my nose!" I grabbed my nose. It didn't hurt much. But getting nailed like that on top of everything else made me a little agitated.

"I said I was sorry," the woman said.

"You don't understand. I'm a nose model. Oh my sweet Jesus!" The woman looked at me, said, "Hmmmmwhat?" and walked away.

"You'll hear from me," I called after her. Then I went inside.

It was more a restaurant than a bar. Tables jammed close and filled with nerdy-looking executives talking to lovely girls in black.

I saw a small bar crammed over to the side, where people waited for a table. Some even drank. I shoved my way in that direction, eyeballing the crowd in search of Timmy. A ballerina type in wedgie shoes and a ten-year-old's party dress touched me lightly on the arm.

"Are you meeting someone?" she asked. Her Cockney accent threw me.

"No. *Je suis* sitting at the bar *pour* to — how you say — zup some drinks?"

"Right then. Suit yourself." She went back to her lectern and closely studied the seating chart. I followed her.

"Hey," I said, "do you know a guy named Timmy Harris? Owns a used bookstore not too far from here?" She looked at her watch and carefully erased a name on the chart before responding to me.

"I don't read," she said.

I inserted myself between a couple on a first date and leaned over the bar to try and get the bartender's attention. He was down at the other end, working the blender. Over the noise of the restaurant, I heard the woman on the date talking. She was saying, "They were supposed to name my brother 'Sean' but when the woman, the administrator woman or the woman that made up the birth certificate or whatever, when she saw that name, she said, 'See-an! What you gonna name your kid See-an for!' So right then they changed his name to Douglas."

The guy said, "Wow. Wow. That's a really funny story."

She said, "Yeah. Yup." They both looked around. They didn't really fit in the place and maybe they realized it. She said, "But I like the name Ira. It's good on you." She smelled like a new office building. And she had made her blond hair huge for the occasion. He peeled the label off his beer bottle. Really worked it. Somehow a tiny piece of label had stuck to the undertip of his nose. But she wasn't saying a thing.

The bartender walked past me and I waved to get his attention. He had red hair so I said, "Hey, Red!" He stopped and came back. "What can I get you?" he asked.

"Tim Harris been in tonight?"

Red shook his head. "Have not seen him."

I drummed my fingers on the bar. "The thing is," I said, "he owes me a drink and I'm a little short. Can you spot me a fast shot of cheap vodka and dump it on his tab?"

The bartender looked at me like I had just stolen Christmas and walked away to fool around some more with his blender. I guessed that meant no.

45

I turned to leave and came face to face with first-date Ira. The piece of paper still stuck to his nose. As I was pushing past him, I paused. I said, "You have part of your beer label stuck to your nose and I'm afraid it might be ruining your chance of having sex with that woman later."

"What?" he said. He started rubbing his nose furiously. I left.

I decided to return to Timmy's place. Going bar to bar seemed like a waste of energy. The way to find him was to plant myself in his path. Sooner or later he'd get sleepy.

A block away from his house, I saw a deli/liquor store and went in. I nosed around the beer section for something to keep me company while I waited for Timmy. Picked up a forty-ounce bottle of malt liquor and brought it to the counter where a young Korean guy sat reading *Auto Trader*. I asked, "You ever drink this stuff?" He looked up, looked at the bottle, nodded. "How is it?"

"Makes you crazy."

"Fine," I said. He rang it up, and with my change I bought a Tootsie Pop. He bagged the stuff for me and said, "Drink fast. Once it gets warm, it's unpalatable."

I went back to Timmy's place, knowing he wouldn't be there. Knowing I would have to sit around with the ducks and drink my malt liquor and lick my lolly. Even though the place was dark, I rang the bell on the chance that he had come home and gone to bed. Nothing. It must have been around nine-thirty or ten. If he stayed out until last call, it would be a wait, all right. And if he picked someone up . . . well, I was counting on the fact that he'd bring her here to show off the house. I was counting on a lot of things.

I went around to the canal side and looked for a place to wait. A narrow cement walkway ran between the patio and the water. I found a relatively crap-free spot and I started to lay out the paper bag from the liquor store but decided I would wrap the bag around the forty instead to try to keep it cool. The ducks stirred but laid off quacking. I dumped my backpack and sat cross-legged and uncapped the bottle. I started with one long pull and when I stopped to breathe, I felt as if I had just eaten a loaf of bread.

The canal had the look and feel of a trial-size swamp, but there was a jasmine bush nearby and it made the night smell fancy. I could see into a couple of the neighbors' houses. I saw kids and sometimes adults lined up on couches watching TV. In the house directly across the canal — a big palazzo joint — a family was watching some comedy show and I could hear the fake laughter on TV and then the family would laugh back and it made me think of being in a church. Instead of "Amen," they said, "Haha."

I kept drinking the forty, though I developed an instant hangover. I thought that if I had a phone I would call my sister in Boston. I owed her a call. She'd left a couple messages for me lately. But it would be late there, and she always went to bed early. Like the big guy in the baseball cap. Early to bed, early to rise. I tried to figure out why the guy was so familiar to me. If he lived nearby, I guess I could have seen him around the neighborhood. But I didn't want to think of him as a neighbor. I really didn't want to think of him at all. I wanted to flatten that dwarf for getting me wrapped up in the whole thing. And for putting the bookstore in jeopardy. I really disliked this kind of shake-up. It had taken me a long time to find a routine I liked. A nice, simple life.

I took another long drink and tried to figure out what show the gang across the canal was watching. I was pretty sure it was a show about this kooky Italian-American family that always gets into trouble together. The grandfather's senile — thinks he's a lemon.

I hadn't talked to my sister in a couple months. The hell with waking her up — if I had had a phone, I definitely would have called her. I didn't usually like talking long distance. I had to be in the right mood for it. My sister had gotten in the habit of talking to my answering machine as though it were me. She'd fill the tape. She knew I was there listening. Her dog chewed up a bra, she made Law Review, she was having red cabbage and chicken for dinner. She had gotten pretty good at not asking what my plans were. Both of us went through a bad time four years back. There wasn't much point dwelling on it. Our mother had cancer and died very slowly. Until the end, of course. That was fast. Pretty fast. The whole thing shook me up a bit. I don't mind admitting it. I just didn't like to talk talk talk about it all the time. Or, even worse, make a point of not talking about it. Some relative of mine would get on the phone. Some old friend. And literally ask about the weather. It was like carving up a little kid for dinner and no one mentions it doesn't look like a turkey. Also, it had just been the two of us there at the end. My mother and me. There were things the others didn't know about and wouldn't get if they did. Those were the things to be put aside. It left me different.

When we were kids, my sister was the tough one. No

48

nonsense. My uncle once referred to her as goal oriented. That still fits. Good for her.

I unwrapped my Tootsie Pop and lay on my back and looked up, but thanks to the light pollution and the regular pollution, the stars were nil. I put the Tootsie Pop in my mouth. It was chocolate. There's something, some rule about not sucking on things when you're lying down. Or when you're running, maybe. I pointed my feet up at the sky and scissored my legs back and forth. Did the bicycle. I said, "Ladies, you too can have thinner thighs in thirty days. It's as simple as baking a cake. You know how to bake a cake, don't you? Well then!" It was hard to enunciate with the pop in my mouth. The ducks began to put up a fuss. I said, "Aw, quit your quacking you fine feathered freaks!" Then I shut up. I just lay quietly with my hands folded over my belly. If I had had more makeup on, I could have passed for a corpse.

49

The sound of a car roused me and I brushed the dirt off the back of my legs and picked up the forty and headed around the house. Timmy was sitting in his car in the driveway. An old convertible. I couldn't tell what make.

"Hey!" I said. His head jerked up.

"Wha— Sally?" he said. He put a hand up to his brow as though he was shielding his eyes from the sun. A reflex, I guess.

"It's Jill."

"Who?"

"Jill, from the bookstore. From Bitter Muse Bookstore."

"Jesus, you scared the bejesus out of me. Man oh man." He started to get out of his car. He locked both doors and checked the handles, even though the top was down. "I thought I was getting mugged," he said. "I've been mugged a bunch of times."

"Sorry," I said.

"It was like — whew! — I couldn't believe I was getting mugged again. Boy oh boy." He leaned against his car.

"I should have approached you more gradually," I said. His jeans hung low on his hips. He didn't eat enough — that I could tell.

"So what's going on?" he said.

I said, "Well, here's the thing . . ."

"Hold on," he said. "Let's go inside so we don't have to stand outside, you know?"

"Sure," I said. I followed him to the door, where he fiddled with his keys and locks. Turned the bolt one way, then tried the knob, turned the bolt the other way, tried the knob. I get really impatient when people can't open a door. He said, "I can never remember if I bolted it."

"That's okay," I said. He finally got it. He stepped inside and turned on the kitchen light and I followed. He looked at me and frowned. He said, "What have you got there, a lollipop?" I nodded. He said, "I thought it was like, this thing, coming out of your mouth." He went to the sink and got a glass of water and drank it. I put my bottle on the counter. The kitchen was homey and surprisingly neat. Blue-and-white tile. A wall clock shaped like a chicken. Some dried flowers in a mason jar. I half expected to see pies cooling on the sill.

"Do you have a trash?" I asked.

"Under the sink," he said. I was going to throw away the rest of my lollipop but just then I got to the Tootsie Roll in the middle so I didn't. Timmy looked at me like he was waiting for me to put something in the garbage but I just stood there. Chewing.

"So," he said, "Jill who goes up the hill."

"Uh huh," I said.

"So what's going on?" I held up my hand because I couldn't talk while I was eating the Tootsie Roll. He stood with his arms crossed and smiled at me. Then he got bored and poured himself a drink. Rum with some instant piña colada mix. He made one for me too. By the time he was done, I had swallowed the Tootsie Roll. I tossed the stick in the garbage.

I said, "I know this is going to sound crazy and annoying but I need the book back." He handed me the drink and I took a sip and realized I couldn't swallow it. It made a putrid combination with the Tootsie Pop. I walked over to the sink and spat it out. Then I dumped the rest of the drink and rinsed the glass, swilled some water around my mouth and spat that out also. I said, "Excuse me."

"You're sort of gross," he said. He smiled shyly when he said it.

"Sorry," I said. "I can't drink sweet drinks."

"This is the only stuff I like." We both stood there silently and I figured he had already forgotten what I had said about needing the book back.

"So I need to take the book back," I said.

"Whoa! What?"

"I need the book back. I'm sorry." I began to fish in my back pocket for his check and the wad of cash. "I have all your money," I said. "I know it's a pain but something very

51

strange happened and I need to get it back." I held out the check and the money and I thought of the dwarf, miserably offering up my crumpled twenty.

"All right. Hold the phone. First of all, let's go sit in the living room." He started to walk away. I just stood still with my hand out. He stopped. "C'mon," he said. "It's right down the hall." I picked up my malt liquor and followed him.

We sat on a bright green couch. I took off my clogs and tucked my feet beneath me. He drank his disgusting piña colada and I drank my disgusting malt liquor. His check and his money sat slowly unfolding on the coffee table where I had left them.

52 The living room had a jukebox and some lithographs of illustrations from children's books and a chair made out of corrugated cardboard that must have been worth plenty. I had started to sit in it but he said, "That chair's not for sitting," so we both ended up on the couch.

"How long were you waiting for me?" he asked.

"A while."

"'Cause I was out."

"Yes you were," I said. "So," I said, "is the book here?"

"Yeah. The book. Let's talk about this a bit." He put down his drink and clapped his hands and looked at me intently. "You say you need it back?"

"Look, I didn't expect anything like this to happen. But I really need it back. It's not even like I just decided I wanted it back. I actually need it back."

He rubbed his hands together like a bum standing over

a barrel fire. "Well, right now the book is with my signatures guy. I don't have it here. But if it's, like, a question of money, I feel like I gave you a good deal."

"It's not money. It's not the money. It's that the original owner is demanding it back."

"The guy that had the garage sale?"

"Right."

"Well that's not right. You bought it fair and square. He can't just take it back. That's like, Indian giving."

I opened my mouth, then closed it. Rubbed my eyes until I saw red blooms behind my lids. "It's a long story," I said. "The guy having the garage sale stole it and the guy he stole it from wants it back."

"Some guy stole it so he could sell it at a garage sale?" He looked at me, blinking. I twisted the paper bag tight around the malt liquor and with one colossal effort, finished what was left in the bottle. I set it down on the wagon wheel coffee table and half swallowed a belch. "Pardon," I said.

"Yeah," he said, "you're just a little bit gross."

"Can you just please tell me you'll give it back to me?"

Timmy had finished his drink also and began chewing slowly on an ice cube. Then he jockeyed around so that he was lying on the couch on his stomach with his knees bent and his feet in the air. Like a teenage girl talking on the phone in her jammies. It was a long couch.

"Where are you from originally?" he asked. His voice was gentle and it gave me a strange, tickling feeling in my throat. I realized that we were both the kind of people who could be dead drunk and not show it.

I sighed. "Connecticut."

"Connecticut! You probably grew up riding ponies."

"No," I said. "They don't allow ponies in the suburbs. Zoning laws."

"When I was a kid, I was an actor. I had to learn how to ride a pony for a movie I was in."

"*Jiminy Livin'*," I said.

"Oh man you've seen it." He buried his head in his hands.

"Jiminy Booth saves Aunt Harriet's farm with help from his pony, Shortstuff."

"Oh boy," he said.

"It was a real birthday party favorite when I was growing up."

"I'm embarrassed," he said. But I knew he wasn't.

"No," I said. "You were good in it."

54

"Sometimes I forget that I did all that stuff." He stood up. "I'm going to get another drink but I won't get you one." He headed toward the kitchen. Bounced off one wall in the hallway but recovered pretty well. I yelled, "Do you have any aspirin?"

"I'll bring you some."

He came back with aspirin and water, and when he sat down, he said, "Give me your foot."

"What?" I said.

"It's to get rid of a headache. No kidding. Give it." He sat right next to me on the couch. I looked down at my feet for a moment, thinking. "C'mon," he said.

I leaned back against the arm of the couch and put my foot in his lap. He pressed hard against the insole. Kneaded it with his thumb. And my head began to feel better, I guess.

"So do you want to own a bookstore someday? Is that why you work for Paul?"

"No," I said.

"Well, are you . . . what? a writer?" I shook my head. "You just like to read," he said.

"I read a lot," I said. "I like it . . . a lot."

"Did you go to college?"

"Yes."

"Really? Did you graduate?"

"No. Almost."

"Hey! Me either! Though I only made it through a semester. I was a sucky student, I'll tell you that. And in addition, I just wasn't used to regular school. I had always had uh . . . tutors, you know, or my mother."

"My mother was a teacher," I said. "A professor." **55**

"Well, no wonder you didn't like school. That's the worst! Although in my case, it was that my mother had played a teaching nun in a movie so then she decided that she, like, knew all there was about teaching. So she would try to teach me herself. It was actually good for me because half the time she forgot she was supposed to be doing it." We sat silently and he stared at the wall and stopped rubbing my foot. Then he laughed suddenly. "Ha HA!" A loud parrot laugh. He turned back to me and said, "What?"

"I didn't say anything," I said.

"Oh," he said. "So, you don't want to do anything? Just sell used books?"

"It's a very good job," I said.

"Yeah but you don't want to be some, like, eighty-year-old woman saying, 'Here's your book, sir, sniff sniff cough

cough, time for my prunes.'" He used a high-pitched English accent and pinched his face up.

"That's good acting," I said. "You must be a professional."

"It's just not all that ambitious is what I'm saying. It's a little nowhere."

I took my foot away. And after I thought about it for a second, I said, "Fuck you."

"Whoa! Whoa! I'm not judging. It's fine. It's not important to know what you want. Give me your foot. Give it back." He reached for my foot and stroked the bottom of it. "What does that do for you?" he asked. "Do you like it?"

I said, "Actually, no."

"Oh," he said. It came out a little petulant. And I don't know why I had stopped him, because it felt nice. He took a sip of his drink.

"I regret not going to more college," he said. "I should have stuck it out."

"So?"

"So?" he said. "So? Sew buttons."

"You're strange," I said.

"*You're* strange! But I have to say, you are incredibly sexy." He leaned over and kissed the top of my foot.

Now, I don't care that he was an actor and that he was full of crap. Hearing that from someone you've had your eye on for a good six months, someone you've actually thought of shoving against the Travel section and kissing until you both fall down, well, it's pretty tough to resist. Not to mention that it had been about a year since I had had sex.

"Hey!" he said. "Want to see my ducks?" He set down my foot and walked over to the French doors at the end of the room. He flipped a switch and the patio light came on.

"I saw the ducks," I said. "Before, when I was waiting for you."

"C'mon," he said. "You've gotta meet them properly." He stepped out onto the patio and waved for me to follow. I shook my head and he shrugged and closed the door behind him, but I could hear him talk to the ducks. "Hey guys!" he said. "Hey! Hey there!" He walked among them like a politician in a preschool, bending occasionally to stroke one on the head. "Whatcha been doing, huh? Just sleeping?" I stood by the door watching, and because of the light I could also see my own reflection. Barefoot and tentative. I mussed up my hair. I'm sort of small.

Timmy waved again for me to come out. His arm flicked at my reflection like a spirit tongue. I smiled and shook my head again. I said, "You are fucking loony toons." He couldn't hear me through the glass. The ducks gathered around him and he pulled a few of them into an embrace. Buried his head in their feathers. When he looked up at me again, he was Jiminy Booth and he and his pony, Shortstuff, had just won the thousand-dollar derby. I smiled back at him. And I kept smiling while I pulled my top off.

57

5

I dreamt I saw the book at the bottom of a pool. The pool was in a library and two obese librarians were asking me to leave because it was closing time. I dove in the water, but couldn't find the book. I batted a duck out of my way. A librarian said, "If you bother that duck one more time, I'm going to break you." The book lay on the steps in the shallow end. Soggy and enormous. I pushed open the cover and inside, of course, was my mother and she was dead.

In the middle of the night, I woke up thirsty and I went to the kitchen and drank some water. I snooped around a little and found a pretty pink box half full of brownies and I ate one. In an office down the hall I looked at movie stills from Timmy's acting days. The place was lousy with them. Also, pictures of little Timmy posing with celebrities. Little Timmy standing on a chair next to Burt Reynolds. Little Timmy getting a kiss from Julie Christie.

Little Timmy with Johnny Mathis and a very young kid I didn't recognize. The other kid had his hands behind his back and Timmy was eyeing him unhappily. I didn't see any pictures of his mother, though — the late and beautiful Jennie Harris.

I took one of his business cards and a couple of pens because we never have enough pens at the bookstore. I came across a package of recently developed photos and they were all shots of the ducks. I took one for myself, and on another one, I drew a little talk bubble next to a duck and wrote in "I'm tasty!"

I put the stuff in my knapsack and went back to bed. Timmy was a mumbler. He said all sorts of things in his sleep that I couldn't make out. Rolled around like a malaria patient. The sheets were hot and twisted. They had pictures of cowboys and ponies and trains on them. I opened a window. Tried sleeping again. I had finally gotten Timmy to promise that he would call his signatures guy first thing in the morning and tell him to hold tight to the book until one of us came to get it. But it still made me edgy. I wanted the whole thing done with. I didn't like getting caught up in someone else's game. It made me feel cut loose, a little unsprung. After my mother died, I had spent a long time trying to pin myself down. This town, with all of its craziness, had somehow done the trick. Until this.

I turned over my pillow for the hundredth time. Timmy had left on the patio light and the tree outside the window made a shadow forest on the ceiling. After a while I gave up on sleep and started stroking Timmy until he rolled toward me.

59

When I woke up in the morning, I heard Timmy talking on the phone in another room. I lay in bed trying to hear the words. The walls muffled all of it except "Oh my carumba!" The digital alarm clock on his bedside table said nine-twenty. I had to open the bookstore at eleven. His bedroom was much messier than the rest of the house. Clothes all over the place. I wondered if he stood in front of the mirror trying on a dozen jeans and T-shirt combos before deciding on the one that was just right.

I walked naked to the bathroom and used his toothbrush while the shower heated up. After a shower, I found a clean T-shirt in one of his drawers and put it on with my own shorts. The T-shirt had a picture of the Belgian cartoon character Tintin on it. My mother read us those books when we were kids. Later, I read them to her. It didn't bother me to wear the shirt, though. Since I don't look at myself, I wouldn't even know I had it on.

In the kitchen, Timmy was eating a bowl of cereal and drinking a Coke. "Hey, beautiful," he said. He had on a pair of jeans but no top. I squeezed one of his nipples.

"That's nice," he said sarcastically.

"Whatever," I said. I found a bowl in a cabinet and helped myself to cereal. When I sat down, he said, "You know, that was excellent last night."

"I enjoyed it," I said.

"Hey," he said, "you're wearing my shirt. I was going to wear that shirt."

"Sorry," I said. "First come, first served."

"No, seriously. I'll get you another shirt. I sort of need to wear that today. But I have plenty." He stood up and walked toward his bedroom. "I'll even give you one you can keep," he said.

I said, "Captain Generosity of the good ship Magnanimous." He gave me an old pink T-shirt with a picture of a windsurfer. I hate pink. But the cotton was soft from so many washings and I didn't complain. While I switched shirts, he tried to start something up again. I would be late for the bookstore if we had sex again, so I kept things strictly above the waist. He sat on a chair and I sat on his lap facing him. After a minute, I mashed my face against his neck and became still. Today he smelled like a soap I used to use at summer camp. I pressed my eyes hard against his skin until white spots appeared in the darkness of my closed lids like credits on a movie screen. I could have stayed that way for a while.

He let go of my breasts. "What are you, falling asleep?"   **61**

"Hey," I said, pulling away from him, "how are we going to do this thing with the book? You'll have to get it and bring it to the store."

"Yeah," he said, "I can do that. No problem."

"So you'll do it early?" I said.

"*Tout de suite,* baby," he said. "Hey, do you ever close the store for lunch? Maybe we could go in the back and have, like, a little lunch date?"

"Christ you're horny," I said. "Am I your first or something?"

"I don't know," he said. "Maybe it's seeing you in my shirt. I think that turns me on."

"Well that's pathetic," I said. I held his chin in my mouth. Then I got off his lap and gathered my stuff together. "I'll see you in a couple hours, right?"

"Right."

When I got to the motorcycle, I saw it had a ticket on it. Placed neatly on the seat. It could have blown off so easily. I decided to help it along a little. I blew on it and sure enough, it tumbled off into the dirt. I walked the bike to a flat spot and started it up. No one had stolen the helmet.

I took Venice Boulevard. Past all the two-story apartment buildings where old women laid out their cast-off clothes like a distress signal. They would sit around in beach chairs waiting to sell wrinkled muumuus for two bucks a pop. Past the strip malls with the five dollar manicure places. Past Donut Heaven, Donut Time, Winchel's Donuts, Time for Donuts, I Love Donuts, Falafel and Donuts, Jimmy's Donuts, and Dough-nutty. Past the Hare Krishna temple. I had gone there once for a free vegetarian meal. They asked me to leave before serving me. You have to chant before you can eat and I kept saying "Hairy Hitler" instead of Hare Krishna. The girl praying next to me blew the whistle. I was hungry and I shouldn't have been such a wiseass. I've heard the food is pretty good.

I cut north in the direction of the hills. You couldn't even see them because of the smog. There's a big bush near my apartment building and the leaves are a half-inch thick in dirt. Just the stuff that falls from the air. I can't look at that bush.

It was hot again. I was sweating through the T-shirt into Debi's leather jacket. I braked for a light and a middle-aged Mexican guy crossed in front of me. He stopped to show me something. "Fi' dollas," he said. "*Bueno*. Fi' dollas." I took a closer look and saw he was holding out his teeth. Selling his plates for a bottle or some lunch or whatever.

I said, "Thanks but no." I pointed at my own teeth apologetically.

"Fo' dollas," he said. "Is *bueno*."

"If I didn't have these, I would definitely want them," I said. He stuck out his tongue at me and blew. A Bronx cheer, as they say. "Oh yes, that's much better without teeth," I said. "Lovely." The guy behind me honked and I realized the light was green.

When I arrived at the bookstore, it was just shy of eleven so I got a couple bucks from the register and bought some cat food and treated myself to a good cup of coffee from a coffee place down the block. A double iced latte to go. I went through the motions of opening the store and sat down with my coffee and Harry Dean Stanton live on the radio. He sang a beautiful Spanish ballad but when he spoke he sounded as if he was just coming off a three-day drunk.

63

Some guy came in and bought eighty bucks' worth of used Franklin Mint classics — those leather-bound beauties they advertise on late-night TV. The first one's only ninety-nine cents, the next fifty will run you a couple thousand dollars. The guy kept smelling the leather. He smelled every book he bought. Snorting until his nostrils closed up. Then he would say, "AaahhhhI'll take this one, too," and add it to the pile.

A woman and her grown-up daughter came in. The woman's whole face looked torched. Like someone had tried to boil up her head for dinner. She told me she had just had a face peel. She was overweight and balding. Had the gravel voice of a lifetime smoker. She showed me a glossy of her that had been taken twenty or thirty years ago. She said, "After it heals, I'll look like this." The daughter didn't pay attention to her. The woman would call to her and the daughter ignored it. Just kept looking through the Fiction section. The woman walked over to the daughter with a book. "You should read this, Sue. It's good, Sue." The daughter didn't look up. I strolled over to see what book the woman was talking about. It wasn't a very good book but I agreed with her that it was. The woman asked me if we had anything about Brigitte Bardot. When she was young, everyone mistook her for Brigitte Bardot. I said, "I can picture that."

I took it easy waiting for Timmy to show up. I thought about the sex. It had been okay. Splendid, considering he was drunk. He had a nice lanky body. And he didn't bore me. I wouldn't mind repeating the process. Yeah, it might be nice to spend a couple months getting messy with him on his cowboy sheets. I had an open schedule.

Whenever someone came in, I jumped. I was edgy thinking that the Joke Man might change his mind about the time frame and pop on by. With a stack of old magazines and a gas can. It wouldn't take much to get this place going. That worried me more than anything.

The cat was feeling chummy. It wanted to spend a little time in my lap. The weight of it gave me a stomachache and it made me sweat even harder. But I let it lie there. No one would hurt a girl with a cat in her lap. Or at least it was nice to think that way. Then the cat got restless. Started doing that push-push thing with its front paws. Stretching its claws and pinching me with them. They were long claws — Paul didn't like to trim them. Push, claw, push, claw. Those talons went right through Timmy's shirt. I tried to get it to calm down. I said, "Whoa there, cat. Lie down, cat. Who's a good cat." But it was on a real roll. Purring and pushing and clawing and rubbing up against me. Then it got me in the breast, bad, and I decided enough was enough. I tossed it into the middle of the store and it gave me a dirty look and headed for the back. Probably to execute a revenge crap on the duplicate paperbacks. "*You're* the one with the attitude problem," I said.

Around one o'clock I began to get very antsy. I called information again for the number of Timmy's store and then I called there. One of the guys who works for him answered. He had a German accent and I figured it was the guy that often came with Timmy to buy books. Young guy with a droopy mustache. Always wore sandals. Nodded his head and said, "Ya, ya, ya, ya," the whole time you talked to him.

"Tim Harris please," I said.

He said, "Oh ya, he iss out for moost off za day."

"All right. Never mind."

"Ya, ya."

"Or maybe you can help me," I said.

"Ya, ya."

"Do you have a copy of . . ."

"Ya, ya, ya."

". . . *Yellow Rivers* by I. P. Daily?"

"Ya, Daily iss D-A-L-E-Y?"

"Right." I got wise when I was unsettled.

"Ya, I look." I hung up.

The mailman came in, surprisingly late. And one of his socks wasn't pulled up all the way. I said, "My God, look at you. You're a mess." He slapped the mail down on the display case and did an about-face. I flicked the top letter onto the floor and his neck jerked, but he managed not to turn around.

At two o'clock I started shelving books just to be doing something. I moved books that had been in the New Arrivals section for a couple months onto the main shelves. I organized the Travel section by country. I dusted off some of the art books. I changed the display window. Put away the gardening books that had been there since spring and put out a bunch of former bestsellers — beach reading. Then to keep busy, I made an elaborate sign that said "Beach Reading" and put it in the window with the books.

At three-thirty I called his house and left no message. "Don't make me hate you," I said after I hung up. And later **66** I said, "I mean it." I called his store again and asked for the name of the signatures guy that they used. The German said that as far as he knew, ya, they didn't haff a signatures man. That rankled me. I sat by the phone, jiggling my foot. "Don't do this to me, Timmy," I said. "You should call and say you're late. Be polite." A young woman browsing nearby said, "My boyfriend does the same thing to me all the time. It drives me nuts."

"You should kill him," I said.

"Yeah, right? Wouldn't that be nice."

"No, I'm serious," I said. "You do mine and I'll do yours. That way they'll never catch us. They'll never make the connection." She laughed a little nervously. "What's your boyfriend's address?" I asked.

"Is that the actual time?" she said, looking at the clock above the desk. "I am going to be so late."

I said, "Come back whenever and we'll talk."

When she left, the store was empty and I turned up the music and paced around. Sort of hopped and paced. I put in a tape of the Muffs, a very good L.A. band with a great female vocalist. Really knows how to scream. I closed the front door and jumped and danced around crazily. For some reason, jumping relaxes me. After a couple songs, I sat down hard in front of the fan. Lifted my shirt up over my head to dry my chest. Lifted my bra as well.

The door opened and I whipped my shirt down a beat too late to avoid flashing the cyberdork that entered. He had a copy of *Wired* magazine and a screen tan. Pasty white.

"Oh, sorry," he said.

"Don't sweat it." I stood up and adjusted myself. Went to the door and looked up and down the block.

"You're really pissing me off, Timmy," I said.

67

"Do you have any William Gibson books?" asked the dork.

"Try looking under *D*," I said, distracted. In no mood for dumb questions.

"Under *D?*" His eyes kept darting down to my chest and then rebounding away. Like his eyeballs had come unsprung.

"I said under *G*. As in Gibson, you techno-doofus." I knew he wasn't listening. He looked helplessly around the store.

"Where is *G?*" I brushed passed him and checked Fiction — there's no Sci Fi section in the store.

"We don't have anything right now," I said. "Try Book Boodle by the movie theaters."

"Isn't that just new books?" he asked.

"Yeah."

"You can buy his stuff new?"

"What are you, nuts?" I asked. He was now casually holding the copy of *Wired* down over his crotch area. A goofy, moony look on his face.

"Do you like William Gibson?" he asked.

I said, "All right, Boner Boy, go buy your book. Get out of here."

He giggled a little hysterically. "What do you mean?" he said.

"Good-bye," I said, pointing toward the door.

"It was nice talking to you," he said.

I was getting that helpless furious feeling down in the pit of my stomach. I started to wonder what would happen if Timmy never showed. If he ducked out on me. Maybe he still thought I was just being money hungry. That I had found a higher bidder. He didn't know the stakes. He thought he was dealing with mere garage-sale shenanigans. Didn't know what would happen if I sent Happy Man and his one-dwarf circus out Venice way. I wondered if I should phone the big guy up and try to stall. I decided I had to give Timmy until five-thirty.

I just couldn't believe he hadn't called.

I sat at the desk, jiggling. My sweaty thighs making kissing noises against the chair. My stomach a wreck. The phone rang and I dove for it. It was Paul.

"Hello, Jill, this is Paul," he said. He had an unmistakable voice. Soft and high. Like a ten-year-old in the final round of a spelling bee. But he always announced himself.

"Hi, Paul," I said.

"How's it going there?" That was his way of saying, "How many books did you sell today?" I told him about the Franklin Mint man and he was happy. There were days when the whole take was no more than ten bucks. Brutal days. Those were the days I took home books instead of my regular salary. Paul told me his van had been stolen in San Francisco. He had left it overnight in the Haight and when he got to it the next morning, there were six people in it. He asked them to leave and they asked for a ride to the Phish concert. He said no and they dug in for the long haul. Sat there passing around an industrial-size can of ravioli. At that point Paul probably said something like, "C'mon, you guys, that's not really fair." Eventually he went to find a policeman. When he got back, the van was gone. All this had happened about half an hour ago.

"So I want you," he said to me, "to find out all the places in California that the Phish are playing in the next week. And I'll call you back around seven."

"Oh," I said. "Sure."

"Bye-bye," he said. "Talk to you later." He hung up.

"Kee-riced!" I said. It was idiotic for me to be doing this legwork. But Paul liked to feel like he was getting his money's worth out of me. He knew that, most of the time he was away, I sat around reading and dipping into the candy bowl.

So now I had to call Ticketmaster and find out Phish's show schedule. It would pass the time, or at least three minutes of it. I got depressed thinking of Paul skulking around the parking lots at the Phish concerts. Asking the T-shirt and hummus hawkers if they had seen an orange VW van. The only guy wearing a bow tie. He was a very sweet guy. But bad luck followed Paul around like a fifth-grade crush.

I hauled out the phone book and found the number for Ticketmaster. They put me on hold right off the bat. Every thirty seconds, a recorded voice interrupted the music to tell me how important my call was to them. A real person finally picked up after about ten minutes. He said, "Ticketmaster, how may I help you," and then Timmy came in the front door and I racked the phone and jumped for him.

"Where the fuck have you been?" He held a book-size bag which was a good sign. I hit him anyway. Hard on the arm. A guy gave me some fighting lessons at a party one night. Guy that used to do some bare-knuckle boxing. That's why I don't hit like a girl.

"OW!" said Timmy. "Oh, man!" He rubbed his arm.

"Well I've been fucking sitting around all day waiting and you didn't even call to say what was going on, that you'd be late, or what!"

"I know," he said. "I'm sorry. I'm sorry." He did a visual tour of the store. Stood on his toes to look over the center bookcase and see that the place was empty. "The whole thing is crazy," he said.

"You should have called me."

"Yes, I know. And I have a really long explanation."

"Eh, shut it," I said. "Is that the book?"

"It's the book." I took the bag from him and opened it. Gently removed the book and flipped to the inscription page. There it was. 'Dear Francis' etc. etc. I closed the book and pressed it to my forehead for a second before returning it to the bag.

"So here's why I'm so late," said Timmy. "It's really good. I mean, it's quite a good reason."

"Skip it," I said. "It'll just annoy me." I got behind the

desk and picked up the phone. Before I dialed, I turned to Timmy. "Please browse or something," I said. He inched off a couple of baby steps. "Like in the Poetry section," I said. That was at the back of the store. He obliged.

The phone rang for a while before someone picked it up. I said, "May I speak with the, um, Joke Man?"

"He's not disposed at the moment, can I take a message?" That was something I hadn't expected.

"I'm um calling about a book? That I have to return?"

"Oh, hi," said the voice, "it's me."

"The, uh, Joke Man?" I asked.

"No, me, Adam."

"Oh, the, um . . . are you a bit short?"

"Yeah, " he said. "It's me. So you got the book back?"

"I have it. I got it back."

"Ooh that's great," he said. "That's really terrific." He spoke to someone else in the room. "She got the book back," he said.

"Good!" replied a voice. Probably the Joke Man. I heard a television. The theme song from an old cop show. Through the phone lines, it took on a sad flattened quality. "Ask her if she's at the store," said the voice in the room. And the dwarf asked, "Are you at the store now?"

"Yes," I said.

"Yes!" said the dwarf to the voice.

"Tell her someone will be by soon," said the voice.

"Someone will be by —"

"I heard him," I said.

"Oh," said the dwarf. "I didn't know." There was an awkward silence.

"So. Well 'bye then," I said.

71

"Good-bye," said the dwarf. I hung up, feeling like I had just called home from camp and the gang was thrilled to hear that I had earned my Canoe Chief badge. If the back of the store didn't still smell like burned hair, I might have thought that the whole incident was some two-bit magician's trick.

Timmy popped up in front of the desk with a small book in his hands. "Hey, look what I found," he said. "e. e. cummings! I've been trying to find this edition for like a year."

"Good for you," I said. "You can pay for the book and beat it."

"Hey, hey, what's that about? Let me tell you why I'm so late. I swear it's good."

"I told you I don't want to hear it," I said. I placed the London book in one of the desk drawers. Didn't look Timmy's way at all.

"You don't want to hear it? It involves a dog."

"Look. I've already got you figured for a liar." I coughed hard because my voice was getting a catch to it that I wasn't interested in hearing.

"What do you mean?" The corners of Timmy's kisser took a long trip south.

"I talked to Hansel at your store and he said you don't use a signatures guy." I pretended I was looking for a pen.

"Who, Kurt?" he said. "Kurt. Kurt doesn't know we have a signatures guy because *he's* supposed to be the signatures guy. But he kind of sucks at it so I use this old friend of mine." He leaned across the desk and pushed my hair back away from my face. "C'mon," he said. Softly. Almost a whisper. "C'mon. I got it to you, didn't I? Better late than

72

never?" He touched my neck, my ear. "I told you I'm a nice guy. You have to just trust me."

"No I don't," I said. I didn't move away. "I don't have to at all. I guess that's the good part." I kissed him hard.

We unclenched after a moment and he said, "Mmmm oh *oh!*" He kissed me again, softly. Touched my lip with his finger. "Chapped," he said.

"From riding a motorcycle," I said.

"Motorcycle! Sexy!" He made a noise like a cat. "Rrar!" Then he said, "So they're coming for it right now?"

"Yeah," I said.

"Yeah, well, I need to get going anyway. I haven't been to my place all day." His beeper went off. It sounded broken. An electronic warble like a cry for help.

"You have a beeper?" I said. "All right, use the phone but make it fast."

"Naw," said Timmy, "it's probably . . . oh look, yeah, it's just the store. I'm going to head out." He flipped the ring of his car keys around his index finger. Flip, flip. . . . "I guess I'll see you," he said. The keys flew off his finger and hit the wall. "Oops," he said. He retrieved them and headed for the door. "Okay, I'll see ya."

"Yeah, I guess so," I said.

"We'll go see a movie or something."

"Oh," I said. "All right. I guess we will." As he was stepping outside, I said, "Hey!"

"Wha —!" He spun around.

"You have to pay for the book."

"Oh, right, um, put it on the hold shelf, will you? I'll come back for it. I don't think I have any money on me."

"Fine."

He gave a little half wave, a lackluster salute. Took off flipping his keys again.

I called Ticketmaster while I waited for someone to show up for the book. Held the receiver slightly away from my ear to try and avoid the music. This time when a live person answered, the dwarf showed up. He was wearing a ten-gallon hat low over his brow. A sweat suit. Same old patent leather lifts. I racked the phone.

"How's business today?" he asked. I eyeballed the doorway and the street but saw no sign of the Joke Man.

"It's just you?"

74

"Just me, myself, and I," he said. Under the brim of the hat, his eyes were glassy. He was definitely on something. Painkillers, no doubt.

"I just sort of expected the other guy," I said.

"I think it's — ooh — it's a little test," said the dwarf. "For me. You know, to make up for things."

"O . . . kay," I said. "Well, here's the book." I opened the desk drawer and held out the bag with the book. He took it gently and tucked it under his arm.

He said, "I'm sorry about the inconvenience of everything. But it seems to have worked out for the best."

"I wouldn't exactly say for the best," I said.

"Oh, pooh, you know what I mean."

"Don't you want to check and make sure it's the right book?" I asked.

"Boy, I'm glad you mentioned that." The dwarf unbagged the book and read the title. "*The Cruise of the Snark* by

Jack London." He giggled. His little jelly body rocking, his hat nodding up and down like he was riding the electric bull at an urban cowboy joint. "It's a silly title, isn't it. It's silly! You can't tell from the title that this is an important — a *big deal* — book, now can you? I mean, who can blame a guy!"

I said, "You're not planning on operating any heavy machinery, are you?" That cracked him up even more.

"Nooo, pardner!" he said. The laughter subsided slowly. "Hehe, hoho, haha haaahhhhh," he said.

I said, "You are pretty loopy." While I had him in such a good mood, I was tempted to ask what the story was behind the book — why it was such a big deal. Then I realized that I wasn't too interested in turning over that rock after all.

"Well," he said, "gotta mosey. What's your name, anyway?"

"Lucile," I said.

"Well, Lucile, you're a good kid. It's been nice meeting you. I guess I'll see you around."

"Oh, Christ, don't say that," I said. He winked at me. It gave him some trouble. Looked more like a spastic blink. Then he took a business card from the holder on the desk. He said, "For my collection." After a brief search for a pocket, he tucked it inside the waistband of his sweat suit and walked out.

When he was gone I said, "Oh, phew!" And that didn't cover the half of it. I was back to the shitty beginning — no money and soon no motorcycle — and it was a huge relief. Come to think of it, I never got my twenty-five bucks from that damn dwarf so I was behind in the game. Still, I was ecstatic.

I had an hour till close and I decided to celebrate a little. I slapped a "Back in 2 min." sign on the door and jogged to

75

the mini-market. Picked up a tall beer and a bag of chips. I also bought one of those single serving vitamin packs. It made me feel better about my eating habits. The Korean guy stapled my bag shut again so I couldn't pop the beer in the store. I had been branded.

Back at the bookstore, I put my feet up on the desk. The cat ambled over and I gave it a couple potato chips. It sat chewing and nodding its head and spraying crumbs around. I poured a little beer into my hand and held it cupped under the cat's mouth. The cat sniffed and then backed up a couple paces. "Smart cat," I said. I lapped the beer off my palm.

I picked up the phone and dialed the Ticketmaster number again. Stuffed a handful of chips into my face. Said, "Cat, I love chips!" I decided I would call my sister after I got off with Ticketmaster. Paul could hold back a bit on my paycheck to cover the charges. It would be nice to talk to her. Just talk about boring things.

A skinny guy came in the store. I stashed the beer under the desk. "Hi!" I said. He nodded to me and set his backpack down near me and started in on the Fiction section. The type of guy who will read every title A through Z and maybe discover one book.

The hold music ended. "This is Tony at Ticketmaster, how may I help?"

"Oh," I said. "Do you sell rolls of tickets?" I was feeling giddy. Lighthearted.

"I'm sorry?" said Tony.

"If I wanted to have a raffle, like to raffle off some ice cream or some old shoes, do you sell rolls of tickets for that?"

"No," said Tony. "We sell concert tickets."

"So if I was going to have a concert, like in my backyard, you could sell me a bunch of tickets to use?"

"We sell individual tickets to major concerts, ma'am. We are not a ticket wholesaler."

"Oh," I said. He seemed on the verge of hanging up. "Wait! Don't hang up!" I said it so loud the browser gave me a dirty look.

"Yeah?" said Tony.

"I need the dates and locations of all the Phish concerts in California, starting today." Tony put me on hold again while he called the information up on the computer.

The browser in the store held up a book and said, "How much is this book?" I told him that all the books were priced on the upper right-hand corner of the first page. A moment later he held up another book. A crappy mass market paperback. "How much is this book?" he asked.

77

"Fifty bucks," I said. The browser stared at the paperback in his hands, turning it over and over.

Tony came back on the line and started to drone out dates and places. I told him to wait a second while I got something to write on. The browser asked, "Why's it so valuable?" I pointed at the phone to show him I wasn't in a position to explain. The phone made a clicking sound, indicating that there was another call coming in. I said, "Tony, that's my other line, can you hold on a second?" He grumbled an "all right" and I hit the flash button.

"Bitter Muse Bookstore?" I said.

"It's the wrong book." It was the dwarf talking. I could recognize the voice now.

"What are you talking about?" I said.

"You gave us the wrong book. You thought we wouldn't notice? That you made a switch?"

"I don't . . . what do you mean? It's got the inscription . . . you saw . . ."

"It's fake!" said the dwarf. "You're in trouble." Then another voice chimed in in the background.

"Who are you talking to?" it asked the dwarf. It was the same background voice as before. The Joke Man, I assumed.

"I'm talking to her," said the dwarf. "I'm telling her how she's in a lot of trouble."

"You don't tell her over the phone! You go there directly! YOU GO THERE!" I heard a thwack, and the dwarf yelped. "Now hang up that phone and let's get going!"

"I'll see you soon," said the dwarf.

78   "Don't say that! Just hang up the phone!" Sound of a receiver being slammed home. Nothing.

I looked at the phone. Held on to it with both hands and looked at it. I said, "Oh . . . my . . . God. . . ." I was half laughing. "Oh my God." I hung up the phone. Then I pushed it away from me. When I pushed it, the receiver fell off and I heard a tiny Tony voice saying "Hello? Hello? I'm still holding." I hung up the receiver again.

I stood up and looked all around me. "Okay," I said. "Okay." The browser approached me.

"So why is this book—"

"I'm closing the store right now," I said. I grabbed my backpack and searched for my keys. "You have to leave. I'm closing up." Started putting on Debi's leather jacket. Hit the "no sale" key on the register, took out all the big bills and stuffed them in my pocket.

"It says on your door that you're open until seven," said the browser.

"It's an EMERGENCY!" I yelled. "LET'S GO!"

"Don't get that tone with me," he said. He planted his feet like he was ready to hang around a couple hours on principle.

"Oh Christ," I said. "You're going to fight me on this?"

"Well," he said, "you be nice. That's all I want."

"My mother is dying," I said. "She's dying as we speak she's dying in a hospital in a terrible accident she's bleeding all over and I have to see her."

"I don't believe you." He stood with his hands on his hips. One hand held the book he had asked me about. "I heard you asking about a concert. You just want to close up early to go to a concert. That's not fair."

"Take the fifty-dollar book," I said.

"That would be dishonest," he said. "Besides, I found a price that says it's only a dollar twenty-five." I shouldered my backpack and put on my helmet.

"In that case," I said, "I'm leaving and I'm locking the door behind me. You can spend the fucking night and READ EVERY GODDAMN BOOK IN THE GOD-DAMN STORE!" I walked toward the door and flipped the light switch rapidly on and off a couple times. Jangled my keys. "THIS IS IT!" I said. "IN OR OUT!" I went out the door and began to close it. He grabbed his bag and skittered past me, still holding the paperback. I locked the door and jumped on the motorcycle. It started on the third try.

6

I went straight to Scott's place. They passed me a block away from the store. The Joke Man driving the big Caddie. The dwarf kneeling next to him in the front seat. Holding the dash. If his tongue was out, he would have looked just like one of those car-happy mutts, out for a Saturday spin. I shoved down the sun visor on my helmet. They weren't looking in my direction.

I took side streets up to Laurel Canyon on the chance that they might start driving around the boulevards for me after they saw I had skipped the store. I was going too fast for my skill level and I almost ran over an Orthodox Jewish kid. He said, "Hey, hey, hey!"

"Sorry," I said. He was all shaken up. He said, "Oh yeah? Oh *yeah?*"

After that, I calmed down a little. Stopped at stop signs. They weren't going to find me. Not right away.

I tried to make sense of my unbelievable predicament.

The book I gave back to them had seemed identical with the one the dwarf sold me in the first place. For a second, I wondered if the Joke Man wasn't looking for a different book entirely. A fantastic mix-up. But then, the dwarf had said they recognized the book as a fake. They were looking for *The Cruise of the Snark* all right. Just not that *Cruise of the Snark*.

As I was pulling into Scott's driveway, I realized that I had made a mistake. I should have headed straight for the beach — straight for Timmy. He had pulled a switch on me, the lanky two-faced son of a bitch. No wonder he had spent so long with his signatures guy. Good forgery takes time.

I got off the bike mad as hell and threw the helmet as hard as I could against the ground. Jesus, I had been stupid. "You fuck!" I said. "Mister fucking trust me nice guy fuck!" Scott's neighbor across the street was watering her five blades of grass and looked up at me, clearing her throat noisily.

"Excuse me?" she said.

I opened my mouth to say something. But I was at a total loss. Just headed into Scott's house, slamming the door behind me. As long as I was here, I needed to take a little time to get hold of myself. And I needed someone to keep me from falling, falling apart.

Scott lay asleep on the couch in front of the TV. Nellie stood on a chair in the dining area between the living room and the kitchen, pushing her Barbie doll through a stack of chocolate donuts. A couple of glow-in-the-dark Band-Aids drooped from her finger. When she saw me she said, "Oh!" and got down off her chair. She ran over and held my leg with one arm. With the other, she held up donut-trapped Barbie.

"Kiss Barbie!" she said. "Then you'll have a chocolate kiss."

"Let go, Nellie," I said. I pulled away and went to slap Scott on the bottom of his feet.

"Then you'll have a chocolate kiss!" squealed Nellie. I slapped Scott hard.

"No, Nellie," he said.

"Scott," I said. "Get up." He growled and rolled onto his stomach. I knelt by his head and parted the hair over his ear. He smelled like cigarette smoke. "SCOTT!"

"Oh, shit!" He sat up, grabbing his ear. "You broke my eardrum. You broke my frigging eardrum." Nellie jumped onto the couch next to him. Donut crumbs flying off Barbie like leprous skin.

"Kiss Barbie," she said to Scott. She shoved donut Barbie in his face.

"Scott," I said.

"Kiss Barbie!"

Scott stood up and backed away from us. Staggered backward like he had an arrow through his gut.

"What is happening? What the hell is going on? What do you all want from me?" And I realized that I had been ready to spill my guts to Scott for a little sympathy. But I didn't really want to bring him into it. For one thing, I tend to handle matters on my own. And I didn't want to feel responsible for Scott or anyone else getting mixed up in my business. For another, he was useless.

"I've got to use your phone," I said. I was better now. Contained.

"That's what all that was about? You never ask if you can use it." I walked into the kitchen. "You just use it!" he called after me.

"KISS BAR-BEEE!" Nellie roared.

I dialed 911 and the operator picked up and asked the nature of my emergency.

I said, "Yeah, hi. There's a bookstore I really hate. I'm really pissed off at this place and I'm going to burn it down or something. It's called Bitter Muse Bookstore and I'm going to burn it down or something, just so you are aware."

"What was that name?"

"Bitter Muse Bookstore," I said. "On Third Street. You better send someone over to watch the place because I'm on my way there now."

"So what exactly are you saying?" said the operator.

"Just that you better watch out! Bitter Muse! I'm not kidding!" I hung up so they wouldn't have time to trace the call.

Scott came in the kitchen and got a natural soda from the refrigerator and started poking around in the closets. He wore cut-off pajama bottoms as shorts.

"You bringing the bike back?" he asked.

"No," I said. I took the soda from him and drank about half.

"Nellie, where does Mommy keep the Dustbuster?" Scott yelled over his shoulder.

I asked Scott, "Does Debi still own a gun?"

"Ayshhhh!" Scott said. He put his index finger up to his lips. Pursed up like a librarian. "Nellie's scared of guns. She doesn't know about it."

"I need it."

"What is going on with you?" He cocked his head and leaned toward me.

"I just need to borrow it. It's for a costume party. I'll return it when I return the bike."

83

"No way," he said. "Not if you were the last person on earth."

He finally found it in a shoe box on the top shelf of her closet. Behind a stack of *Playboy* magazines.

"In *her* closet?" I asked, indicating the magazines.

"You know, for the hairstyles," said Scott.

"Uh huh," I said. Scott unzipped the gun's soft carrying case and removed it gently. It was one of those flat black jobs. Pretty small.

"What am I doing?" he said. He bounced his hand slowly up and down to feel the weight. The way people always do with guns. "I'm going to hell."

84

"What kind is it?" I asked.

"It's got to say somewhere," he said. He turned it over. "Oh. Colt. I think those are supposed to be pretty good. Don't they have a factory in Connecticut?"

"Is it loaded?" I asked.

"Yeah, they definitely do. I drove past it once when we were at school."

"Scott, is it loaded?"

"I don't know," said Scott. "I never deal with it. Maybe there's a booklet somewhere."

"Oh Christ," I said. I looked in the shoe box to see if there were any bullets lying around. A clip, as they say. Nothing but some old tissue paper. I took the gun from Scott and checked out the safety. Clicked it off, then on again. That, at least, was obvious. I zipped the gun back into the case and put it toward the bottom of my backpack.

"Holster?" I asked.

Scott said, "Who are you, Harry Connick Jr.?"

"Harry Callahan?" I said. "Dirty Harry?"

"Right," he said. "Who are you, him?"

"You're high as a monkey," I said. But I was lucky he was. If he had been straight, my chances of conning for the gun would have been squat. And I really wanted it along for the ride. For when I met up with Timmy. Or whoever. It would cut through the bullshit. Give me a little control over the situation. And help put a finish to this nonsense.

"I have to borrow a pair of Debi's jeans," I said.

"Oh, don't do that," said Scott. "C'mon. Haven't you taken enough? I mean, you just take and take."

"Scott," I said, "she has thirty pairs of jeans. That's too many jeans. And it's cold riding the bike in shorts at night." Scott mumbled something and left the room. I found a pair of jeans that fit me. Debi's weight yo-yos up and down so she had a variety of sizes. I also took some socks and a long-sleeve shirt that I put over Timmy's T-shirt.

Scott walked me out. Looked over the bike to see if I had done any damage yet.

"You know the gas gauge doesn't work," he said. "You should just fill it up because I have no idea how much is in there."

"Great," I said. He stuck his hands down the front of his shorts. They had no pockets and he's a real pockets type.

"Hey," he said, "I know you don't like to talk about stuff. About your problems." He pulled his hands out of his shorts long enough to make quotation marks in the air with his fingers when he said "problems." "But if you want to . . ."

"Yeah, I know," I said. "But no thanks."

He had been a psychology major. "Well, whatever you're gonna do, don't be stupid about it."

"It's just a costume party," I said. He grabbed me and sort of gave me a hug but I backed away from it. "C'mon, I'm late," I said. I got on the bike and pulled the helmet down low over my forehead. He stood, his hands down his shorts again. Shoulders hunched as though a cold wind was blowing down through the hills instead of the eighty-five-degree Santa Anas.

As I was revving the bike, I said, "Where's Cox?"

"I think he ran away," said Scott.

86 It was past closing time at Timmy's store so I headed for his house. The place stood dark and empty. I thought about breaking in and looking around for the book, but I had a hunch I wouldn't find it there. Timmy would have it with him. And I felt certain that he would try to unload it as quickly as possible. Pocket a couple thousand and play dumb with me. Or hope that no one had noticed the switch in the first place.

I rode over to his store. Turning my head every mile or so to check out the cars behind me. They all looked like Caddies. My helmet was too big and kept going askew so I would jerk my head to reposition it. Like novice royalty.

When I wasn't imagining the Joke Man directly on my tail, I pictured him finding my apartment. Busting up some stuff looking for the book. At least I didn't own anything I cared about. I was more worried about the bookstore. If anything happened to old Bitter Muse, I figured I would just about explode.

Timmy's store was called Doolittle's, I guess for Dr. Doolittle, though as far as I knew, Timmy had not had a role in that particular kiddy flick. Doolittle's sat right off the main drag between Venice and Santa Monica. I had been there a couple times just browsing. During the day, they hang a bunch of colorful handmade kites out front and that attracts the tourists. In addition to rare books, they sell the kites. The store was bigger than Bitter Muse, but still tiny by the new mega-bookstore standards.

As expected, the kites were down, the lights off. I pressed my face to the glass and saw a glow coming from the back, **87** from behind a large bookshelf. I knew that back there were a couple of desks — a sort of open office area. They might leave that light on to keep the book thieves away. Or it might be Timmy. I worried that he would spook if he saw me. I pushed the bike a little farther down the block. Then I pounded hard on the front window, bolted across the street, and squatted behind a bush.

A figure popped out from behind the bookshelf and walked toward the front of the store. He wore shorts and he had a huge droopy mustache. And he definitely wasn't Timmy.

I walked back across the street, waving at him. I motioned him toward the door where he pointed at a closed sign. I shook my head, yelled so that the sound would travel through the glass.

"I'm Timmy Harris's cousin!" I said. "Is he here?"

German Kurt shook his head back and forth. "Ya, ya, he iss not here!" he yelled.

"Please!" I yelled. "I have to go to the bathroom!" Kurt looked me up and down. His mustache twitched back and forth as he thought it over. "I came straight here from San Francisco to surprise Timmy!" He slowly withdrew a large key chain from his pocket and unlocked the door. As he ushered me in, I said, "Oh thanks so much. You must be Kurt. I've talked to you on the phone."

"Ya, ya," he said. "I sink I remember. I look at you through the vindo and I sink you look like Tim, you must be hiss cousin."

"Oh come on," I said. "You probably think all of us Americans look alike." He laughed a big beer hall laugh.

"Ya, ya, zat issn't true!" he said. We stood in the half-dark.

"The store looks great," I said.

"Ya," he said, "here iss some light." He flipped a couple switches by the door and I covered my eyes for a moment. "Come," he said, "I show you vere iss za restroom." I followed him to the rear of the store. The place was all done up like a Dickensian library. Hardwood floors with old Oriental carpets thrown around. Faded velvet armchairs. End tables with casually stacked books. And somehow the kites blended in okay, too. I heard a Hollywood set decorator had designed the place. Timmy really understood the way that this town feeds on fantasy. He understood how to sell old books.

As we passed the office area, a young blonde stood up from one of the desk chairs with half a sandwich in her hand.

"Oh, ya, zis iss Tsandy," said Kurt.

"It's really nice to meet you," she said. She spoke with the voice of a beauty pageant contestant. A runner-up Miss Jacksonville.

"She iss just bring me somesing to eat."

"That's so incredibly great!" I said. Kurt pointed out the bathroom and, as long as I was in there, I used it. When I emerged, he stood up from his desk picnic and Sandy put down her sandwich selfconsciously.

"Please go ahead," I said. "Eat while it's hot."

"Oh, it's just sandwiches," said Sandy. "It's not hot."

"So, Kurt, do you know where I can find Timmy? I really can't wait to see him. Last time I saw him, he gave me this shirt!" I lifted up Debi's shirt so they could see the T-shirt underneath.

"Oh, ya," said Kurt, and Sandy said, "Ooh."   **89**

"Vell, you know you haff za very bad timing. I know zat Tim iss avay but he does not tell me vere. He goes only for two days. He vill call me but he doss not say vere he iss."

"Oh fuck," I said. Sandy giggled. "Are you serious?" I said. "He left no indication at all where he was going?"

"He vanted some time to redisscover himself," said Kurt.

"I like to go to the desert for that," said Sandy. "Maybe he's in the desert."

"Oh," I said. "That's a good thought." He wasn't in the desert. He was pawning the book somewhere. Maybe even in the city. "Um, Karl . . ." I said.

"Kurt," said Kurt.

"Ay, I'm sorry," I said. "Kurt . . ."

"Ya, Tim doss za same sing," said Kurt. "You must be related!"

"Say, Kurt, part of the reason I wanted to see Timmy was that I'm doing a paper for school about modern-day book collectors — mostly people who collect Jack London. And I was wondering if you guys deal with anyone who's a big Jack London collector." Kurt was still standing as though at attention. But his eyes would drift down to his sandwich every so often.

"I'm in school, too," said Sandy.

"You vould haff to ask Tim because, you know, I cannot give such information."

"Well can you just tell me if there is a Jack London collector in Los Angeles?"

"No," said Kurt. Sandy started to dip into a bag of chips but the bag crackled and she withdrew her hand quickly. Like it had been burned.

"No you can't tell me or no there isn't one?"

"No I cannot tell you."

"Shit," I said. Sandy giggled. "Please excuse my profanity, Sandy," I said.

"Oh I don't mind," she said. "Sometimes I do it too." She shrugged her shoulders and crinkled her eyes as if she was the most full-of-mischief gal in the world. "Though, usually when I'm alone."

If I had thought Kurt was holding back on me, I might have tried waving the gun around a little. But his story made sense. Timmy would want to disappear until the book had also. He couldn't risk leaving Kurt with a forwarding address. I decided I would have to go break into Timmy's place after all and look for a clue to where he had gone.

"I guess I better go find my other friends and see if I can stay with them tonight," I said. "Boy this is really too bad.

Timmy's always been unreliable. I bet he's a lousy boss, too, huh, Kurt?"

"Oh ya, you know . . ."

"But if he didn't know you were coming . . ." said Sandy.

"Oh, Sandy," I said, "you're right! You're right. I'm too judgmental." I reshouldered my backpack. "Well, have a nice dinner you guys!" I said. Kurt followed me to the door.

He said, "I don't know eff Tim vould like zat Tsandy iss here," he said. "But she luffs to eat vith za books around her."

"Don't worry, Kurt," I said. "I'll only tell him if I actually talk to him." Kurt swung the door in and held it open for me. A big wooden frame job with a glass center, much like the door at Bitter Muse. And, as at Bitter Muse, they used the glass center of the door to post the store hours along with some notices. One of them grabbed my attention. I recognized it from the one that had come in the mail. The Antiquarian Book Fair in Las Vegas. Starting tomorrow. Dealers would be there, and collectors. The big spenders. I stuck my arm around the door and ripped off the notice.

"Oh, hey," said Kurt.

"There was a bug on it," I said. "Wouldn't Timmy be at this?"

"Oh you know he goes most years but he tells me today on za phone zat he von't go. Zat eff somevun vants to know, he must haff a qviet veekend to redisscover himself. To be alone vit . . . hiss . . . soughts."

That cinched it. The bastard was in Vegas.

7

A couple of blocks from Doolittle's I passed a diner and I made a U-turn and pulled into the parking lot. I needed to sit and think a minute. And since it looked like I would be riding to Vegas, I needed some coffee. The place was pretty empty so I took a booth to myself. I ordered coffee from an old waitress in a pink uniform with a stuffed bunny pinned to the waist. She hobbled a little when she walked, but I'm sure she didn't need me to tell her that she was in the wrong profession.

I took off Debi's jacket and stretched out. A guy in the booth next to me was yakking on and on about something. I rubbed my temples and tried to concentrate a little. It was rare for me to sit down and really work my mind. Usually my aim was to distract it. Books were good for that. Alcohol did a nice job too. I didn't like thinking about my life too much. I had gotten used to feeling a little foggy. During my mother's death, I had started to get the idea that the air around me was heavier than it was around other people. Tight and heavy like one of those old orange life preservers. It dulled things. Gave them a dreamlike quality. If I pushed it, I could feel as if I was sleepwalking. *Somnambulate* was the word, if you felt like getting technical. To walk while asleep. It made things less essential. But that feeling was difficult to sustain if a dwarf and a giant geek were out to get you.

I thought about Timmy double-crossing me. It pissed me off but it destroyed me a little, too. I should have seen it at the store when he showed up with the book. He was acting. He wasn't even good at it anymore. Unfortunately, I had let all the moochiness blind me. My face against his neck and all that. I had let myself forget he was an actor.

The guy in the next booth was very loud. He was destroying my thought process. He kept jabbering on and on about a screenplay he was working on. I had a couple sips of coffee, which was weak. It was an uplifting story about a kid with MS who really wants to drive Monster Trucks. All the other Monster Truck kids make fun of him because of his MS and his parents tell him he can't do it but he's really dying to prove to everyone that he can be the greatest Monster Truck driver in the world. So he meets this guy — a former Monster Truck superstar who's now just a drunk working as the night watchman in a junkyard because, see, he ran over a kid by mistake once during a Monster Truck rally and he hasn't been able to get in a cab since — and the MS kid starts sneaking out at night and going to the junkyard and he and the old Monster Truck drunk start fooling around with parts and before they know it, they're building a Monster Truck out of different junked cars. And then one night the daughter of the owner of the junkyard comes out

93

there because she had a fight with her boyfriend (who's in with the bad Monster Truck crowd) and she starts helping them because it turns out that in addition to being pretty, she's also a great welder and together in a montage they make the Monster Truck even better. And the Monster Truck regional rally is coming up and this whole time the MS kid is overcoming his handicap and the old Monster Truck drunk is learning how to feel again —

"Shut up!" I turned around in the booth and yelled at the guy. I took the saucer from underneath my coffee cup — a heavy porcelain job — and waved it at him. "Shut up about those frigging Monster Trucks or I swear to God I will smash this saucer on you," I said. The dozen or so other people in the diner all got quiet. The young screenwriter and his friend just blinked at me in shock from behind their glasses. They both had glasses with tortoiseshell frames. After an uncomfortable silence, some wise guy sitting at the counter said something like, "Well, I guess it's time for *her* to switch to decaf." I swung my arm toward him and said, "You shut up too! That 'time to switch to decaf' joke — that's a terrible joke. Terrible. Everyone always says it and it's never funny." Then the old waitress appeared next to me and said, "Okay, honey, put the saucer down." I put the saucer down. "Do you want a piece of pie?" she asked. I shook my head. "Are you sure? It's on the house." The screenwriter guy in the next booth said, "What — you're giving her free pie? You should be kicking her out and giving me free pie!" And I picked up the saucer again. Pulled my arm back like I was ready to hurl it at him. He said "Ack!" and both he and his friend ducked under the table.

94

"Put it down," the waitress said to me, "or I *will* kick you out." I drank what was left of my coffee and I threw two bucks on the table and got my stuff together.

There was a gas station across the street and I stopped to fill up the bike. When I was paying for the gas, I asked the guy behind the counter if he knew how to get to Las Vegas. He said, "You buy a map."

"How about if I just look at a map?" I asked. And the guy moved his lips back and forth from one side of his face to the other and rolled his eyes around and then he said, "Yeah. Okay." I looked at the map. The Santa Monica Freeway east and then Route 15 all the way to Vegas. I figured it would take me at least half the night to get there and then I would still have to find Timmy, get the book, and come back. There was no way I would make it in time to open the bookstore in the morning, and that really pissed me off. I didn't feel good about the bookstore being closed during business hours. And I knew Paul would be very unhappy. I thought about calling Scott and asking if he would cover for me but that wasn't such a good idea. He'd have Nellie with him and he had never worked a cash register before. I couldn't talk him through everything over the phone. Then I thought of Mike, the boozer that I had replaced. He was a friend of Paul's and even though he made a lousy full-time employee, he would be all right for a day. He knew the routine. And he was not currently working.

I didn't feel sufficiently wired from the one weak cup of coffee I had had at the diner. The gas station was attached to a convenience store so I filled up a large Styrofoam cup with coffee and I added a packet of hot chocolate mix for the sugar benefit. Then a half-dozen creamers so it would cool off and I could drink it fast. I went to use the pay phone out by the street. Stood in that tepee of light with my back to the boulevard and got Mike's number from information. He picked up after four or five rings and I could tell right off he was drunk. He was one of those sloppy drunks, too. Slurring and weaving and loving everyone after only a couple shots.

"Mike," I said. "Hey Mike! It's Jill from the bookstore."

"Hey! Jill! Hey house my old replacement, you wacky pack. Hey you wanna go see this guy with me tonight? He plays guitar and makes up the funny stuff. From my building." Mike always made plans to go out but he rarely got past his front door. If you were supposed to meet him somewhere, you just showed up at his apartment instead.

"Mike," I said, "listen. Can you work tomorrow at the bookstore? Maybe not even the whole day. Just open up and hang around until I get there."

"Hey you know Paul fired me the last time I was there." Then he said, "Ow, don't do that, you nogoodnik. Hey, Jill, did you hear I got a Lassie dog?"

"Yeah, I heard you got a dog." I had heard from Paul how Mike and a friend of his went drunk to a mall one day and the friend talked him into buying a purebred collie at the pet store for $899.99. He was already behind on the payments.

"He keeps trying to . . . I don't know . . . round me up or — OW! — something."

"Mike," I said. "C'mon. You gotta do it. It's an emergency. Just open up and feed the cat and hang around until I get there."

"Ho ho ho, the cat!" said Mike. I forgot that he had a theory that the cat was plotting to kill him. Mike said, "He is clever, that one, but not as clever as I!"

"Are you gonna do it? I'll pay you for the whole day no matter when I get back." I figured he could use the dough to make a dog payment.

"Okay," he said. "I'll do it."

"Great." I could hear him wrestling with the dog. He said, "That's my butt. Not something to eat. It's my butt. Go away. Go find Richie or Billy or whoever."

"Hey Mike!"

"What?"

"When Paul calls, tell him I'm sorry and that it was an emergency and then, oh shit — you have to call first thing in the morning and find out the dates and places of all the Phish concerts in California so you can tell Paul. Call Ticketmaster first thing when you get to the store."

"Okay."

". . . And Mike!"

"What!"

"This is very important. Take down all the notices about the Antiquarian Book Fair. There's one on the door and on the bulletin board. Take them all down."

"Anthill Bookfarm," he said.

"No. The Antiquarian Book Fair."

"Paul doesn't like Phish, I don't think."

"You still have your key?"

"Uhhh yup."

"Great. You should go set your alarm right now. And write yourself a note and pin it to your shirt so you don't forget in the morning when you wake up. Write down the part about the Phish shows."

"That's actually a very good idea," he said. "Hey, Jill, let me tell ya something else. What I know now. We — I mean *all of us* — we need dogs. We *need* them." I hung up quick so he wouldn't get to talking. It was all right. He'd blame the disconnection on the government.

The coffee had cooled down quite a bit and I drank half the cup. Except for the cars going by, it was quiet. L.A. is a quiet place at night. All the noise happens behind closed doors. It's like living with a couple million agoraphobics.

I braced myself and dialed up the Joke Man. After a couple rings, an answering machine picked up. It took me by surprise. An electronic voice saying, "Please leave a message."

"Listen," I said, "um, I going to get your book back for you and I'll call as soon as I have it. I didn't know the other was a fake but I'll get the right one. There's going to be a guy working at the bookstore tomorrow and, you know, he wouldn't be there if he knew anything about this stuff so you should just leave him alone. . . . This is all my thing. I should have the book by tomorrow and I'll call you. So, um, bye."

I finished the rest of the coffee, threw the cup away, and got on the bike.

I made it out of the city fast. Traffic was light and I handled the freeway pretty well. I just kept a good distance between myself and the cars. Changed lanes as infrequently as possible. Talked myself through the rough parts. Once I got used to it, it was easier riding the bike at sixty-five than at thirty.

I figured I had a good chance of getting to Timmy before he sold the book because most of the major players would arrive in Vegas tonight and not start making the rounds until the book fair officially got under way in the morning. It drove me nuts that I hadn't inspected the book more closely when Timmy brought it by Bitter Muse. He must have had his own first edition lying around somewhere and had just added the fake inscription. And there must have been something about the original that made it worth Timmy's screwing me over. Not to mention that he would now be selling a stolen book, which was a major risk. If word **99** got out that the book was hot, some dealers would turn him in flat. He would have to find a buyer carefully, but he had the connections. And there were always collectors who got an extra thrill from owning something that they weren't supposed to.

I got past downtown and slowly began to leave behind the car dealerships and chain restaurants and motels that ooze away from Los Angeles like an old stain. The consumer no-man's-land before you hit the sticks. I passed Forest Lawn cemetery where a bunch of the great stars were buried, rotting side by side with the average Joes. I prefer cremation to burial. That way no one can spend nights thinking about you stuck under all that dirt. Lonely as hell.

I hadn't been out of the city — really out of the city — since I had arrived almost exactly a year ago. After my mother's funeral, I drove around the country for two and a half, three years with no particular destination in mind. I stopped in different towns, different cities. Waited tables. Answered telephones. Helped out on an artichoke farm. Worked the parking lot at a national forest. Did research for a guy trying to get an orthopedic foam pillow business off the ground. Nothing lasted more than a couple months. I thought it would help. It didn't. When I reached L.A., I got into a big crackup right off the bat and totaled the car. There was a bicycle shop next to the garage where they towed the wreck, so I bought a bicycle and rode around until I found an apartment. Later, I looked up Scott. Got a job at the bookstore. It had been the same thing ever since. The routine was good for me and I was relatively content. Before all this business began.

100

Once on Route 15, the traffic really fell off. Mostly tractor trailers. Some of the drivers rolled down their windows and whistled at me or tried to make conversation. Anything to pass the time on the road. Lone women on motorcycles were a rare sight. I didn't pay much attention to them. The helmet kept tipping back off my head so I had to push my chin down to my chest and use the wind to keep it in place. It made it harder to see where I was going. When there were no other cars around, I rode the lane divider. Miles and miles of connect-the-dots.

After about an hour and a half, I stopped to pee at a rest area. There were two gas stations and two restaurants. Hard to tell if the place called itself a town. I pulled into the parking lot of the nearest restaurant and went inside. A handful of truckers were eating eggs. A young couple drank coffee and shared a piece of pie and a cigarette. Looked at the walls instead of each other. She said, "But if you thought that all along, why didn't you say something?" She was eyeing a buffalo painting over his head while she said it.

I used the bathroom and then stood in front of the hand dryer for a couple minutes, smacking the button whenever the thing shut off. The desert got cold at night and I had no hand protection. I gave every part of my body a turn at the vent. While I was holding my right leg up there, one of the waitresses came in.

"It sure is cold in the desert at night," I said.

"I know," she said. She was a plump Hispanic girl. She withdrew an eye pencil from the pocket of her apron and pulled down her lower lids to line the top of them. On the wall next to the mirror, someone had written, "Jesus, I love you so much it hurts."

101

As I walked back to my bike, I saw a guy with a cast on his arm hanging around, smoking a cigarette. He approached me and asked if I would help him lift his infirm mother out of the car. He gestured toward the far end of the parking lot. She couldn't get out by herself and he was having trouble lifting her because of his cast. She wanted to move from the front seat to the back seat or the back seat to the front seat or something. He wiped his face with the sleeve of his jacket. Sweating in fifty-degree weather. I said, "Get the hell away from me."

He said, "W-won't you help me? It will just take a minute, a second."

I said, "Listen, bub. You look to me a lot like a serial killer." I said this over my shoulder as I hot-footed my way to the bike. "And," I said, "the last thing I need right now is to be serial killed." I jumped on and got it started. I had parked so that I would not have to back up.

"I'm not a serial killer," he whined. He began to jog after me. "I'm a minister! A Presbyterian minister!"

I said, "That's what a serial killer would say!" I accelerated quickly and left him far behind.

The next couple hours on the road passed without incident. I didn't think about much. Just concentrated on not crashing the bike. It didn't occur to me to develop any sort of plan for getting the book back. For a while, I remembered how it felt to rake leaves. There were very few leaf-raking opportunities in Los Angeles. It was something I missed. I could rake for hours. Make big piles and jump in them and throw the leaves in the air. Say, "Whoopee." If it was overcast and drizzling, that was even better. They stuck to your face, your arms. Deep inside the pile you could find a dry place to hide away. Make your breathing small while the others ran around. Where is she? Where is she? When I was done, my mother would make hot chocolate. She would look out the window and say, "Isn't it wonderful, all of it? God, it's just great. What a gift." The thing about my mother, she loved living.

I started to feel sleepy and I had to pee again so I pulled over to the side of the road and squatted by some tumbleweed. When I was done, I walked around stretching and jumping up and down and slapping my hands together. The temperature had dropped way down. Debi's clothes kept me pretty warm but my hands were freezing into a permanent clawlike position. I dug around in my backpack to see if I had any gloves. Pretty certain that I did not. But that backpack is so full of junk that I'm frequently surprised. Once I found a stethoscope in there. I have no idea where it came from.

I didn't find gloves but I pulled out the gun and took a look at it. I used the headlight of the motorcycle to see. Hunched over in case a car came by. I had never shot a gun before and I figured I should try it once so I could look like I knew what I was doing, even if I only intended using it for threat purposes. Also, if the gun was empty, this was a good way to find out.

Beyond the road, a dirt sea crawled off into the dark. Not much going on there but scrub. No danger of hitting something inadvertently. The stars would give me enough light to shoot by, so I walked away from the highway. There was a wire fence ten yards out, and I ducked through it. Cars and trucks passed infrequently. I shuffled along, weaving between the cactus and the scrub. Holding the gun out and down. The way you're supposed to walk with scissors. Then I stopped. I stood there but I didn't shoot right away because I felt too small to move. A tiny piece of scrap on the universal landscape. "Fuck you," I said. "You think I care?"

I clicked off the safety and looked back at the road. Waited for a truck to pass. The noise of the shot worried me. I didn't want to attract the attention of some cop taking a snooze around the next bend. Or any curious motorist, for that matter. I aimed straight out using both hands to hold the gun, like every good cop does on their prime-time beat. Right before firing, I started coughing as loud as I could to muffle the sound just in case someone was coming. Then I squeezed the trigger. When the gun went off, I staggered backward but I didn't fall. Not that there was that much recoil. I just wasn't as ready as I thought I was. The noise filled up the night like a scream from a neighbor's apartment. Unexpected and terrible. And when it was over, you passed it off as a dream. That gun could do a lot of damage. They don't seem to do much damage in the movies. A thousand bullets and maybe one hits home. This was different. A genuine shock. I stood in the dark a second, listening to my heart. I put the barrel of the gun in my mouth. My teeth clicked against the metal. It tasted like chicken.

Back at the bike, I took Debi's socks off my feet and put them on my hands. Then I was rolling again.

At the Nevada border, I passed a pocket of casinos along the highway. A fake mining town, a show boat. They were enormous. Lit up like prisons. On four-story-high electronic signs, words burst open and then faded. "Prime Rib Dinner $6.95!" One place advertised that they had the world's tallest roller coaster. It seems like every roller coaster in the country is the tallest or oldest or scariest or made from the most wood. This coaster had running lights, so I could see it looping through the dark like a low-hanging constellation. It didn't look very tall.

I had been to Vegas once before, on my cross-country trip, and I wasn't thrilled with the idea of being back there. It was all that carpet. It depressed the hell out of me. I didn't mind the old ladies with the big yellow hair plugging their rainy-day money into the slots like it was their job; I didn't mind the comb-over club at the crap tables; or the overweight couples in matching golf shirts waiting for someone to restock the shrimps at the buffet; or the kids hemorrhaging snot into the swimming pools. I wasn't bothered by the fake-o rainstorms and volcanoes and trips down the Nile and talking Roman statues, and I could even get over the pervasive smell of overcooked beef — Christ, truckloads of the stuff arriving day and night, a carnage caravan, ready to reward the winners and console the losers with all the meat they could eat. But that carpet. Miles and miles of it in happy wacky colors and patterns. Reds and purples and greens and golds. Star patterns and crown patterns and jungle patterns and fans and big bloody flowers blooming along the border. It drove me nuts to look at it and to feel it beneath my feet. To imagine all the people who had walked across it and spilled stuff on it and lost things forever against its great sucking surface.

I did not like that carpet.   **105**

8

It took another half hour to reach Vegas. I saw the halo of light from miles away. And the single perpendicular ray from the Luxor hotel, skewering the place to the desert like a giant beetle run through with a push-pin. I took the first exit for the Strip and passed the airport and some construction. The big hotels loomed ahead, each with a thousand-plus rooms, and I thought for a minute how peachy it would be to stretch out on a lumpy anonymous bed, punch a couple pillows up over my ears, and sleep for ten hours. But that wasn't an option.

I pulled into a gas station by the Luxor and parked away from the pumps. Even at this hour, everything on the street was go-go-going. People were out walking from one casino to the next. Feeling lucky or unlucky. Jingling coin cups. Wearing Bermuda shorts with sweatshirts that advertised what they had seen on previous vacations.

I sat on the bike and took another look at the flyer for the book fair. The fair would open at 9:00 A.M. in the Las Vegas Convention Center. I didn't own a watch and I had no idea what time it was. Somewhere around 3:00 A.M. was my best guess. A drunk guy walked past me — danced, really — singing the Muhammad Ali song. "Muhammad, Muhammad Ali, he floats like a butterfly and stings like a bee. They call him the black Superman, I'm Aaaa . . . aaa . . . lee, catch me if you can dododo dododo dodo dodo do." I said, "Hey, fella!" He stopped and looked at me. A goomba in a tuxedo. His jacket and shirt were open and his red bow tie was hanging out of his pants pocket like the rip cord of a parachute.

"Oh, hey! Hey, how are you!" he said. He walked over my way.

"I'm good," I said. "Um, do you know what time it is?"

"Hey, this is *Las Vegas!*" he said. "There's no time in *Las Vegas!* You know, I'm glad I ran into you," he said. He put a hand on my shoulder. It was conspiratorial but he also used it to steady himself. "I really — I wanted to give you a bigger tip. I felt like you deserved a bigger one." He dug into his pocket and pulled out a roll of bills. "This is a little something extra," he said. He peeled off a fifty and tucked it into the pocket of my jacket. "Buy yourself something nice, hmmm?"

"Okay," I said. "Thanks." Maybe Vegas was my town after all.

"We all deserve something nice once in a while," he said.

"That's true," I said.

"And I'm gonna come back and sit at your table again 'cause you're my luck charm," he said. "In fact, I wonder — I bet I could fit you in my pocket."

"No, you couldn't," I said.

"I bet I could," he said. "You're so little and cute. You're pocket-size."

"Okay," I said. I started the bike, but I had parked facing a curb and I had to back up to get out. The guy took hold of one of my elbows.

"C'mon," he said, "don't you wanna be my little pocket-size girl?" He was having a jolly time. He sang a little tune. "Hey, Pocket! Whadda ya say! You're my pock pock pocket-size girl!" He shook my elbow back and forth and the movement was so sudden and forceful that it threw me off balance. It pulled me down sideways and the bike landed on top of me and stalled.

"Well that really hurt," I said. I got out from under the bike. My leg and hip throbbed, but I could tell nothing was broken.

"I'm sorry," he said. He tried to help me up. "Are you hurt?"

"You severed my spinal column," I said, "you banana head." I brushed the gutter junk from my jeans. A woman approached us. She had been sitting on a piece of cardboard on the sidewalk nearby. She looked pretty strung out. Wore ratty corduroys and a Care Bears T-shirt. She said, "I just want you to know that I saw him going after you if you need a witness. I'll tell it in court that he made the bike fall on you. It was like he assaulted you with that bike."

"Hey," he said, "What's this? We were kidding around. I didn't make that bike fall on her. Here," he said. He bent over and picked up the bike. "Good as new," he said. The kickstand was up and when he released the bike, it began to fall again but I threw my weight against it and put the stand down.

"Uh huh, you did assault her," said the woman. "You better just give her some more of that money so she doesn't sue your ass." The guy looked back and forth from the woman to me. Then he got out his roll of dough and pulled off a hundred bucks and held it out to me.

"Well," he said. "I don't think I did nothin' wrong but here's some good faith money."

"Uh uh, you better give her more than that," said the strung-out woman.

"You buzz off!" said the drunk guy.

"Okay, you threatening *me* the *witness?*" said the woman. She pointed at herself with both hands. "What are you, begging to go to jail?"

"No but . . ." The guy sighed and peeled off a fifty and looked at the woman. The woman shook her head and the guy peeled off another fifty and the woman nodded. "Lookit that wad," she said. "You're gettin' off easy. Now you can just go away somewhere. Go lie down." The guy walked off down the street. Then he turned and yelled, "I'm going but I'm not going to lie down, I'm going to go do whatever I WANT!" He shouted a couple unenthusiastic bars of the Muhammad Ali song. Then he stopped. Just kept walking with his shoulders slumped.

I was holding the bills in my fist like a bridal bouquet. I guess luck hustles around this town so wildly that it shows up in all the wrong places. It made me a little nervous. I didn't want to use up any of my good fortune prematurely — I would need all of it to find Timmy.

"Not bad," said the woman in the Care Bears T-shirt. I handed her the hundred and one of the fifties. She put the money in the front pocket of her corduroys. "You didn't have to give me *that* much," she said. "I was gonna take fitty percent but I'm not complaining."

"Do you know what time it is?" I asked. She shrugged.

"Feels like it's around three," she said.

The Convention Center would be locked up tight and Timmy could be anywhere. I thought about trying the hotels right around the Convention Center. But Timmy was a gambler, which meant he had been to Las Vegas before. Many times before. He wouldn't stay in a place for convenience, he would stay at his regular hangout. So I had to ask myself, if I was a goof like Timmy, where would I want to go? I looked down the Strip, and the Excalibur caught my eye. A giant cartoon castle for kids of all ages. It seemed like a good place to start.

I left the bike where it was and walked toward the Excalibur. On a nearby corner, two guys were handing out pamphlets. I took one because the sooner they got rid of them, the sooner they could go home. As I crossed the street, I flipped through it. A couple glossy pages of naked women with pink stars and bars added to cover their nipples and genitalia. Phone numbers and captions like, "I'm Rachel, call me. I'm available anytime for V-ROOM service." There were Missy and Sissy the bad-girl roommates. Busty Betsy. Latitia the Wild Woman. And Jim. Discarded pamphlets littered the sidewalk. I put mine in the pocket of my coat.

The Excalibur looked pretty good at night. The spot-lights made the white towers and the primary-colored tower-tops seem new. Like candy. From one of those towers, a big plastic Merlin cast his gotta-gamble spell on everyone who went inside. In front of the entrance, a guy in an aging jester's outfit was hopping up and down, trying to stay warm. He wore black high-top sneakers. Socks with reindeer on them. The rest was jester. His jester's hat had a rip, and some white cotton stuffing was easing its way out of the crack. He helped people lurch their way into taxis. One guy he helped looked a little weepy. But he held his head very erect.

I walked in and the noise of the slots hit me. And the colors. And the carpet. The Excalibur has fake stained-glass windows running along the ceiling. Similar pattern as the carpet. It was killing me.

111

To the left, I saw a block-long reception desk shaped like a castle turret and I walked over to it. There were only two people working and they were both busy. I waited for one of them to finish up with a Japanese couple checking out. The Japanese man was trying to tell the desk clerk that their room had smelled bad and that they shouldn't have to pay the full amount. The clerk was saying, "Yes, I understand that, Mr. . . . ." He referred to a piece of paper in front of him. ". . . Mig-, Mcrow-, Mr. Migron-, Mignowi? Mr. Mignowi. But what you have to understand is . . . ."

I turned to face the casino action. Most of the people playing the slots this time of night were women in their forties and fifties. Smoking a cigarette and drinking a drink. There was so much color and noise and fake armor and fake vines and smoke that it was hard to really see anyone. They got lost. The Japanese couple finished up and walked sadly toward the exit, shaking their heads. They must have been thinking that, in their country, things were different.

I turned to the reception desk. I put my elbows on the desk and leaned forward and smiled winningly at the desk clerk.

"Hi," I said. "How are you this morning?" He had some acne scars on his face and I could see that he used pancake makeup to try and cover them up. It gave him a real wax-museum look. He took a slurpy sip from a coffee mug.

"Yes," he said, "and what can I do for you this evening?"

"Well," I said, "I sort of messed up. Real bad. My fiancé was trying to surprise me with a trip to come here and I started a fight with him — well, you don't want the whole story. So. His name is Timmy Harris."

112

"I can tell you if he's here but I can't give out his room number," said the wax man. He said this while he tap tap tapped on the computer keys. Over in the slots area, a young woman squealed with laughter. She was sitting on some guy's lap and he was jiggling his knees up and down so that her whole body jounced around. He said, "Woooo! Woohooo!" and her limbs and head jerked in all directions and then her breasts leapt out over her scoop-neck T-shirt and she squealed again and tried to stuff them back in. He kept jiggling her while she was stuffing them and then she yelled, "Stop, stop, I'm going to be sick," and she got up and ran away. Her pony-ride stayed seated in the chair looking confused. Then he put a quarter in the machine in front of him and pulled the handle.

"No, I'm sorry. No one by that name."

"Oh," I said. "How about Booth?" I asked. "Jiminy Booth."

"Jiminy Booth?"

"It's a pet name," I said. "You know, it's what I call his penis." I covered my mouth with my hand.

"Fine," said the clerk. "Checking for a Mr. Jiminy Booth . . . sorry, nothing."

"Could you try Doolittle? Because that's another word I use for it."

"Is this . . . are you just having fun?" asked the clerk. He had that look. Like he had been razzed all his life. Pizza Face. Did you get the license of the truck that ran over your face. You're so ugly they should shave your ass and teach you to walk backward. . . . The sadness and fury of the last kid picked.

"No, I promise," I said. "It's just, he was really mad at me so I thought he might have used one of those other names to avoid me." After a pause, the clerk checked the computer.

113

"No Doolittle," he said. "You know, if he doesn't want to see you, he doesn't want to see you."

I walked through the casino, looking left and right for Timmy. It was almost four in the morning and the crowd was sloppy. Except for the chumps who were down, way down, and trying to turn their luck around before dawn. They hunched over their chips like cons eating Sunday dinner. Slid them forward with quick precise movements and then glared at them. Willing them to come back at the end of the hand. The sloppy players had lost too much to worry about it anymore. Or they were actually winning.

I got so turned around, I couldn't tell if I had checked out the whole casino or just a couple feet of it. Every area looked the same. Lots of entrances, lots of elevators. I was dizzy and tired and in need of a pick-me-up. I found the door I had come through originally and stood near it, watching the people walk in and out. Many tourists, zero Timmys.

My attention shifted to a roulette game in progress nearby. An elderly man wearing a short-sleeved shirt and a tie sat alone at the table. I remembered that on my previous trip to Vegas, I had started gambling late at night and when I stopped a couple hours later, having lost only fifty bucks, I had been too wired to sleep. It was the adrenaline. And the free booze.

I picked up my coat and helmet and walked over to the roulette table. Had a seat facing the doors. A motherly woman with dark frizzy hair took my fifty-dollar bill and converted it into fifty bright green chips.

"Good luck," she said. Her name-tag read "Maureen."

I sat out the first couple spins to see what came up. I was also looking around for a cocktail waitress. The old man in the tie kept laying down the same bet — a chip directly on number two and then four more on the borders. You had to bet a minimum of five dollars inside or out. He wasn't landing anything and his pile kept getting smaller.

I flagged down a cocktail waitress who was wearing some sort of medieval getup that barely covered her ass. I could see the control top portion of her pantyhose. She looked beat and she had a run but she smiled nicely at me. I ordered a Bloody Mary and then I was ready to bet. I put down ten chips on random numbers across the board. Maureen sent the ball and I stood up and yelled, "C'mon, twenty! Or twenty-one or twenty-two! C'mon, fifteen, you old bastard! Let's go thirty-four, -five, or -six!" Nineteen came up. It was one of my numbers. "Ha HA!" I said. Maureen swept aside the losing chips and pushed over my winnings. The old guy laid down five more chips in the same configuration and I blanketed the board randomly again. "C'mon, you dirty dogs!" I yelled. "Mama needs a new bag!" Fourteen came up and I had it. I jumped up and down. "Mama gets her new bag!" I said. I turned to the old guy. "Can you believe it? Mama finally gets that new bag. She's wanted that bag for so long." It was that unstrung feeling that made me want to chat people up. Interact a little. Make like I was a different kind of person altogether. The guy smiled tensely and placed his bet. I threw down some more chips and watched Maureen do her stuff. I liked watching her flick the ball and send it circling. She did a good job. I also liked the way she passed her arm gracefully over the table, like a blessing, to indicate "no more bets." I guess I was getting a little punchy from lack of sleep. I felt like I wanted Maureen to be my best friend. Eleven came up and I jumped up and down. "Whoopee! Eleven! Mama gets a new dress!"

115

"You don't have eleven," said Maureen.

"Oh. Oops."

The cocktail waitress brought me my drink.

"I'll have another one of these when you have a chance," I said. I tipped her a chip. The old guy was almost out.

"I have to stay here until six," he said.

"I'm doing my best," said Maureen.

The old guy removed his wallet from his pants pocket and carefully laid out three twenty-dollar bills, which Maureen converted into chips. A fat silver chain linked his wallet to his pants. He was at that point, I could tell, where he knew his number had to come up soon. Had to. The law of averages dictated. It was that law-of-averages business that really messed you up. He put five chips smack on number two. I put my chips all around number two and those numbers started coming up. "That number two really sucks," I said. "You've got to get off it." He didn't say a word. I realized he had the hairiest ears I had ever laid eyes on.

The cocktail waitress brought me another drink and I quickly finished the first so I could give her the empty glass. It was a good salty drink. Not too weak. I tipped her another buck.

I put everything I had won so far — about thirty bucks — in stacks all over the board. The old guy bet on two. Maureen flicked the roulette ball and passed her arm dreamily over the table. "C'mon, you stacked-up pieces of crap!" I said. The old guy flinched and slid down a seat.

"I'm going to have to ask you to calm down," said Maureen, "for the sake of the other players."

I whispered, "C'mon, you stacks. Mama needs a new Winnebago. Mama needs it bad!" Nine came up. "Oh, Mama," I said. "I'm sorry, Mama. Now you won't even get your bag. I'll never bet again. This time I mean it." I cashed in and gave Maureen a five-dollar tip. I said, "Thanks, kid." The old gentleman pushed five more chips onto number two. I tossed back the rest of my drink. Then I turned to the old guy and said, "Baby, I'm going to kiss your big hairy ear for luck." And I did.

116

9

On my way out of the Excalibur, I stopped at a newsstand and bought a small bottle of aspirin for almost four bucks and some Vivarin. I would take the Vivarin when I started to feel tired again. I wasn't feeling tired now, just a little drunk. At the counter, I tossed a package of tiny powdered donuts onto my pile of goods. I ate the donuts as I walked over a pedestrian bridge toward the MGM Grand. It seemed like the next best place to look for Timmy. I think one of his starring roles had been in an MGM flick. Maybe he got to stay there for free.

Donut powder snowed down my chin and jacket. I finished them fast and balled the wrapper in my hand. On the other side of the bridge, the same two guys I had seen earlier were passing out girlie pamphlets. I eyed them, still feeling chatty. High now, too. My sense of urgency dulled. I was experiencing that brief window of time when the alcohol laid its hands all over me gently. Before it turned nasty. Before it started to squeeze.

I stopped and stood shoulder to shoulder with one of the pamphleteers. "Look, I have a question," I said. I kept my eyes on my feet. "I'm interested in Missy and Sissy, the bad roommates. I want to know, would they do bad things to me?"

One guy stopped passing out pamphlets. "You mean you want something going on with two other women? Something you'd be involved with?" The other guy kept passing out the pamphlets, but he kept an ear cocked in our direction.

"I want bad roommates," I said.

118 "Well, if you call the number, you'd, you know, work something out. It might not be those two particular girls in the picture. . . ."

"But could I definitely get bad roommates?"

"Yeah, whatever, you could work something out like that. You gotta call the number."

"Would they, for instance, um, if I asked, would they *squeeze* my, um, toothpaste from the top of the tube?" I kept my voice hushed and looked all around before speaking. "I would want something like that. Or if they got some of their bad-girl hairs on my, er, soap, ahem, or drank all my . . . *milk*, that would be good."

"Listen," said the guy. He had the hood of his sweatshirt up and pulled tight around his face. All I saw was a nose and a mouth. The sweatshirt had a picture of a state seal on it with the words "Historic Pennsylvania." "You gotta call the number, right?" he said. "I just give these things out. I don't really have any hands-on connection to what goes on when you call the number. That aspect of the business, that's not my thing. But I'm sure they can fix you up."

"All right," I said. "I'll give it a try."

I walked into the giant gold-colored lion that acted as the entrance to the MGM Grand. Inside, life-size Wizard of Oz dolls greeted me from their Emerald Forest perch. A woman in a wheelchair was getting her picture taken with the Oz gang in the background. "Am I blocking anybody?" she asked. The guy taking the picture said, "Move a little that way. I'm not getting Toto." He gestured with his right arm and she wheeled over so she wouldn't be blocking Toto. She held up a big plastic cup full of quarters so I figured she had had a lucky night.

I found the reception desk and played the same game I had played with the clerk at the Excalibur. If Timmy was staying at either place, he was staying under a name I couldn't guess. I asked for the time and the clerk told me it was four-thirty. Then I asked if I could use a room for just an hour or so, just to take a shower and relax a bit. She said I would have to take the room for the night and the only thing they had left were the miniature suites which ran $139. She was very no-nonsense. Reminded me of a grammar school teacher I had once. One of her legs had been about twice the size of the other. I was dying for a shower, but it wasn't worth $139 dollars to me. I asked the woman if I could leave my helmet and coat with her while I walked around for a little while. She said no.

119

I went to use the bathroom. There were old movie posters all over the walls. I wet down some paper towels and gave myself a prostitute shower. Face, neck, and armpits. I stripped down to my bra to do it. I wasn't surprised when someone came in to use the bathroom. Someone always comes in when you want a little privacy. This someone was a young married type. All gussied up in a pink lace dress. Permed hair. She made a beeline for a stall and tried not to look at me. When she came out, I was covered up again.

"I like your dress," I said.

"Thank you," she said. "It was only twenty-two dollars when I bought it."

120   I walked slowly around the MGM Grand casino, looking for Timmy. I thought I saw him sitting at a blackjack table and I rushed over and grabbed his shoulder, but it was just a guy with the same hair.

"Sorry," I said. "I'm looking for a guy."

"That's okay," said the guy. "I am a guy. It's a logical mistake."

"Well, I'm actually looking for an asshole."

"Hey, *I'm* kind of an asshole," said the guy. "There you go." Another guy at the table said, "Are we playing or flirting?" The guy looked at me and said, "It's up to you, am I playing or flirting?"

"Playing," I said. I walked away, still hauling around my coat, helmet, and backpack. I dragged Debi's coat and since I was sick of carrying the helmet, I stuck it on my head. The chin strap flopped against my neck.

I tried New York New York, Bally's, Caesars Palace, The Mirage, and Treasure Island with the same lousy results. At The Mirage, I played roulette again so I could have another drink. I lost and the drink ended up costing me twenty-five bucks. I followed the signs to see the cavorting dolphins but the area was closed off at night. When it was open, they charged you three bucks. Then I followed the signs to see the white tigers that Siegfried and Roy use in their magic act. There I found a placard that said, "The White Tigers are not available for viewing while we refurbish their habitat. The Mirage apologizes for the inconvenience."

Slowly, the time was passing. And I was getting tired. Bent and empty. A beer can beneath a back porch. I realized that I wouldn't find Timmy until the book fair opened but I had to fill in the hours somehow. I walked back to the MGM Grand. The Timmy look-alike was still playing blackjack. He had a good-size pile of chips in front of him. I put my stuff down next to him and waited until he looked my way. He did a double take. Hadn't expected to see me again.

"Oh, hi!" he said. "Did you find your asshole?"

"Are you staying in this hotel?" I asked. He smiled slowly.

"Yeeaah? Why?" He turned to the dealer. "Deal me one out," he said. He turned his chair around to face me. He did look a lot like Timmy. Tall and skinny. Longish hair and a face that was all angles. He was younger, though. Closer to my age.

"Can I use your room to take a shower?" I said. "I won't disturb anything. I won't steal anything. All your money is

121

probably down here. I just want to have a shower and sit for an hour or two. Is all. You won't even know I'm there." He raised his eyebrows and looked me over.

"What are you, homeless?" he asked. I realized I still had on the motorcycle helmet. Probably looked like one of those rubber room cases that cover their head to deflect the mind-sucking rays. I took off the helmet and smoothed my hair. "I have a home," I said. "I just want a shower."

"Are you, like, a pro?" he asked. Mumbled.

"Fuck you," I said. I started to pick up my stuff.

"Don't get me wrong," he said. "I'm interested!"

"It's not an option," I said. I walked away but I heard him cashing in his chips behind me. He ran and caught up.

"Wait a second," he said. "Hold on. Just what are we talking about here?"

"A shower!" I said. "Just a goddamned shower."

"Well, am I supposed to watch? Is that the idea?"

"No," I said. We had stopped near the Emerald Forest, and overhead some laser lights were creating a twister effect.

"So — okay, I'm just trying to get a handle on this — so you just want to shower in my room and that's it?"

"You got it, mister," I said.

"Okay. Okay. Well what if I do want to watch?" I thought for a minute. Looked him over. I didn't care if he saw me naked. But I didn't want to get him excited and then spend a half hour fending off some sloppy pawings.

"Naw," I said. "Forget it. If you saw me take a shower, you'd probably want to fuck me."

"Oh. Well, I guess you're right," he said. "I probably would."

"So let's forget it," I said.

"Hold on," he said. "All right. What the hell. Why not. I never do stuff like this. But, yeah, what the hell. Okay. Let's do it. You can have a shower and I'll . . . well, you can lock the bathroom door."

"But you're going to come up there with me? Be in the room?"

"Sure. But I won't try anything. I'll just keep an eye on my stuff."

"I don't know," I said. "Now it feels a little fishy. I'd really rather you just stay down here and play. I'll bring you your key when I'm done."

"No," he said. "No. I have things in my room."

"Oh fine," I said. What did I have to worry about. I was the one with a gun in my backpack.

123

He stopped at the front desk and asked the lady to put his winnings in the safe. I said to her, "Sure, you'll hold on to his money but you won't hold my helmet."

She said, "It's so nice that you found your friend." At the elevator banks, a guard checked the guy's plastic room key before allowing us to go up. He looked young for the job. His uniform had creases in strange places. Like it was fresh from its original wrapper. While we waited for an elevator, I asked the guard when his shift ended. He said he was there until nine. I said, "If I don't come down by then, send someone up."

"Really?" he said.

"Write down the room number," I said.

"You don't just want a wake-up call?"

"If I don't come down," I said, "it means I'm in trouble."

"Oh," said the guard. He gave my new friend a hard look. "I guess I could do that."

"Same goes for me," said my young friend.

"Same goes for you?" said the guard. "Okay, I guess. Same room number?"

"Yeah."

On the elevator, the guy said, "You know, you shouldn't discount the idea of our really hitting it off."

"Just a shower," I said.

"Well, I won a bundle and I plan on ordering up some champagne to celebrate. So if you feel like joining me . . . It's up to you."

124   "How much did you win?" I asked.

"Five hundred bucks."

"Nice going." We both watched the red digital numbers count off the floors.

"First I lost eight hundred. That wasn't so good."

We got off on the seventeenth floor.

"It's down this way," said my young friend. I followed him along the yellow carpeted hallway. There were some room service carts outside the doors. The remains of fifty-dollar late night snacks. I picked a tiny unopened jar of strawberry jam off one of the carts and put it in my back-pack. A tiny jar of honey. An unused tea bag. The guy watched me.

"I hate waste," I said.

"Oh," he said. Toward the end of hallway, he opened a door and stepped aside for me to enter. "*Voilà!*" he said. I dumped my stuff and looked around.

"It'll do." The MGM Grand was pretty new so the room still had a crispness to it. No shabby spreads or carpet stains. None of that smell that builds up after the three thousandth occupation. The smell of sex and food and fights and vacation blues. He walked over to the telephone and dialed up room service. Ordered a bottle of champagne.

"Are you hungry?" he asked.

"Sure."

He spoke into the phone. "Hold on a second, I'm going to order some food also." He tossed the room service menu in my direction.

"Do they do the prime rib at this hour?" I said.

"Oh," he said. And then, into the phone, "Umm, do you have prime rib now?" And to me, "Yes, they always have the prime rib."

"In that case, order me some croissants. And a bowl of strawberries."

"And prime rib?" He had his hand over the mouthpiece.

I shook my head with disgust. He ordered four croissants and two bowls of strawberries and butter and jam. And an extra bottle of champagne.

"They ordered that in some movie," he said. "I remember thinking it looked good."

"What movie was that?"

"Actually, I think they did it in a couple different movies." He walked over to the window and opened the curtains so we could see the view. The sun was up but low.

The city looked wasted. Postapocalyptic. All the color had been sucked away with the night. "Nice," I said.

"Uh huh," he said. We looked at the city. Both of us with our arms crossed over our chests. "What's your name?" he asked.

"Mary," I said. "What about you?"

"Luis."

"You don't have to give me a fake name," I said.

"It's not. That's my name," he said.

"Well you're a very white guy to have a name like that."

"My mother was born in Mexico," he said. "I'm more of a Luis than you are a Mary."

126 I showered for a long time. The hot water made me realize how dead I felt. I sat down in the tub beneath the stream but I caught myself falling asleep and got up and ran the cold tap until I said, "Stop it." Then I got out and toweled off. I used the complimentary moisturizer and talcum powder. I had a brush in my backpack. I poked through Luis's toiletry kit and gargled with his mouthwash. Used his deodorant. I felt hazy. Not sharp. But I was saving the Vivarin for when I really needed it.

Out in the room, Luis was sitting on the bed, drinking champagne from the bottle and watching a movie on television. Something about a mischievous little kid. Throwing water balloons at workmen. Kicking the grumpy old neighbor in the ass.

"This is really a piece of shit," said Luis. "Want some champagne?" He held out the bottle and I took a long hit. It was good stuff. Dry and cold. And I don't like champagne. I handed the bottle back to him and started eating a croissant.

"I have to start eating better," I said.

"You're not worried about your weight, are you? Because you're skinny."

"No," I said. "Although I'm not crazy skinny." I lifted my shirt and smacked my belly. It made a nice thwacking sound. I thwacked out a beat with both hands. Croissant dangling from my mouth.

"'Girl from Ipanema'?" asked Luis. The dangling part of the croissant dropped from my mouth and landed on the floor. I picked it up and took another bite.

"My own composition," I said. He had muted the TV but the kid continued to wreak havoc in silence. Blew up a doghouse. Reaction shot of the adults shaking their heads. Kid grins wildly. Looks at the camera and shrugs his shoulders.

Luis watched me watching the TV. "They just don't make them like they used to," he said.

"Let me guess," I said. "You're in the movie business."

"No. Well, I write for TV."

"Oh Christ. You went to an Ivy League school?" I took another hit of the champagne and held on to the bottle.

"Actually . . ."

"Ah crap. Well we know some of the same people. That's great."

"Really? But I didn't —"

"Why can't I ever meet someone that doesn't know someone that I know, you know?"

"No."

"I don't want to talk about it, see? I'm liable to go nuts and tear up the joint."

"I just . . . I don't think I understand anything you are saying."

"I'm just being goofy," I said. "I'll go back to smacking my belly." I put down the champagne and uncovered my belly and smacked out a tune. This time it was "The Girl from Ipanema." When I was done, I took another slug off the bottle and handed it back to him. Then I said, "Oh boy," and lay down on the other bed. I plumped up the pillows and leaned back with my hands over my face. I felt like I was scattered all over the room. Pieces of me crawling around, looking for an out. Looking for a way to die. It always came on fast like that.

"Are you okay?"

"Nah," I said. "But it's nothing new." I sat forward and put my head between my knees and hugged them close to me.

"Are you going to throw up?" he asked.

I shook my head. "It's just that my mouth is in love with my knees," I said. I let out a small, sad laugh. "I have to give them a little time alone once in a while. You know?" I sat very still and quiet for a minute and so, it seemed, did Luis. I heard the tiny whisper voices of the television. The volume wasn't off altogether, just low. A muffled explosion. A nothing scream.

"Do you want a wet towel?" I lifted my head and came back to it all. The *Singin' in the Rain* poster. The white-hair blue-face print of Marilyn Monroe. The unfrozen strawberries sinking into one another on the room service cart. The carpet.

Luis held the bottle by the neck with both hands and squinted at me.

"A wet towel? Jesus, that sounds awful. Why would I want a wet towel?"

"Oh I just thought . . . if you felt sick . . . well, you know how they're always doing something with a wet towel. . . ."

"I'm not sick," I said.

He drank from the bottle and some of the champagne spilled down his chin and onto his T-shirt. "Shit," he said. He pulled his shirt up toward his mouth and sucked the champagne out of the collar.

"What does your T-shirt mean?" I asked.

"It's the logo for my friends' film company. They don't have any films yet. Just T-shirts."

"C'mere, please," I said. He shuffled a little closer to me. **129**

"What," he said. I took his hand and held it a moment. I held his hand and his forearm very tightly while he stood over me. "What," he said. I let go of him.

"That's all," I said. "Thanks very much."

"Oh," he said. "Um, you're welcome very much." He took a swig of champagne and held the bottle toward me. I took it and drank.

I said, "You know, you're nice. You're nice to let me take a shower in your hotel room. You're probably just one of those nice guys. I've known guys like you. Nice."

"I guess," he said. "Although"— he took the bottle and had a swig — "there are a lot of people I hate. Who, in theory, I would like to kill. A friend of mine came up with an idea for this gun. The twenty-four-hour gun. You could shoot someone and they would die for just twenty-four-hours.

Then they'd be fine but they would know that they had done something that was so annoying that someone would want to kill them."

"You should be more tolerant," I said. "You should love everyone like crazy. I know I do."

"But that's the point, I am tolerant."

I spread my legs and leaned out over them, stretching like a ballet dancer. "What if you actually had to kill someone," I said. "Do you think you could kill someone?" I said "kill" with a bit of a French accent.

"What do you mean, like in a fight? Or someone said, 'You kill that guy or we'll kill you'?"

"No, like if someone asked you to kill them." I leaned toward the room service cart and picked up the bowl of strawberries. Drank the juice out of the bowl, making a mess.

"If someone asked me?"

"Someone begged you to do it."

"Someone begged me? Do I know them?"

I nodded my head. Juice all over my face like a clown mouth. "Napkin," I said. He gave me one.

"I don't know," he said. "I guess if they really wanted it. . . . Why wouldn't they just kill themselves — uh, themself?"

"They tried. They couldn't."

"Oh, like they're a vegetable maybe?" I looked at him. A nice guy, though I'd been wrong before.

I said, "Maybe something like that. Or they just need some help."

He sat down beside me on the bed. "I suppose if they begged me. . . ." He was getting a little slurry. Champagne works fast. "Are you asking me to kill you? You're not, right?"

"Would you do it if I was?" I twisted on the bed and looked him in the eye. No one's used to being looked in the eye anymore. It's a big deal and they get quite serious.

Luis shook his head. "No," he said. "No, I couldn't kill you. Maybe if I knew you better . . . but then maybe I'd really like you, so . . . no."

"What if I got you all tanked up first?"

He made a snort noise. A guffaw. "No."

"It's okay," I said. "Don't worry about it. It's hypothetical."

"Okay."

I lay back on the bed again. He had passed me the champagne and I tried balancing the bottle on my belly. "Luis," I said, "I miss my mother." I was a little drunk and I said it out loud so I could hear the words. It was all right to say stuff like that to a stranger.

"You wanna call her? You can call her."

"No I can't. Because she's dead."

"Oh." Someone banged around in the room next to ours. A door closed. A voice yelled, "*Where?*"

"How'd she die?"

I hit the bottle against my stomach and laughed a hateful and bitter laugh. "With difficulty," I said.

"Oh," he said. "I see. I think I . . ."

I sat up again fast. "So were you hoping I'd change my mind about the sex?"

"Sure, why not. Who wouldn't."

"Yeah. Well tough."

131

"Eh, whatever. It's all right. Anyway, I don't think I really care that much anymore. About the sex. And anyway, I have a girlfriend in L.A."

"Why didn't she come?"

"She was going to. And then she didn't." He offered me the bottle but I shook my head. He tipped it back and then realized it was empty. "You know," he said, "I'm going to drink this other fucking bottle." He opened it up and drank. Spilled down his shirt again. "Piss," he said.

"Maybe you need a glass."

"You know in movies when people pour champagne or some other food all over them and then they have sex? Or they have a lot of cash somehow and they have sex all over the cash? None of those appeals to me."

132

"That's another thing we have in common," I said.

"Right," he said. Then, "Wait, what was the first thing?"

"Bupkis," I said.

"Oh, I get it."

We both sat back on the bed and watched the muted movie for a while. Passing the bottle.

"What time is it ?" I asked. He looked at his watch.

"Seven-fifteen." After a minute, he said, "Do you want to talk? Or do you just want to watch the movie?"

"Watch the movie," I said. He unmuted the television.

In this dream my mother and I were sitting at a table. We were in a seamen's bar that also happened to be her house. She looked healthy and beautiful and drank from a tin goblet. She said, "It won't be hard. You put the bag over my head. Then wrap the tape." Later, she bounced off the walls and pawed at her face. When she had made a hole in the plastic, she cried, "Why did you do that? Weren't you listening?"

We both awoke to a pounding on the door. A muffled voice. "Hello in there. Open the door. Hello?" Luis bolted upright.

"What the hell — ?"

"Open the door, you guys. I'll be forced to use my personal key. If you don't open up." Luis rubbed his face. "Arrh," he said. He stood and walked toward the door like a first-time skater on rotten ice. "What? What the hell is it?" He yelled it at the door-crack.

"It's nine-oh-five in the A.M. Is there some sort of problem in there?" By now I was up. Nine-oh-five. Fuck. The book fair was open.

"What do you mean, problem?" asked Luis.

"It's the security guard," I said. I got my bag out of the bathroom. Stuffed any belongings into it. Luis was fighting with the locks, saying, "Hold on. Just a second." I got on my clogs and Debi's jacket. Shouldered my pack. Luis opened the door and the young guard pressed forward.

"Everything okay in here?" he asked. "No problems?" I shot past him out the door.

"Motherfuckers," I said, to myself more than anyone.

"Whoa!" said the guard. I had shoved him a bit in my hurry.

"Where are you going?" asked Luis. He followed me out into the hall. "Don't let that door close," he said to the guard.

133

"What?" said the guard.

Luis trotted behind me down the hallway. "Do you want to make some sort of plans to get together later?" he said. "Do you want to come by when you're done doing whatever you have to do?"

"I don't think so," I said. "I'm pretty tied up with a project right now." We reached the elevators. A family of five was waiting to go down. The oldest kid kicked at an ash stand with his sneaker. His mother said, "I'm not going to tell you again."

"We should get together in L.A.," said Luis. "Just do whatever. You could, uh, use my shower. I have a good shower there."

"In L.A., I have my own shower," I said.

"Yeah, I know," he said. "I'm just talking." The elevator arrived and we all got in. "I'll just ride down with you. Then I'll come back up." The elevator zoomed down the floors. None of us said a word. Then we were at the lobby. I got out and Luis stayed on. He said, "What's your real name?"

"Jill," I said. "What about you?"

"Luis," he said. "Luis Goldberg." Some other people got on the elevator and the doors closed.

10

I picked up the motorcycle and rode over to the Convention Center. The day too hot already. It had the smell and feel of an attic in August. Couples walked the strip with sun visors and baseball caps. Some wore those mini-umbrella hats. A couple blocks farther, I stopped at a light where the guy was selling them. He said, "Get out of the sun, baby! That bad sun is killing you." He said this to a heavy grandmother fanning her face with one hand. Waiting to cross. "Five bucks buys your own shade." She ignored him. From her expression, you could imagine he was telling her she had a nice ass.

I rode into the Convention Center parking lot and left the motorcycle next to a bike rack. I left the helmet on the seat. Jogged to the entrance with my backpack bouncing against my back. Two steps through the automatic doors and the air conditioning had me freezing. I buttoned up Debi's jacket, bypassed the information booth, and went right into the convention hall. But something was off. There were no booths, no books — just a lot of people wandering around with plastic drink cups. Kids everywhere. I turned a full circle looking for some sort of clue and there, above the doors, I saw a huge banner. "Gulick Family Reunion." I grabbed the sleeve of the nearest person.

"I don't understand," I said, "you're all Gulicks?"

"Nearly so," he said. He looked around. "Yup, just about."

"But where are all the books?" I asked. "The old books?"

"How's that?" he said. I left him and jogged to the information booth in the lobby. The woman in the booth was giving someone directions to a Denny's restaurant. I said, "Excuse me, isn't this supposed to be the Antiquarian Book Fair?"

"That's in the B wing," she said. "Out the door and to the left." Out the door and to the left I saw a giant sign. I had missed it before. "Antiquarian Book Fair." I headed for the entrance. A young woman in a red blazer stopped me at the door.

"Ticket?" she said.

"Ticket?"

"Are you a dealer?"

"Okay."

"Do you have your resale card?"

"Not quite."

"There's a five-dollar entrance fee. You can buy a ticket over there." She gestured at a kiosk nearby.

"I'm just looking for someone," I said. She shook her head back and forth. "My boss said no exceptions of any kind."

I growled at her. Then I went and bought a ticket for five bucks and I was in.

The books were there, all right. The place was lousy with them. A hundred or so mini-bookstores all under the same roof. Because it was still early, the place wasn't too crowded. Dealers were still putting things out, sipping coffee, and eating donuts and egg sandwiches. I looked for the names of L.A. stores, figuring the L.A. booksellers would be the most likely to know Timmy. None of the names rang a bell, but over to the left I saw a booth that looked like it specialized in children's books. A woman in a big Dr. Seuss hat and appliqué flowers on her shirt was fiddling with a Nancy Drew set. I beelined in her direction.

"Excuse me, do you know Tim Harris of Doolittle's in Los Angeles?"

She had a piece of beef jerky in her hand and she chewed on it slowly. "I think I've heard of them," she said.

"Never mind," I said.

I moved quickly through the hall, giving everyone the once-over.

An enormous guy sat perched on a stool, engulfed it really, and watched a tweedy nerd flip slowly through a first edition of *The Jungle*.

"It's more than I had planned on," said the flipper. The big guy sucked air into his mouth and labored it back out.

"It's a very sexy item," he said.

Over in the corner, I spotted a sign for Jonathan Samuelson Booksellers — an L.A. joint. I walked over and nosed around while the guy manning the booth finished up with a customer. I kept one eye on the small crowd slowly making the hall. The browser took off without a purchase and I approached the salesman. I recognized him from the times he had come into Bitter Muse. I thought his name was Eliot, but I wasn't sure.

"Hi," I said.

"Oh hello! Hello. Now how do I know you?"

"I buy a lot of books at your store," I said. "I'm sort of a budding collector. Larry McMurtry? Remember?"

"Ah, right. Yes, of course, how are you! Yes. Yes of course. Well you know I brought some Mr. McMurtry, it just so happens. It just so happens . . ." He began to look through his stock.

"Well, truth be told, I'm not even really looking yet," I said. "But I wonder if you can help me — do you know Tim Harris?"

"Hmm?" said the seller. He was making a neat pile of all his McMurtry books. "Yes, sure. Tim Harris. Yes, I know him."

"Do you know if he's here? I was supposed to see him about a certain book. . . ."

"Oh here it is! A signed first *Moving On*. It's well priced, too."

"So have you seen him?"

"I know he's not doing a booth this year," said maybe-Eliot. He held out the book with both hands. Altar boy to priest. I made no move to take it from him.

"But I heard he was, in fact, here," I said. Maybe-Eliot sighed and began looking through the book himself. To prove it was a worthy gesture.

"I saw him last night. I haven't seen him this morning but I guess he's around somewhere."

"Thanks," I said. "I'll come back and take a closer look at that McMurtry."

"Well if you are interested at all you had better move fast," he said. "It's a very sexy item."

I cruised the hall twice with no sign of Timmy. "Please don't be off selling the book somewhere," I said. "Please be sleeping or gambling. Don't be selling the goddamn book." Having no better ideas, I decided to stake out the entrance to the hall and wait a little while. I popped two Vivarin to keep alert and put on a show of looking at books in a booth near the front doors. The place was getting more crowded and for a while I was left alone. Eventually the guy manning that booth got chatty, so I moved to another. After an hour, I was dying to go to the bathroom. But I worried I would miss Timmy and the hall had gotten pretty full — he would be tough to sight if I had to make the rounds again. I crossed my legs and held it awhile. Finally I said, "Ah, fuck," and went out the doors. The ticket taker pointed out the bathroom a hundred feet away. I was quick. When I came out, I stood a moment and surveyed the lobby. Some guy coming out of the men's room bumped me from behind. I didn't turn around, didn't even react. I thought I had seen Timmy at the opposite end of the lobby and I was focusing everything in that direction. When I started to walk, so did the guy that bumped me, so that we jostled again. This time I turned to swear and I got an eyeball full of Timmy. Right there.

"Oh, shit!" I said.

"Wha —? Oh yikes," he said.

Before he had time to react fully, I heaved my weight against him and pushed him back into the men's room. I kept on pushing and we crashed through one of the stall doors. Timmy stumbled and landed on the toilet. I locked the door behind me. There had been a guy at the urinal, but things had happened too fast for him whip around for a look. Probably figured someone was just in a big hurry. I sat facing Timmy on his lap and I wrapped my legs around his torso, hooking my feet onto the pipes behind him.

"All right," I whispered, "you lying bastard. You 'I have a good excuse, it involves a dog' piece of shit. I'm now going to need you to give me the book. The real book. And if you say you don't know what I'm talking about, I'll be tempted to pop you."

"Wha—, what do you mean the book? I gave you the —" I leaned back and punched him in the face. I felt my ring connect with his cheekbone. But overall it was a pretty lame punch. The angle was all wrong.

"OW!" said Timmy. "Jesus! What are you, crazy? That hurt. I have an unbelievable hangover."

From the main part of the bathroom, I heard the guy at the urinal say, "Excuse me, are you speaking to me?" I looked at Timmy and shook my head. Timmy said, "No," then he cleared his throat and said it again — "No."

We sat in silence for a moment, waiting for the guy to leave. Instead, a couple new guys entered. The pissing, flushing, and hand-washing sounds covered our conversation. I continued at a whisper. "You'd be smart to sit and listen quietly for a minute," I said, "because you are potentially in a lot of fucking trouble. And I don't mean from me. I'm

140

talking the law. The real owner of that book is a D.A. And when he discovered the book you gave me had a fake-o inscription, he went nuts. He was ready to take measures."

"— a D.A.?" said Timmy.

"District attorney, you numbnuts."

"No, no, I know what it is, I just can't believe —"

"Listen," I said, "he was very anxious to have your bookseller's license revoked. At the least! I had to spend three hours getting him drunk and convincing him that I could get the book back and we could forget the whole thing. Lucky for you, my mom was a D.A. so the guy was inclined to cut you a little slack on my behalf. Though God only knows why I didn't just let him throw you in the clink. In other words, mister, you owe me a big fucking favor." I tried to keep my voice low and easy. Not bust apart like a short-pants kid. The tougher I talked, the tougher I felt.

141

Timmy sat silent for a moment. He looked down at his shirt and fiddled with a button. I hadn't thought he owned any button-down shirts. Then he said, "I really don't know what you're talking about." He said it without enthusiasm. "Although I guess it's possible that my signature guy made a switch."

I grabbed his face with both hands and forced him to look at me. I said, "Tim, don't do it this way. It's over. One way or another, you've got to give it back."

He tried averting his eyes and I saw a single tear well up and fall slowly toward the corner of his mouth. "What if I didn't have it anymore? And then giving it back would, like, not even be an option?"

"You've still got it. You better hope to Christ you've still got it. Because if you've already sold it, you're going to be

holding tight to your soap for the next five or so years."
Timmy lightly batted my hands away from his face. Then he
rubbed his eyes with his fists. When he looked at me again,
he seemed surprised that I was still there. That he hadn't
banished me like a bad dream.

"I don't understand that image," he said. "Is that supposed to be, like, some sort of allusion to prison?" Someone
entered the stall next to us and I heard the rustling of a
newspaper.

"Look," I said, "I've got to get comfortable. Where are
you staying?"

"The MGM Grand."

"Under what name?"

"Uh . . . Augustus Gloop."

"Oh boy."

He shrugged his shoulders. "I like it."

I reached into my bag and poked around until I found
my roll of duct tape. I tore off a couple feet and held Timmy's
hand and taped his right wrist to my left one. Using my right
hand to loop the tape up and around.

"What are you doing?" he said. I didn't bother to answer. He seemed slightly dazed by the whole business and he
didn't try to fight it.

When we left the stall I said, "Surprise," to the bathroom
populace. I waved like the queen.

At the bike, I realized that it would be dangerous to try and
ride taped together that way. It would throw my balance,
and Timmy could easily send us crashing if he felt like it. So
I found my Swiss Army knife and held it in my teeth while

142

I pulled out the tiny scissors. I used them to cut the tape. It took a little while. The scissors aren't meant for that kind of job. When I pulled the tape off Timmy's wrist, a patch of his hair came up with it.

"This is all nuts," he said. "It's nuts."

"Get on the bike," I said.

"I want the helmet," he said. I plopped the helmet on his head. He got on the bike and I got on in front of him with my backpack sandwiched tightly between us. I started the bike and told him to hold on to my waist, praying I had mastered the thing enough by then to ride with a passenger. We started to move and he must have decided to hop off the back and make a run for it but he waited too long. He took a hard fall. I stopped the bike and he was lying flat on his back a couple yards behind. He slowly sat up and cradled his left hand. "Fuck!" he said. "Fuck fuck fuck fuck fuck. Fuck!" He tried putting his hand in his armpit and then he said "Fuck" again. A Gulick walked by and said, "Jeepers, are you okay?" I helped Timmy up and, with the Gulick watching, I started the tape on Timmy's back, then stood in front of him and looped it across my belly. The Gulick said, "What are you doing, taping him to you? So's he won't fall off?"

"That's right," I said. "You win the trip to Hawaii." I couldn't reach around behind Timmy for another pass with the tape, so I asked the Gulick for assistance. He happily walked around us, unrolling the tape and palming it against our clothes as he went. He said, "I'm going to tell someone about this because they won't believe me."

When we got to the MGM Grand, I cut us apart and taped our wrists together again for the walk through the

143

casino. I kissed his arm, his hand, whatever, so it would look like some moochy honeymoon business. Timmy had a room on the seventeenth floor. Other side of the hotel from Luis's. He opened it up and then made me walk back to the ice machine with him to get some ice for his wrist. His good hand was attached to mine so we both leaned deep into the machine to harvest what was left in the bottom. We managed to wrestle free one big chunk, which Timmy balanced on top of the ice bucket. Back in his room, I cut us apart one last time. Then I moved a chair over near the door and sat down. Timmy made himself a screwdriver from the minibar and tried to break up the ice by stomping on it. It whizzed around the room.

"Put it in a towel."

"I might put it in a towel." He put it in a towel and banged at it with a pink ceramic lamp, which cracked. Then he went into the bathroom and swung the towel against the wall. That worked. He came back out and sat on the bed and iced his wrist.

"All settled?" I said.

"This is so . . . nuts."

"Where's the book?"

"It's just so nuts, is all. Stop scratching your arm!"

"Don't tell me what to do!" I put my hands in my lap.

"You're going to end up with a scar."

"If you don't give me the book, you're fucked. Don't you realize that? That if you don't give me the book you're fucked? You're going to lose your store for a lousy thousand or so bucks? Do you see how that logic is a bit faulty?"

"I'm fucked either way," he said. He pressed the towel of

ice against his head. Then back to his wrist. He removed a piece of ice and ate it. Said, "Oh mother." He walked to the window and adjusted the blinds to block the sun. The light separated, making a shadow fence across the room. "A thousand dollars? Did you just say a thousand dollars?"

"Well, give or take."

"Man, are you out of the loop. A thousand dollars?"

"What, five thousand?"

"I'm insulted that you would think I would steal a book for a thousand dollars. For a paltry thousand dollars. If I did, in fact, steal it."

"Ten thousand? What?"

"Man, my wrist really hurts. I think I may need X rays or something." He held up his wrist to inspect it. "My ass, too." He pulled a pillow from underneath the bedspread and sat on it.

"What about the book, Timmy?"

"It's funny that you call me Timmy. People haven't called me that since I stopped making movies. I almost changed my name altogether. To Seymour, if you can believe that."

"The book," I said. He sighed and looked at his wrist again. Then he walked over and squatted down in front of me. Rested his chin on my thigh. Dust motes staggered around his head.

"Don't," I said. I pushed him away with my leg. Not hard. He kneeled on one knee as close as he could get. Like a football coach. Like a suitor.

"What if we could figure out a way to keep the book. Well, to not give it back. Do you feel like making a lot of money? Like a ton?" He blinked rapidly. Dark eyelashes, dark eyes.

145

"Is the book here in the room?"

"Listen . . . Jill. Listen, Jill, I want to work with you. I feel like we have a real thing between us . . . a connection. We can make a good team." I returned his gaze as blankly as I could. "I like you, is the deal. I do. Have you ever heard of the Grautzweller books?" I shook my head and began to feel around for my backpack. It was behind the chair. "Well, Lincoln Grautzweller. Worked for the Macmillan Company from 1907 through 1912. A bookbinder. Okay, an unhappy fellow. He got a kick out of screwing up the pages of one book in each printing. He wouldn't mix all the pages up — just about fifty or so. Each shuffle was some elaborate code which formed a dirty poem about the author. Each code was different. Only a couple of the known Grautzweller books have been unscrambled — you know, like . . . decoded. He worked for the army during Double-u Double-u One. Or so they thought."

I eased my backpack closer and unzipped it. Felt around inside. Timmy broke character and looked down to see what I was doing.

"What are you looking for?"

"Cigarettes."

"This is a nonsmoking floor," he said.

"I'll just sniff them," I said. "So basically you're telling me that this book is worth more than ten thousand dollars?"

"This book is the only signed Grautzweller in known existence. This book is worth — well it's probably worth about two hundred thousand but in real money it's more like one fifteen." I had located the gun inside my backpack and I was trying to unzip the case. "It's hot in here," Timmy said. "Aren't you hot?" He stood abruptly and walked to the thermostat. I pulled my backpack onto my lap and unzipped the gun from its case. I held it rested on the arm of the chair, pointed in Timmy's general direction.

"Hey," I said.

"Hold on, I'm figuring out the thing."

"Hey."

"I'm no good with technology. Technology and names."

"Hey!"

Timmy turned around. It took him a second to notice the gun. His face went a little screwy.

"What? What the hell is that?"

"It's a gun."

"Yeah but — what are you doing with it? Are you pointing it at me?"

"I'd say it's aimed in your general direction, yes."

Timmy's ice towel dripped onto the floor. The water hit the green and yellow carpet with a thwapping noise like it was counting off the wasted seconds.

"Well, why?"

"Because the fact that this book is worth that much money just makes it clear that you are not going to give it up without a little encouragement. And you may think that if you talk long enough, you can convince me to go in on this thing with you, but I know that that's never going to happen. I need to return the book. And I'm in a hurry. And fifty-five thousand dollars isn't going to change that."

"Fifty-five —? Whoa, I never said anything about splitting down the middle."

"It doesn't matter, Timmy, is what I'm saying. I just want the goddamn book." Timmy walked over to the bed that was farthest from me and sat down.

147

Then he said, "Don't shoot. I'm just going to sit down."

"Is it in the room? In the hotel?"

"I can't give it back."

"You sold it?"

"Yes, let's say I sold it."

"You didn't sell it."

"No, let's say I sold it." He squeezed the towel. A stream of water splatted onto the bedspread. He slid away from it.

"Why are you doing this? You're in what is referred to as a no-win situation. The only option you've got is to return the book."

"I can't return the book," he said. "I can't, I can't, I can't!"

"Why not?"

"If I return the book, I'm dead. I lose everything. I lose the ducks." He balled a part of the bedspread in his good hand.

"Come again?" Out in the hallway, some people walked by talking loudly. One said, "I am the master of the wheel, baby. I am the master!"

"My house, the ducks, probably the store. Definitely the house and the ducks. I need the money. I need it. I can't lose those guys. It would be hard to explain but . . . they're very important to me. You saw what they're like."

Suddenly, the radio on the bedside clock came on at high volume. Some previous occupant's wake-up call, still programmed. Timmy and I both bolted like we'd been goosed. I was relieved I had left the safety on the gun because my hand tensed up as a reflex. The Carpenters were singing "Top of the World." The song had been a favorite of my mother's and hearing it in this context threw me a bit. Last time had been the day before the night she died. I was puking in the bathroom. My mother whispering in her bed. Saying "It's all right" and "Please" and even "Be strong."

"Jesus, that scared the life out of me," said Timmy. He leaned over and lowered the volume a bit.

"What are you doing?" I said. "Turn it off! Turn it all the way off. I don't want to hear that shit. We're talking about something important here."

"All right! Boy!" He messed around with the clock-radio for a while.

"What's the problem?"

"I told you. I'm lousy with technology." He finally turned it off and sat back down. "Music can sometimes relax people. That's all I was thinking," he said. "I wonder if maybe you're being extra hostile to me because you feel this whole incident is like a betrayal of our lovemaking? Because let me tell you, it's not. I think because you're smart, you may be overanalyzing this whole thing. But that's a whole separate issue for me. And I am still really attracted to you."

"All right, shut up with that. Okay? It's ridiculous. It's . . . there's nothing there. All right? Zip. So forget about it. But so now, are you telling me that you have to sell the book because you're going to lose your house and the ducks from — what, let me guess — gambling debts?"

"Yeah, yeah, gambling. Stupid, stupid . . ." He squeezed out the towel above his head and let the cold water fall on his hair, his face. Then he shook himself like a dog.

"Why don't they just break your legs?"

"What? No. They don't want my legs. They don't care about my legs. What's that going to do for them? They want

149

money. More than they want to hurt. They'll take the house. They're businesslike."

"Well, just find an apartment that allows pets."

"No, you don't understand. The ducks go with the canals. They can't be separated."

"Okay, now that I think about it, I realize I don't give a shit about any of this. About you and your ducks. I don't even know you. What I care about is the book. So stop being an idiot because the only way out of this is to give it to me." I was incredibly thirsty. I darted my tongue around like some bug-happy gecko.

"Jill," he said, "I have a buyer, the buyer has the money. It can be done within a couple hours." He stood up and paced around a bit. Jerked his head to flip the hair off his face. "You can have ten thousand. There's no way for that D.A. to prove that he had a Grautzweller because the Grautzweller *Cruise of the Snark* has never been reported before. I mean, it was known to exist, but no one knew where it was or who owned it or what. That's why I assumed that the person you got it from didn't know what they had." He kept pacing jumpily, squeezing the water from the towel. Making a trail of dark spots on the carpet.

I said, "Why don't you calm down for a second and get me a glass of water." I waved the gun a bit. "Please." I didn't want to leave my post by the door. He was liable to bolt. Timmy went into the bathroom, got a glass of water, and stalled his way back toward me. Stopped a couple feet away to inspect a glossy poster of Fred Astaire.

"Man, that Fred Astaire," he said. He looked over toward the beds. Stood frozen. I held out my hand for the water. "Water?" I said. The clock-radio went off again. This time the noise was deafening. Timmy threw the water in my face and roundhoused me with the towel of ice. My head snapped sideways. I was down but not out. The feel of his hand on my gun-hand, trying to unlock my fingers, brought me back. Enough to say, "Oh no," and kick out blindly. I got lucky and caught him between the legs with my clog. He groaned and knelt down on the floor in front of me. Prayer position. He grabbed my calf with his good hand and bit down hard. The thickness of the denim stymied him. I kicked out again, this time connecting with his lame wrist. He screamed and rolled over into fetal position. I pushed myself up so I was squatting on the chair, facing him. I flipped the catch on the gun and yelled, "The safety's off! The safety is off! Do you hear me? You jerk you fucking jerk? It's fucking off!" I let out a single sob, then held it all in.

151

11.

I was making good time until I ran out of gas a couple miles outside of Baker. Some local kids picked me up and gave me a ride to Aldo's Auto where I bought a gallon of gas and a container to put it in. Aldo himself gave me a ride back to my bike in his tow truck. A nice guy in his late forties. Traces of an accent. He blasted the air conditioning, which was fine with me. He aimed the vents in my direction. Said, "Okay, now we're going. Now we got some stuff coming out." During our short ride, he told me that his son was in jail for counterfeiting. The son had bleached one-dollar bills and used some sort of color copying system to make one hundreds. Aldo gestured with both hands when he spoke. He held the wheel steady with his knees. He said that he was not pissed off that his son had done something illegal, he was pissed off that he had done a sloppy, half-assed job of it — that he hadn't taken personal pride in the quality of his work.

He didn't charge me for the ride.

I stopped in Baker to fill the bike all the way and then I walked across the street to Bun Boy for some food. When the waitress came to take my order, I said, "I want a burger but I'm trying to eat better."

"Burgers are our specialty," she said, "but everything's good."

"All right, I'll have one rare with fries and a Diet Coke."

"We can't serve them rare anymore on account of the bacterial scares," she said.

I said, "Bacteria is the last thing I'm scared of." I had to settle for well done anyway.

While I was eating, I felt into my backpack for the book. I did that twice. Just to be sure. **153**

The book had been in a safe in Timmy's hotel room. I guess room safes were the norm in Vegas. Timmy continued to hold out after our scuffle but we both knew he would give it up eventually. And in the long run, it wasn't his fear of being arrested or disgraced or even shot. It was my threat to kill every single damn duck on those damn canals. He had revealed his Achilles' heel. And he couldn't take the chance I was bluffing.

I left him duct-taped to the toilet. Pants down. A "Do Not Disturb" sign on the door to his room. I figured he would be there until the next morning at least. By then, the book would be back in the right hands.

Before I left, he asked me to kiss him. He meant it. I should have said something equally nasty but I just shook my head and turned my back on him.

I ate my burger and looked around the restaurant. A bunch of families. A bunch of couples. I couldn't remember the last time I had sat across from someone in a restaurant. I didn't dislike people. Actually, I liked a lot of them. They were funny, did crazy stuff. I just got edgy making connections. I had gotten to the point, it was bad, where I would rather fib my way around, even if the truth was easier. And Timmy, God bless him, proved I was right. That it wasn't worth getting too chummy with anyone.

After I ate, I went into the bathroom to inspect the bruise on the side of my head. It faded into my hairline. The visible half was purplish and puffy. I touched it and laughed. Pressed my forehead against the mirror and laughed silently for a minute or so. When someone came in, I left.

154   The helmet really aggravated my bruise. I popped some aspirin and strapped the helmet to the back of the bike. What the hell, I'd risk the ticket.

An hour or so later, I got real spacey and almost plowed headlong into a Volvo station wagon coming the opposite way. The driver laid on his horn, we both swerved, and I fishtailed for about twenty feet before regaining control of the bike. I pulled over but the Volvo kept going. I saw a couple of kids in the way-back, staring out the window at me. Their tongues pressed against the glass. I put my helmet on, strapped it tight, and swore my way back to L.A.

A couple miles from Bitter Muse, I stopped at a donut shack and ate a cruller. Then I called Mike at the store. He picked up after six rings.

"Yo!"

"Mike," I said. "It's Jill. What's going on?"

"Oh hey! Hey! Nothing."

"Well, did everything go okay?"

"Sure, sure. No problems. I was a little late. I brought the dog."

"Did anyone come by looking for me?"

"Oh, um, let me think. Yeah. A kind of a kid. Asked about when you — ah! cheater! — when you, uh, work. Wanted to talk to you more about somebody."

"A kid? You sure it wasn't a midget?"

"Naw, naw, he was five-six or something. He patted the dog."

"Nothing strange has happened today? You haven't gotten any weird phone calls or been beaten up? Was anyone hanging around out front of the store?"

"Naw. Oh, well, there was something with the cat." He lowered his voice, made it conspiratorial. "I'd rather not talk about it on the phone, though."   **155**

"Well, I'm coming over now anyway," I said.

One of Mike's buddies was sitting across the desk from him. They were playing a card game called Slap Jack. The friend was talking on the phone. Had it wedged between his ear and shoulder. He said, "Tell them it's the whole load or no load . . . whole load or no load!"

Mike's collie barked furiously. I could see him tied to the vacuum cleaner in the back room. He made it halfway to the front of the store, dragging the vacuum cleaner. Mike said, "No, Champ. No, Lassie!" He didn't look up until he had finished the round of Slap Jack. Two cans of beer sweated on Paul's desk.

"Hey Mike," I said, "C'mon. What's this?"

"It's after five," he said. "Paul doesn't care if you drink after five." It was bullshit but I didn't feel like arguing. I picked up the can nearest Mike and finished it. I put the other one on an issue of *Publishers Weekly*.

"Naw, no more of that faux rococo shit," Mike's buddy said into the phone. "You want that faded stuff, am I right? Distressed! Yeah, that shit. They're eating that shit up."

"I need to use the phone," I said.

"He'll just be a second," said Mike. "He's handling a big important thing."

I walked toward the dog. "Did you get Paul the information about the Phish concerts?"

"Huh? Oh, he never called." The dog jumped at me and managed to land its front paws on my stomach. Its tongue strained to connect with bare flesh.

"Great. You haven't been answering the phone, right?" I noticed what seemed like a ribbon around the dog's head. It was one of those headbands you strap on for Halloween. Little red devil ears poked up behind the dog's real ears.

"I didn't always get to it in time," Mike said. I took the headband off the dog and led him to the back room. Minus the vacuum cleaner. Tied him to the handle of the back door. The cat's collar and a small triangle of its ear lay next to the water cooler. The dog sniffed them. His tail wagged like a furious metronome. I was beat.

I walked into the bathroom and locked the door behind me. A multitude of factors had conspired to give me some intestinal problems. I unshouldered my pack and made myself comfortable. While I was sitting there, I felt for the book and withdrew it from the backpack. I carefully opened it and began flipping through to find the Grautzweller pages. They started on page ninety and ended on one forty-five. Completely jumbled. Here I was sitting on a toilet, holding a book worth two hundred thousand bucks. And for what? Some nutty guy's whim back in 1911. I thought about Grautzweller. A lonely guy spending his nights writing dirty poems and thinking up codes. But he was smart, that Grautzweller. It was a good prank. He figured out a way to be remembered. Obsessed over, really. I flipped the pages, watching the numbers scoot by. No one who owned this edition would care about London's words, only about Grautzweller's. The hidden life within the pages. And the only one in the entire world. You could spend forever trying to crack his code. There was as much meaning in doing that as in doing anything else. It was like owning a combination safe full of dough, only you don't have the combination. Looking at those scrambled numbers got me a little tingly. I was thinking like a collector. And that was no good.

I finished up and came out of the bathroom, still looking through the book. I yelled, "Is he off?" toward the front of the store. As if in answer, the phone rang. There was an extension in the back and I picked it up. Mike's friend simultaneously picked up the other phone. I said, "Bitter Muse Bookstore." The friend said, "Bobby?" I heard Paul on the line.

"Hello? Is this the bookstore?"

"Bobby?"

"Hang up," I said. "It's not Bobby, it's for me."

"Well, okay but don't be long. I'm expecting a very important call right about now."

"Hello? Is this Jill?"

"Hi, Paul," I said.

"Well hello, Jill. This is Paul. What's going on there at the store?"

"It's been a little crazy," I said. "I had a family crisis. I had to ask Mike to work for a couple hours."

"Because no one's been answering the phone, you know," said Paul. "It's very important for people to know that they can call and someone will answer the phone." The dog had a paperback in its mouth. It shook it back and forth as though to stun it.

"I'm sorry, Paul. It really was an emergency."

"Mike's not a very good worker."

"Yeah," I said. "I know."

158   "But there's nothing to be done now, I suppose. Do you have that information for me about those concerts?" I put my hand over the mouthpiece.

"Hey, Mike, did you call and get the Phish information?"

"Naw, because I never talked to Paul!" The dog lay down and held the book between its paws. It ripped off the cover. Before it began to chew it, I saw the title. *Tess of the D'Urbervilles.*

"I'm sorry, Paul. If you call back in fifteen minutes, I'll get you the information."

"People need to know that things that should get done do in fact get done," said Paul.

"Oh, someone's asking me about a book," I said. "Call me back in fifteen minutes." I hung up the phone and took the paperback away from the dog. He whimpered. The cat's ear was gone. I assumed the dog had eaten it.

Heading toward the front desk, I noticed a couple guys talking to Mike. Not browsers. Not the Joke Man. Not the dwarf. I realized I was still holding *The Cruise of the Snark*. I shoved the book in amongst a couple hundred others in the Philosophy section. Mike saw me and waved.

"Hey, Jill," he said, "these guys want to talk to you."

They were fast walkers.

12.

It was my first time in a limo since my mother's funeral. I asked them for a glass of scotch and they gave it to me. I wanted to take some Vivarin, but I remembered that it was in my backpack. Along with everything else I wanted. Maybe Vivarin was the wrong way to go anyway. I was pretty damn jumpy without it.

One guy was very young — barely legal, it seemed — and dressed like a cover boy for *Details* magazine. Except that he wore a calfskin glove on his left hand. Left hand only. His hair was messy in a studied way. But the glove broke the look. The other guy was a typical bodyguard type. From the shoulders up, he was built like an upside-down flowerpot. He had been the persuader. The one who got me outside. The one who poked me lightly with the barrel of his revolver. "Don't let this worry you," he had said. "We're on the same side. It's just to demonstrate how important it is that you come with us." We were in the middle of the store.

Away from Mike and his friend. A foot or so from the book. "But we don't want your pals over there to get messed up in this. Nobody wants a mess," the guy had said. I had told him I would go, but that he better stop poking me because it tickled.

"How much does a car like this rent for?" I asked. "Because my mom's coming into town and I thought I would roll out the red carpet."

Big Neck said, "This isn't a rental. It's owned outright." I sucked down my scotch and held out the glass for a refill. My hand trembled, either from fear or lack of sleep. I shook the glass hard to cover it. Gave the ice a demanding rattle.

"All right," said the glove guy, "keep your pants on." When he gave me the drink, I brought it immediately to my lips. "What kind of movies do you like?" he asked.

I thought for a second. "I like kidnapping flicks," I said.

"Kidnapping flicks," said Big Neck. "I wouldn't say they really constitute an entire genre, but it's an interesting answer."

"I like the postmodern gangster films," said the glove guy.

"Oh, Christ," I said. "Postmodern. That phrase is meaningless in that context. Completely meaningless. It's a description some ex-weatherman idiot film reviewer probably thought up. And it means squat. Postmodern doesn't even make it into the dictionary." I popped a piece of ice into my mouth so I would shut up. Big Neck gave me a dirty look. He reached deep into the recesses of his trench coat. And he withdrew a dictionary. Started flipping through it.

"She's right," he said. "'Postmodern' doesn't make it into the good old American Heritage." He held up three fingers.

161

"What's that mean?" asked the glove guy. "Three what?"

"Third edition."

"Well, it's because it's two words. There's only single words in the dictionary."

"Pickup truck," I said.

"What?"

"Pickup truck? That's two words that made it in."

Big Neck did a little flipping. "She is, again, correct," he said. "Pickup truck is two words. And it's right there." He held the dictionary text outward for the young man to see. Pointed to "pickup truck" with a thumb like a bratwurst.

162 We drove east on Melrose. Because it was rush hour, the going was slow. When we stopped at a light, people held their faces close to the smoked windows, trying to see the celebrity they assumed was inside. We cruised past the Paramount lot, past Koreatown. The glove guy said, "I haven't eaten Korean barbecue in a while."

"Oh, yeah?" said Big Neck.

"Last time was with you, I think."

"That was a while ago."

"Yeah. Maybe it's that I don't like cooking my own food at a restaurant. I want the guy to cook it for me."

"It's a little stressful. Flipping all those little pieces of meat. You have to be good with the sticks."

"Yeah. That's why I don't go anymore."

I just sat and looked out the window and waited. There was nothing else to do.

We passed some bars and a couple blocks' worth of pupuserías. People were out walking, passing a bottle, leaning in doorways. Men sized up women as they exited the food stores with white plastic bags pulling heavily on their arms. They looked like overweighted scales.

"I've never eaten a pupusa," said the glove guy.

"They're pretty good. More of a snack food than a meal."

A guy pushed a shopping cart full of bottles in front of the limo and the driver braked hard. The quick stop threw me forward and I landed against the glove guy. He said, "Well hel*loo!*" I pushed myself off and sat back in my own seat. The driver laid on the horn. The guy with the shopping cart stopped in front of the limo, put up both his middle fingers, and windmilled his arms. The cars behind us began to honk. The guy slowly moved his cart to the side of the road and then turned around and pissed on the limo as it went past him.

"Aw, gross," said Big Neck.

The glove guy cocked his hand into the shape of an imaginary gun and pointed it out the window. "Kaboom," he said. "Kaboom." Then he did a slow-motion imitation of a person's chest exploding. He contorted his face and sunk back against the seat. From his slumped position, he said, "I'm going to go back later and kill that guy."

I had only slept two out of the last thirty-two hours and I was feeling it. I scooped an ice cube from my glass and pressed it against the back of my neck. Closing my eyes for a moment. Memories of the funeral ride popped like flash-bulbs behind my lids. I had been calm. So calm it was crazy. Sitting straight and prim with a little fixed smile. My uncle, drunk, had whispered to my sister, "Well what the hell is the matter with her then?"

We stopped in front of one of those old hotels. Crumbling Art Deco, an orange "Rooms for Rent" banner hanging out a third-floor window. Places like this dotted the city. Once they had been pretty swank. Now they were buildings on the brink of collapse, housing people on the brink of ruin.

The block was lined with RV's, big white panel trucks, guys with tool belts. Anyone who's lived in L.A. for more than a month recognizes the signs of a movie shoot. The boys escorted me out of the limo. We passed a craft service table. A couple of grips milled around, eating bananas and Red Vine licorice. Big Neck plucked a shortbread cookie with his free hand and nibbled on it.

They arm-and-armed me over to a particularly large RV. It said, "Star Wagons." A young woman in jeans and a tailored blazer was waiting by the steps. Holding a clipboard.

"Is this her?" she asked.

"Yes it is," said Big Neck.

"A-duh," said the glove guy. She looked at him with slit eyes. He patted her cheek. "I'm just giving you a hard time," he said.

She turned to Big Neck. "He wants you to help set up at the house."

"Oh. All right. I'll see you both later on." He turned to me. "Buh-bye," he said.

I followed the young woman into the RV. A pretty fancy setup. Sitting area, kitchen, dining area, desk, and, toward the back, a bed. It felt more like a yacht than an RV. The cabinets were made of high-gloss wood. The chairs, navy blue with white piping. Some prints of ships lined the walls. Schooners maybe.

A man lay stretched out on the bed, surrounded by papers. Next to the bed was a stair machine with a red ribbon around it and a big red bow.

"John?" said the young woman.

"Oh, good. She's here." The man on the bed jumped up and walked toward me, tucking in his shirt. He was tallish with sandy-colored hair. Fifty or so but could have passed for younger. He wore a pressed denim shirt and jeans. Suede moccasins. He was John Malcome — actor, director. I recognized him easily.

"Welcome," he said. "Welcome. I'm John." He held out his hand and gave me a weak handshake. Didn't even get past my fingers. He turned to the young guy. "Seth-o. Good work, pal." It occurred to me that the young guy, Seth, looked a good deal like John Malcome. Probably his son. "Let's sit down. Why don't you have a seat right there, Jill." John Malcome indicated a seat at the dining room table. I sat down.

John Malcome addressed the young woman. "Uh, Amy? I guess I ought to have my shake now. Is that right? What time is it? Six? Yes, I better have it now." He turned to me. "I'm having a kind of a protein shake, if you'd like one. They taste pretty good considering they're really just a lot of guck." Amy moved to the kitchen part of the camper and began to fiddle with a blender.

"No thank you," I said.

"Oh, you're sure? What will you have, then? Some sort of snack?" I shook my head. "A drink?" Again, I shook my head. The two limo scotches had made me a bit groggy.

"I don't suppose you have any amphetamines," I said.

"Ah! Um, Amy? Do we have any type of amphetamines?" He had to raise his voice because she had turned on the blender. She turned it off to answer him.

"Someone in the cast might."

"That's all right," I said.

"We have coffee candies," said Amy. "The kind you take when you're driving a long time. They give you a jolt." Amy spoke with authority. A former debater. The type that ran for class president but was too much of a suck-up for the popular vote. Now she was on the Hollywood fast track. In a year she would have her own assistant. John Malcome turned to me.

"Well?" he said.

"I'll have a couple candies," I said.

"Ah, Amy?"

"Yes," she said. During this exchange, Seth turned on the television in the sitting area and began playing a video game. A pixilated Viking decapitated soldiers with frog heads. With every decapitation, the frog-heads yelled, "Argh! Mon dieu!"

I twisted back and forth in my seat like a kid at a fast-food joint. John Malcome sat opposite me, watching Amy. When she had finished making his shake, she brought it over in a tall fluted glass. Placed it carefully in front of him with a napkin, a long spoon, and a flexible straw.

"If it looks good, I fool myself into thinking it is good," Malcome said. It looked like brain matter.

Amy went back to the kitchen area and returned with four cellophane-wrapped candies on a plate. She put the plate in front of me and placed a napkin beside it.

"Oh a napkin," I said. "That's pretty." She moved to the

desk and began typing on a laptop computer. A quiet mechanical rain. I unwrapped one of the candies and put it in my mouth. John Malcome sipped his shake through the straw. It shouldn't have surprised me that he wasn't very good-looking in person.

"Well," he said, "I'm sure you're wondering. Or perhaps you're not. Does your being here seem absurd?"

"Yes," I said. "But —"

"Uh, Seth-o, turn that muck down, won't you? C'mon, man, it's too loud. Too loud." Seth turned down the volume on his game. Negligibly.

"You were saying?" said John Malcome.

"I was going to say that in the past few days I've really learned to embrace absurdity."

"Ah yes. Embrace it. Hmm." He wasn't listening to me. He was looking over at Seth. For a moment, his lips tucked inward and his eyes turned furious.

I watched Seth play the video game. His hands jerked viciously in the direction of the TV. When I looked at John Malcome again, he had bent his head to concentrate on his shake. One of his hands was pressed fisted against the table top. Amy put on an operator's headset and made a phone call. She spoke in the small voice of a girl with a secret.

"Also," I said, regaining John Malcome's attention, "I'm a bit punchy, so anything goes."

"In olden days," said John Malcome, "a glimpse of stocking was looked on as something shocking, now heaven knows . . ."

From the sitting area, Seth sang out, "Anything Goes!" Then he belched loudly. Then he laughed. He looked over quickly to see our reaction.

167

John Malcome made a face. "Shut up! Please! Pal!"

Seth shrugged and returned to his game.

John Malcome took a long sip of his shake. His blue eyes shut in behind a pair of wrinkled lids. I had to look away. I didn't like seeing anyone with their eyes closed.

"Well," I said, "I'm not usually this rude but I do have things I need to do. So if you could fill me in. . . . Is it about my mom? Is she in trouble again?"

"Your mother? No, this has nothing to do with your mother. Amy, do we know anything about her mother?" Amy shook her head and frowned.

"Because she once mentioned she was thinking of stalking you," I said.

"Oh. Really? Well, no, as far as I know nothing like that's been going on. I've never really been stalked as far as I know. Ah, Amy?"

"The woman in the Peter Pan outfit," said Amy. She didn't bother to look up.

"Oh, right. I forgot. But that was a little while ago. And she was much too young to be your mother." He neared the end of his shake and switched to the spoon, scraping the bottom of the glass. "No, this is about a certain book. A book you know about? Seth! Goddammit, turn that damn stuff down. Now c'mon, guy! I mean it!" Malcome smacked the table and the spoon hopped around inside the glass. "A book that you may have?" he continued. Seth turned the video game down some more. John Malcome finished the contents of the glass and set the spoon on the table. Amy was ready. She whisked it all away.

I smiled and wagged my finger at him. "That book," I

said, "belongs to someone else." Without looking, I folded my candy wrapper into the shape of a bird. One of my college roommates had been an origami freak. I had picked up a couple moves.

"Oh but you see that's not true. That's some misinformation. You've been lied to." He touched one of my hands so that I would look at him. I did. Under other circumstances, I might have been a little more starstruck. I had always liked him. He did a good job playing the guilt-racked sergeant, the quiet genius, the cad with a heart of gold. He was a decent director, too. "You've been lied to," he said again. Intensely, regretfully. As though he could kill the bastard who dared.

". . . and, cut," I said.

"No," he said. "I don't do that." He moved away from **169** my hand. "I don't act in my real life. Ask anyone. Amy?"

"No," said Amy.

"Okay," I said. "Whatever you say. But just give it to me fast and straight. I know I've got to hear all this, but I'm really anxious to wrap things up and get to bed, you know?" I didn't want to sit around and listen to Malcome build up to an Oscar-winning moment for my benefit. Acting the part of gentle mentor to the hilt. If I told him his big-necked errand boy had used a piece to get me in the limo, he would have been shocked, appalled. It was what the role required. But he was doing a better job convincing himself that he was that kind of guy than he was convincing me.

"Well, it's not like I'm not a busy person myself, you know. I am directing a movie." He opened his arms and gestured to the room.

"Right," I said. "So let's move it."

He laughed. "Good for you," he said. "I like directness. I like cutting out the niceties. The B.S."

I stood up and moved toward the kitchen. Amy and Seth stood up at the same time. "Where are you going?" asked Malcome.

"I want a glass of water," I said.

"Amy will get that for you. Please sit down. Amy? Amy? Get her a glass of water so she'll sit down." I sat down. Not because Malcome wanted me to, but because I was having a hard time standing. I was rubber-limbed. My head felt like it had been pumped full of helium and was floating a few feet above my neck. Suddenly, very suddenly, the room seemed warm and a little wonderful. I couldn't believe that coffee candies would give me that kind of buzz, but something was working its way through my system. I looked at John Malcome. The greatest actor/director of all time, wasn't he? Sure, whatever. Amy handed me a glass of water and I drank it. It tasted more like water than any water I had ever tasted. I said, "Thank you, Amy." Now I knew without a doubt that they had slipped me a mickey of some sort. Perhaps Seth had put it in the scotch. I tried swimming out of it, but I felt too damn good. The first day at the beach. Sunshine and lollipops.

"Excuse me," I said, "but did you give me something perhaps? Something to make me feel a little strange?"

"Oh," said John Malcome. "What? Well, those candies do have a good deal of caffeine in them. But it's just caffeine, isn't that right, Amy? Just caffeine?"

"Yes," said Amy. I looked over at Seth. He was smiling at me. Smiling an elfin smile. He rolled his eyes around and pursed his lips like Charlie Chaplin making moony. I understood.

"Oh," I said. "Oh shit, I feel nice." Seth turned back to his video game.

"Well, good," said John Malcome.

"Look," I said, pointing to one of the chairs in the sitting area. "See that chair? I'm going to go sit in it."

"Oh. All right," said John Malcome. "We can move over there." I oozed my way over and sat down. The cushions collapsed beneath my weight, making a small "poof" sound. "What a chair," I said.

"Seth-o," said John Malcome, "turn off the game and have yourself a snack. We're going to talk here now." John Malcome motioned for Seth to get up. "C'mon, I need that chair, pal."

"One sec," said Seth. John Malcome stood still a moment longer. Then he grabbed the game component from the top of the television. He walked it to the door of the trailer, giving a tug on the cables to dislodge them from the television. Seth held on to the joystick, which was attached by one long cable to the game. Malcome opened the trailer door and chucked out the game.

"Hey," I said.

Malcome closed the door on the joystick cable and Seth stood up, still holding the stick as though in midplay.

"O-*kay!*" said John Malcome. He sat in the vacated chair. Seth stood slumped and contrite, looking at his father and working the stick around with his gloved hand.

"So when are we going to talk about that other stuff?" said Seth.

Malcome looked at Seth brightly. "Later," he said. "Later. C'mon now."

"You said later before."

"C'mon. Cut the old man a break. Okay? I need to do this now."

"I just wish that if you said —"

"Oh, for fuck's sake!" Malcome pressed his hands against his ears and spoke quietly into his lap. "Later means later and I'll tell you when now is now! Now is not now right now! All right? All *right?* We'll get to it! All right?"

"Sure," said Seth. "Sure, . . . John." Seth covered the lower part of his face with his gloved hand to hide his smile. I saw it anyway. All over the rest of his face.

I said, "Sure."

"So you want me inside?" said Seth. "Or outside."

Malcome's head snapped up as though he had just been caught dozing. "Outside. That's perfect. All the way outside. Take your thing. Thanks a lot, guy." Malcome reached out and playfully patted Seth on the back of the leg. Seth got a Coke from the small fridge. On his way out, he said, "Have fun." He said it directly to me and he made his fingers into a pistol and pointed them at my head.

"Okay," said John Malcome, turning to me. "This is better. Let's do talk about the book now," he said, "because I'm going to need to work soon."

"Oh, all right," I said. "Lay it on me."

13.

John Malcome's father had given him the book. Given it to him as a child. His father had given him the book on his deathbed. John Malcome's sister was there. John Malcome's sister got no deathbed book. John Malcome's sister got nothing. After a while, John Malcome's sister took the book from John Malcome. She denied taking it. She hid it, hid it well. For forty-odd years, John Malcome thought about the book. Wanted the book. Knew the sister had the book. Nothing he said to her, no amount of convincing, could make her return it. John Malcome hated his sister.

John Malcome collected other books, hoping to fill the gap that one had left. Sometimes John Malcome bought books from Tim Harris. Tim brought the book to Vegas and one of the first people he ran into was Vince, John Malcome's bodyguard and book-scout. Vince didn't know the significance of the book — he just knew it was a book John Malcome might want. He agreed to the buy. Timmy missed the meeting time. When Vince told John Malcome what he had almost had, John Malcome became excited. He never imagined that the book might show up on the open market. He told Vince to find the book. Instead, Vince found Timmy. Where I had left him. Timmy fingered me in exchange for a generous cash reward. Desperate for the dough, I guess. Or just disloyal. And that's where we were.

"Have you ever," John Malcome said, "experienced a real sense of loss? A kind of devastating loss?" I was rubbing my hand on the arm of the chair. Soft cotton, like the sheets on a childhood bed. I fingered the piping. I said, "This tiny roll of fabric, this piping, it pulls the whole piece together. It unifies it."

"I'm talking about loss," said John Malcome. "I'm talking about grief. When my father died, my whole world fell apart."

"Yes," I said. "Yes, it must have."

"I was at sea," said John Malcome.

"'My whole world fell apart and I was at sea.' Those both sound so familiar. Did you say them once before? A movie — some movie?" I rubbed my hands together. I had some lovely hands, that was certain.

"Oh. No, I don't believe so."

"No," said Amy.

"Amy's nice," I said.

"But you need to understand, that book completely represented my father for me. It took his place on a symbolic level. I had the book all wrapped up in parchment, then burlap, then — oh, I think it was some sort of calico. I slept with it. I spoke to it."

"You ate with it," I said.

"Yes," said John Malcome, "Sure. I ate with it."

"I mean with it next to you. I didn't mean to imply that you used it as some sort of utensil."

"And because of the wrapping, you see, I didn't even know she had taken it for a long time. A long time. What she had done was she had switched it with another book. That was what hurt the most. The idea that I spent so long embracing the wrong . . . book."

"You were praying to a false god."

"Yes, I . . . no, not quite. . . . Did you know my father was an actor as well? A child actor? He was very popular."

"Boy, *so* many people are actors. It's something I should definitely do."

"Oh really? That interests you?"

"What?" I said.

"Anyway. So I'm sure that you can understand how important it is to me. Perhaps you've lost someone . . . ."

"Not that I know of," I said.

"Well, for me this loss was indefatigable. No. Is that right? Indefatigable?"

"I'm not quite sure," said Amy. I kept my mouth shut.

"Damn," said John Malcome. "Vince is at the house with the dictionary, isn't he."

"Yes," said Amy. "Should I call him?"

"Yes, yes, call him up. I have to know this." We both sat still a moment. John Malcome said, "Would it surprise you to hear that I'm thinking of running for a political office?"

"No," I said.

"No?"

"All the articles about you say that."

"You're a real straight shooter," he said. "A no B.S.-er straight shooter. I like that."

"So Francis — that was your father?"

"Yes, that's right. How did you know?"

"From the — it's in the book."

"Ah yes, the dedication."

"Inscription."

"Hmm?"

"Dedication . . . that's wrong. The book isn't dedicated to your father, it's inscribed to him."

"Now that is fascinating. There's a difference?"

"Get Vince to show you some time."

"I will. I will."

"What about the mixed up pages? The Gratzinheimer thing?"

"Yes. I heard about that. I never noticed it when I was a kid."

"You didn't read the book?"

"No."

Someone knocked lightly on the door and then entered. A guy with a beard and a baseball cap. He said, "John, we're getting ready."

"I *like* your hat," I said. And I did. It had a picture of a lightbulb on it.

The wardrobe woman found me a black gauze dress with dark blue sequins. I slipped it on. It smelled like cedar. She said, "It's a little big, but they wore them that way." I tried to turn a circle but my balance had gone screwy. She handed me a pair of pantyhose. She helped me put them on.

"Not pantyhose," I said.

"I don't know where you're going to be. It's no good if the camera picks up your bare legs."

"Okay," I said. I wanted to make her happy. She had wine-colored hair. I touched it. The room was filled with clothes. Hundreds of empty sleeves. "Those sleeves need arms. So many arms."

"Uh huh," said the wardrobe woman. She had a pin cushion strapped to her wrist. Deep purple. It looked like a tiny crown.

"I used to read in the coat closet when I was a little kid," I said. "It was small. It smelled good. Sort of like this."

"I was scared of the closet," she said. "I'm going to give you some heels, but you don't need to put them on until they're ready for the shot." I noticed she had some sort of bandage around the wrist without the pin cushion. A tight, skin-colored bandage.

"What happened to your wrist?" I asked.

"What's your shoe size?"

"What happened to your wrist?"

"Carpal tunnel syndrome," she said. "Six and a half? Seven?"

"Seven. Don't people get that from typing too much?"

"I got it from holding heavy hangers."

"Holding heavy hangers. Holding heavy hangers. Holding heavy hangers."

"There's no time for your hair. You can wear a hat."

I looked at myself in the mirror. I didn't wear dresses much. I got a little lost in them. This one was sleeveless. I had a bit of a T-shirt tan from riding my bike everywhere. But if she didn't notice, I wasn't going to say anything. I swayed back and forth, holding the sides of the dress. I sang, "When the moon *plays* peek-a-boo." She stuck a hat on my head. A cloth helmet, really. Also black. One side of it partially covered my face. I looked at myself coyly.

"Cunning!" I said. She gave me the once-over.

"Your boobs are a little big, but I don't think it's worth strapping them down. I just can't strap down another set of boobs today. It's too depressing." She picked up a Polaroid camera and handed me a pair of shoes.

"Hold still," she said. The flash went off. I staggered back against a rack of clothes and fell through them. Feeling those clothes give way behind me was terrifying and I laughed.

"What was that for?" I asked.

178   "You've got to be careful of the dress," she said. She pulled me up and brushed the dust off the back of it.

"Thank you," I said.

"Don't thank me. I'm a perfectionist. I don't want to go to the premiere and see a flapper with a dirty ass. Just be a little careful, honey, is all I'm saying."

"Why did you take my picture?"

"Continuity," she said.

In the makeup chair, I sat on my hands and my arms fell asleep. The guy that worked me over had stiff blond hair. He was very tan. Burnt orange really. When he was done with me, he said, "*Voilà*. My recipe for Instant Flapper Tart." My lips were fuck-me red. My eyes sleepy. "Fasten your seat belts," he said, "it's going to be a bumpy night." He moved off to another section of the trailer, recapping bottles.

I sat there a minute, trying to think. That didn't work too well. I leaned into the mirror and touched my lips. I barely recognized myself all painted up that way. But then I had trouble recognizing myself anytime. I always figured I could walk past myself on the street and not give me a second glance. I could sell myself a book and think that maybe I had gone to school with me and we had had a class together and I had hated myself and my stupid comments.

Seth entered the picture behind me, wearing a tuxedo. He had makeup on, but it was less noticeable than mine. Made his eyes darker. His hair was slicked back. Rudolph Valentino. The calfskin glove was gone. Replaced by white satin. A matching glove dripped halfway out of his jacket pocket. He put his hands on my shoulders and rested his chin on the top of my head. As loopy as I was, the contact bugged me. But I sat still for it. Like a park statue puts up with a pigeon.

"We look cool," he said. He leaned his face closer to mine. "Do you feel good?" I shook my head up and down, then back and forth. "I thought you'd like that little favor. That's some happy-feeling stuff. Everything feels good. Everyone's your friend. And being in John's movie — that's huge! You can thank him for that. It's quite a deal."

"I'm lucky," I said. I did feel lucky, though I had to remind myself why. Right, I was going to be in a movie. A John Malcome film. Exciting. It was hard to think of anything for very long. Thoughts like commuters. My brain the turnstile.

Seth cupped my hat with his gloved hand as though it were a basketball. "Look at this hat. That is a cool hat. If you want, I'll find out if you can keep it after."

"Yeah," I said.

"I'm thinking . . . just thinking . . . that maybe you'll want to do something nice for us. Well, we'll talk about it a little later." He stood up straight and I could still feel the pressure of his hand on my head, though he had taken it away. He held my arm and led me out of the trailer. Helped me down the steps. Braced me. The ground wouldn't play nice with my feet. I said, "I want . . ." I said it softly and the thought passed when the words hit the air.

We walked through the night for a couple minutes before entering the hotel. It was warmer outside than it had been in all the air-conditioned trailers. An old man wearing a bathrobe over his suit pants was talking to a young production assistant. "What's the name of this picture?" he said. "Who's the star?" I had thought he was an actor, but he wasn't. The production assistant said, "Sir, please move back. Move away. It's dangerous." And the old man retied his robe and said, "I just want to know the *name* of the *picture!* I *live here.*"

Going up to the lobby, I stepped on my dress and tore it.

"Oh no," I said. "Oh no."

"You can't notice," said Seth.

The lobby was full of cables and lights. People with walkie-talkies. They said, "Wrre youat, whhts yr pzzition now?" I moved around them like I was filled with unbroken eggs.

We went through some double doors and into a packed ballroom. The place was decked out. Nothing matched with the shabbiness of the rest of the hotel. The whole room had been magic-wanded. It smelled new. New carpet, new drapes, new tablecloths. Silver and gold bunting. The chandeliers threw light around like sparklers at a Fourth of July luau. I felt underdressed until I remembered that I wasn't. All of us were outfitted to dance the Charleston. But it didn't feel like a party. People sat quietly at round banquet tables. Talking without gaiety. I saw one woman reading a book. I tried to catch the title. Something about heaven.

Seth steered me to a table and pulled out a chair for me. I sat next to a beefy guy with a face the color of an underripe tomato. The room was too bright. Hot from all the people and the lights. I was developing a theory that I didn't really want to be there. The beefy guy wiped his brow, then took out a compact and dabbed his face with powder.

Seth wasn't sitting next to me, he was up talking to some young guy holding a bullhorn. They were laughing. I thought about spending a little time under the table. It didn't seem like I would be missed.

"Okay!" said the guy with the bullhorn. He used the bullhorn to say it. It filled the room. The room shut up. Seth covered his ears. "Okay, we're getting ready to get started. Now for the first shot, this is what's going to happen — can everyone hear me?" There was a rumble of noise. Could have been affirmative or negative. "Okay, Kerri Jakes . . . who plays Lilly . . . is going to enter the ballroom . . . and walk . . . toward the dance floor! Now as she enters . . . you people . . . are going to stand up . . . and applaud! But we don't want everyone watching and waiting . . . and then all standing up . . . at once! It's got to look like you're doing it . . . as you realize . . . she's there!"

A woman at my table said, "I wish they didn't treat us like utter morons."

"They just want it right the first time," said the beefy guy.

The guy kept speaking into the bullhorn. He pointed at Seth, who curtsied. I heard the words ". . . so we can practice."

"How long is this for?" I asked no one in particular.

"Hmm?" said the beefy guy.

I picked up a butter knife. Small but weighty. I could see myself in it, funhouse style. The beefy guy said, "I know you weren't here for that part, but they specifically asked us not to touch the silverware. It dulls it. They want everything sparkly." He wiggled his fingers around like a magician getting ready to pull out his rabbit.

"Sorry," I said. I went to pocket the knife but my dress had no pockets. I put it back on the table and the beefy guy repositioned it for me. Someone said something funny. A few minutes later I smiled.

The beefy guy nudged me with his elbow. Everyone was up and clapping. I stood up and held on to the table. Watched Seth vamp his way toward the dance floor. A camera on a dolly led the way. Two guys pulling, one riding.

"Do you think there's a phone somewhere?" I asked the beefy man. He was sweating again. Beads of it budding on his forehead, getting ready to spill.

"A phone?"

"I want to call someone," I said.

"They're getting close to doing it for real, you know. You can't leave now. See over there?" He pointed to the dolly with the camera. "That's John Malcome."

I looked at John Malcome, then up at the ceiling. Someone had painted clouds up there. The kind of clouds you see shapes in, if you stare long enough. Lie on the grass and say,

182

"A ship. That's a dragon. That's a girl with a cat in one hand and a big knife in the other." My mother did it all the time. And said, "There's always something else. Whatever it is you think you see, there's always something else." Toward the end, she had me carrying her out onto the lawn — it was like carrying an empty beach chair, she was that light. She wanted to lie on the grass and look up. The only grass we had was in the front yard. People walking by and looking. Her students sometimes. She didn't mind. She told them to join us and they did because they were all crazy about her.

I felt stupid because I was suddenly choked up over that thought and I never cry about my mother.

Seth clasped my arm. "You can sit," he said. He sat down beside me. I was the only one still standing. I sat.

"You were great," a woman at our table said to Seth. She was wearing a ribbon around her head. "I really believed you were Kerri Jakes."

"Ha!" said Seth. "Thanks."

"Doesn't she have a stand-in?" someone asked.

"Yeah, but she wiped out Rollerblading today. Cracked her skull. I'm Kerri's height. So this is my big break." Everyone at the table laughed too hard. I rubbed my eyes with my hands.

"You're gonna smear," said the beefy guy.

I said, "I don't know what made you decide you hate me."

"Excuse me," he said. "I don't. I clearly don't. I'm just trying to help."

Seth's gloved hand rubbed my shoulder. "This is exciting, isn't it? Your big break, right? I'm in all Dad's movies. You ever see *Fullerton Street?* You know the big car chase? I'm the old lady on the street corner. That was funny."

"Is this a rotating restaurant?" I asked.

"Heh heh," said Seth. "You feel just fine." He leaned in closer. "And you know, I'll tell you this. Coming up in his next one or the one after that it looks like I'll be a pretty major player. We're going to hold out a little while . . . until my acting coach gives the green light."

The guy with the bullhorn was at it again. Introducing Kerri Jakes to the crowd. She waved, they applauded. I had read somewhere that she had her breast implants removed to play a flapper in a John Malcome flick. I guess this was it. She looked pretty flat.

"She dies later," said Seth. "She's got a great death. They shot it earlier today." I looked at the ceiling again. "Isn't this sweet? So, hey, you know you've got to give Dad his book." I felt his breath on my ear. "It would be so cool if you would do that. It means a lot to him. Then someday I'll get it. It's that kind of thing. A, you know, a legacy. I have everything of his. Acting . . . pretty soon I'll start directing. . . ."

184

"Who's the Joke Man?" I asked.

"Who?"

"The Joke Man. The other guy trying to get the book."

"Oh," said Seth, "you mean the guy that works for my aunt? That guy — don't you recognize him? — that guy, Barry Knott, he was an actor for a long time. Little bits. Always played the tough guy. The heavy. My aunt hires has-been actors to work for her. Fucking has-been wanna-bes. He's a prick. I saw him at an audition just a couple weeks ago, he pretended he didn't know me."

"He seemed like an awfully nice fella to me," I said.

"Ehw!" said Seth.

I leaned toward him so that he would back off from me

a little. "So, Seth-ee, uh, Seth-o," I whispered, "what's the story with that glove?"

"Hmm?" said Seth. "Oh." He looked at his gloved hand a second, then casually put it in his pocket. "That hand smells."

John Malcome joined us. His head appeared over my right shoulder so suddenly that I jumped and almost fell off the chair. "Come with me," he said.

"What?" I said.

"I need you for this shot. I want someone to cross in front of the camera right before Kerri enters the room."

"I don't wanna," I said.

"But I want you to," he said.

"I'll do it, Dad," said Seth.

"No, Seth-o, I want her. She looks good." He tugged on **185** my arm.

"We talked about me doing something like that," said Seth.

"Don't be stupid now, Seth-o," said John Malcome. "C'mon, Jill. Hup."

"Go!" whispered the beefy man. "Go, go, go!"

"She's got to change her shoes," said Seth. He leaned down and removed my clogs and I slipped my feet — or at least some feet that claimed to be mine — into the high heels. They were too big. Seth whispered into my ear very softly. "Don't tell John about our secret," he said. "He doesn't like drugs." I stood and shuffled behind John Malcome. I was worried about my clogs. I didn't want to lose them. I turned around and the whole table was staring at me like I had just won the lottery. Or I was covered in crap.

"Be careful with my clogs," I said to Seth.

John Malcome paced me through it a couple times. I had to walk quickly in front of the camera and go sit down. Another guy, the cinematographer I guess, told me exactly where to move. He spoke with an Italian accent. I did a lousy job of following his directions. I was still all fogged up from whatever Seth had given me. And tired. Bone tired.

The young guy with the bullhorn said, "You're at a party, look happy. You're happy!"

"No," said John Malcome. "I like that she looks unhappy. She looks like something just happened to her. She saw her husband kissing another woman in the lobby. Or she's just unhappy about life."

"But, John," said the cinematographer. "She has to walk more rapidly!"

"Walk faster," said the guy with the bullhorn. "You're in a hurry. You have to get your seat. Right away!"

"You have to walk faster," said John Malcome, "but don't look excited."

The room was quiet. Watching and waiting. I saw Kerri Jakes sitting in a canvas chair, drinking mineral water from a bottle. Drinking through a very long straw. She touched her throat with her fingers as though she was feeling her glands. She called Amy over and stuck out her tongue. Amy looked deep into her mouth and shook her head.

I walked in front of the camera three more times. The third time was for film. Kerri Jakes made her entrance. The partygoers stood and cheered. I pitched forward and by the time I hit the new rug I was unconscious.

186

14.

I came to because I was having trouble breathing. I opened my eyes but they might as well have still been closed. The room was pitch-black. My ragged breath sounded like an old woman dying alone somewhere. I felt a little panicky. "Hey!" I said. "Turn on a light." No answer to that. I felt around. I was lying on something soft. I felt around some more and identified a table. Bedside lamp. I turned it on and the light ate into my head. I covered my eyes with both hands. "Shit," I said. "Oh Jesus, my head." I cracked my fingers and had a look around.

The room was all done up in chintz. Stripes and flowers. Like a country house in a British period piece. I was on a bed with a feather duvet. I'm allergic to down feathers. I sat on the edge of the bed. My weepy eyes had bled makeup all over what looked like an antique embroidered pillowcase. "Oh," I said. I scratched at the stain. It got bigger.

A small silver clock next to the lamp told me it was three-twenty. I assumed in the morning. The clock was engraved. I had a closer look. "*Fullerton Street,* 1993." The John Malcome flick. You get a lot of presents when you make a movie. Jackets, baseball caps, maybe sports equipment. Engraved clocks.

I stood slowly. I was still wearing the flapper dress. It brought back a little of the night. The trailer. The ballroom. The whole thing felt like a dream. Like I had fallen off the face of reality for a while. Down the rabbit hole, so to speak. My shoes were gone. So was the hat.

There were three doors in the room. One opened onto a closet, another onto a hallway, and the third, the jackpot, onto a bathroom. I took off my pantyhose and used them on my head to hold the hair away from my face. I rinsed my eyes with warm water, drank steadily for a minute, and then washed the makeup off as best I could with the small pearly guest soap. There was some hand lotion under the sink and I used it on my face.

When I opened the door to the hallway and poked my head out, I heard the mixed-up murmur of people talking. Lots of people. For a second, I thought I might still be somewhere in the hotel. But there was the *Fullerton Street* clock. It was a house. Malcome's house.

To the left, the hall led to a large staircase. The noise made its way up from there. In the other direction, the hall went up two steps and ended with a door. I was betting on the fact that there was another staircase back there. Big houses like this usually had a second staircase for the servants to use so they could slip around unnoticed. Clean up the mess like happy little elves.

188

I walked toward the door. It opened suddenly and a very tall woman stepped out. She had on an emerald green gown and her mouth was enormous. She tripped and fell down.

"I'm all right," she said. She stood up. "I cannot find a bathroom for the life of me," she said. "Oh it's driving me crazy and I'm about to burst." I pointed her to the room I had just left. "You're an angel," she said. I continued up the little steps. "Someone's crying back there somewhere," she said. She flipped her arm in the direction from which she had come.

I went through the door and down a hallway which ended, thankfully, at a narrow staircase. I didn't hear any crying.

The staircase brought me to the kitchen. The room was full of people in white cook aprons, packing up food and washing dishes and generally bustling around. One guy was picking radishes cut into flower shapes off of a tray and tossing them into a plastic bag. A young woman in a white shirt and tie smiled at me as she walked by. Her tie was loosened and her top button undone. She put down a tray of leftover hors d'oeuvres. Shrimp and pea pods. Smoked salmon on tiny toast points. Individual tortellini on long wooden skewers. I stuffed four tortellini at a time into my mouth. Ate the shrimp and salmon and the grape garnish. No one paid attention. I saw a refrigerator at the other end of the kitchen and I went over and opened it. In the door were bottles of fruit-flavored ice-tea. I drank one.

"Can I help you find something?" A guy in a droopy chef's hat.

"No." I glared at him so he would think I was somebody important. The guy moved off, but I was wise to the idea

189

that, in sticking around, I was taking a risk. I didn't imagine Malcome or Seth poking around the kitchen. But Amy was a pretty good bet. I'd rather she didn't see me up and about. It was time to snap out of it and get lost. Go get the book and exit the whole business. I was starting to think that I might leave the book under a tree somewhere, tip off all concerned parties, and let them rumble for it. That ought to end my involvement nicely.

I saw some of the caterers exiting a back door and I joined them. Some trucks were parked up close for loading the dishes and the old food. I skirted around the trucks and followed the driveway down toward the front gate. Cars were parked all along the right hand side. Small lamps crouched around in the bushes.

190   The front gate was closed. It was the kind that needed the weight of a car to trigger it. I didn't feel like hanging around for someone to leave the party so I walked back up to the nearest car and, sure enough, it was unlocked. A Jaguar. You didn't worry much about car theft on a security estate.

It was an older Jag. A stick shift with no power steering. Just what I needed. I got in, put it in neutral, let out the parking brake, and coasted backward toward the gate. About ten feet away I stopped the car and the gate began to swing slowly toward me. I opened the door to get out. But I could see that the house was way up in the hills. The city spread out below like tangled Christmas lights. What the hell. They'd find the car easily enough.

I coasted through the gate and had just enough momentum to back up the street and turn the car nose-first toward the city. Then I began rolling forward. Gaining speed fast.

Whenever I hit an intersection, I took the route with the steepest down-slope. There was no one else on the road and I flew all over the pavement.

At one point the road dipped and on the other side of the rise, a black dog was lying in the middle of the street. I hit the brakes and swerved. Screeched to a halt a foot away from him. He turned to look at me. His eyes demon red in the headlights. I hit the horn. His only reaction was a slow blink. "C'mon, dog," I said. I hit the horn a couple more times. Tapped out a little rhythm. Finally, I put on the parking brake and got out of the car. Went around the front and slowly approached the dog.

"Beat it," I said. "Get away. Shoo. Shoo." The dog whimpered. I moved in closer and gently nudged him with my foot. The whimper became a growl. I said, "Well, what am I supposed to do? What's the problem here, anyway?" I squatted down to his level and held out one of my hands so he could get a good sniff. I touched his head. "C'mon, dog," I said, "I'm sure you have some plush little house around here somewhere." I put my hands under his back and tried to boost him up. He yelped. "Oh, fuck," I said. "Did you get hit?" He licked my hand. He was midsize, skinny. No collar. No tags. I got my weight under him and picked him up. He didn't bite. I carried him to the side of the road and set him down. Good dog. Got back in the car. Then I got out of the car. Popped the trunk. It was filled with crap. Empty bottles, magazines, clothes, and one smelly old blanket. I put the blanket on top of the dog. He just looked at me, the blanket framing his face like a nun's wimple. I got back in the car and coasted a couple of feet. I braked and sat there for a moment. "Shit!" I said. Damn dog. I got out again and walked

191

over to the dog. Said, "Don't even give me that look." I picked him up and rested him on the hood while I opened the back door. Placed him on the back seat. He put on a good face. Didn't struggle or make a sound.

At Sunset Boulevard, I ran out of hill. I made a left and slowly came to a halt on the side of the road. I knew where I was. I was a mile or so from a pay phone. I hugged the wheel and sat still while I tried to figure out what to do. A couple cars passed by. The Jag had a phone. I pushed some buttons. A useless gesture. It wouldn't work unless the car was turned on. My neck and my eyes still itched from the down. And I was freezing. I looked in the trunk again and found an old rabbit fur coat. There was a pair of panties in the pocket. But no shoes or socks.

192   I put the Jag's hood up and waited. A few minutes later, a car stopped. A youngish balding guy got out and walked over.

"What seems to be the trouble?" he asked. He bobbed his head over the engine.

"I can't find my keys," I said. He stood up straight and looked at me. Gave me the once-over.

"That is a problem," he said. "Well, they can't have gone far, right?"

"No, I threw them really hard." I gestured at the stone wall next to us. And the acre or so of lawn beyond, velvet in the moonlight. "I don't think I'll find them. But if you could give me a lift, that would be great."

"Well," he said. "Well. All right. What'd you throw your keys fer, anyway?"

"Oh I just got so mad at those keys," I said.

"Uh huh. You just want to leave your car here, then?"

"I'll have to! I'll get my spare keys and come back."

"I'm just going to around La Cienega Boulevard," he said.

"Great," I said. I walked over to his car with him. "Oh shoot," I said. "Wait one second. I forgot something."

I finally convinced the guy to take me to the twenty-four-hour vet. There was one across from Bitter Muse and I directed him to it. He had me pegged as a loony, but no one throws an injured dog out of their car. He didn't ask any questions. Just drove, tapping the wheel in time to Frank Sinatra.

He dropped me in front and took off. I carried the dog to the door. There was a "Back in 5 minutes" sign taped to it. I looked around. Trying to figure out where a vet would go for five minutes at four in the morning. I sat down in front of the door with the dog on my lap. He seemed stunned. I couldn't see any blood. I felt around for broken bones and came up empty. "What's wrong with you, anyway?" I asked. I huddled around the dog for warmth, scratching my neck. And it felt as though the entire world had packed up and moved to a different neighborhood.

A guy in a lab coat rounded the corner. Dark-skinned. Indian or perhaps Pakistani. He was eating a whole chicken. When he saw me, he put it back in its bag and walked faster.

"Sorry," he said. "I hope you weren't waiting long." He held a key straight out, like a tiny saber. "I sit there every night and no one comes in and I get to thinking about chicken. I don't know why." When he got close to the door, the dog stood up and began to sniff at the bag that held the

193

chicken. The vet lifted the bag over his head and opened the door.

"Down, boy," he said. The vet and the dog went inside and I followed. The place reeked of wet fur and antiseptic — an unpleasant combination. The dog was really making an effort to jump for the chicken, the vet turning circles and holding the bag as far away as possible. "Maybe you want to grab ahold of him," he said.

"I think he was hit by a car," I said. The dog stopped jumping, sat up on his hind legs, did a back flip. Almost. "Wow," said the vet.

194

The vet wouldn't give up his chicken, but he filled a bowl with dry kibble. He checked out the dog while the dog nosed the bowl around, gulping food. The dog didn't have any injuries, he was just malnourished. I guess he had finally called it quits in the middle of that road.

I told the vet I was a little short on cash. He said, "Never mind," and gave the dog a vitamin shot. "You look a little malnourished yourself," he said. He pointed at my bare feet.

"I'm all right," I said. "I'm just thirsty." I helped myself to some water from the water cooler. Aqua Mountain water. Fresh as the springtime that made it, or some such thing.

"Are you a sort of runaway?" asked the vet.

"Nope," I said.

"Are you doing right by yourself?"

"Sure."

"Could you use five dollars?"

"Why not?" He gave me five dollars. I was ready to go. I tried to leave the dog behind. The vet nixed the idea. I told him it wasn't my dog. I was just doing a good deed. He didn't believe me. Finally, I exited the place and closed the door so the dog couldn't follow. The vet pushed the dog out the door behind me.

The dog and I walked toward the mini-market on the corner, which stayed open twenty-four hours also. The Korean guy's wife was working the counter. She and her husband didn't get to see very much of each other, I guess. I imagined they communicated through notes left in the cash register. "Order toilet paper and beef jerky." "Good article in *Los Angeles* magazine, p. 38." "Another request for marshmallows, should we carry them?" "I love you."

The dog tried to follow me in.

"No dogs," she said. I shut the door to keep him out. He scraped at the door. His breath bloomed against the glass.

"Do you sell whole chickens?" I asked.

"No," she said. And then, "We have instant chicken soup."

"That's all right." I picked out a couple cans of dog food and stacked them on the counter. There was a bin next to the counter with bags of Bunny Love carrots. On special. I added a bag to the dog food. "I'm trying to improve my eating habits," I said.

"Why," she said.

I cased the bookstore and saw nothing unusual. Scott's motorcycle was parked out front where I had left it. I walked around to the back. The parking lot was empty. Paul had a spare key hidden on a ledge behind the store. He was always losing his key, locking himself out. Absentminded professor.

I felt around for ten minutes before locating it. Paul had moved it.

I put the key in the lock and discovered that the door was open. It gave my stomach a little jolt. Still, if it was the Joke Man waiting, I could just hand over the book and be done with things. I didn't care about Malcome's claim to it. He and his sister were rich enough to duke it out in court if he wanted it that badly. It would be less messy than a rumble. It occurred to me that I hadn't signed a release for my performance in Malcome's movie. Or maybe I had.

I eased the door open a bit and the dog stuck his nose in. "Okay," I said. "If you want to. . . . Go. Seek." I let the dog inside and closed the door behind him. For about thirty seconds there was silence. Then all hell broke loose. The dog started barking like crazy. I heard a sharp noise, a small gun being fired, maybe. The dog snarling, yelping. I hesitated. Deciding whether to bust it up or just run like hell. Then I heard the cat. I opened the door and turned on the light. The dog and the cat were squaring off. Circling like boxers. The cat's left ear looked like a hastily torn note.

They went for each other screeching and snarling. The cat defending its home for the second time that day. "No!" I said. "Get off!" I tried to insert an arm and I got scratched across the back of my hand. They were all over the store. A pinball of ire. I grabbed a roll of paper towels and went after them, swinging. They stopped for a second and I hauled on the dog by the scruff. The cat made for the open back door. I made for it too, but not fast enough. The cat was gone. Leaving some new blood drops behind. "Oh, cat," I said. Another happy surprise waiting for Paul.

An encyclopedia had fallen onto a small table and broken one of the legs. I figured that was the gunshot noise I had heard. It seemed a safe bet that the fight would have flushed out anyone lurking inside the store. The door had been open, but not jimmied. Maybe Mike had just forgotten to lock it before leaving. He had done it before.

After a quick look around to make sure the place was deserted, I made a line for the Philosophy section to retrieve the London book. It wasn't there. I slowed down and went through the shelves again. Then I checked Metaphysics and Transportation on either side. "No," I said. "No no no no no." It didn't seem possible that someone could have found it without knowing where to look. People aren't that lucky. I checked Fiction, hoping some anal dork had seen it misshelved and moved it. Nothing. The dog nudged my hand and I gave it a pat on the nose. It took me a minute to register that his face was wet. Bloody. I took a look. The cat had scratched his cheek, just missing his eye. "Oh no," I said. "No no no no no." An ugly gash in his black fur. The dog whimpered. "Aw, shit," I said. I scratched behind his ear.

The phone rang and I jumped. I ran to it and then stopped, hovering. It could be news about the book. Or Paul, pissed as hell. Or it could be someone checking up on my whereabouts. I took a chance and answered.

"Ah . . . *si?*" I said.

"Blahah? Blahah Joe?"

"You fucking nutcake," I said. "I am going to kill you. Do you understand? Kill you." I hung up. Then I called Mike's place. Maybe he would remember selling the book. It was busy. Off the hook, no doubt. Mike passed out next to it.

The dog looked bad. "Just a minute, dog," I said. I quickly poked through the hold shelves by the front desk. Someone could have set it aside. No dice. Jesus, if a dealer had spotted it, I was really in the soup.

I went to the back of the store again and looked around for my backpack. That was also missing. The keys to the motorcycle were in it. I turned to the dog and said, "Where's my bag, huh? Where is my goddamn bag?" The dog lay down and showed me its belly. "No," I said, "that's not my bag."

I looked around for something to hit or throw. I picked up a copy of *West with the Night*. But I like that book and this particular copy was an unblemished hardcover so I put it down again. I searched around until I found a lousy twenty-five-cent mystery and started to rip it in two. By then, my heart just wasn't in it. I said, "C'mon, you mutt." The bag with the carrots and dog food was by the door and I shouldered it on the way out.

Seth was waiting for me in the parking lot.

"Hey, mama," he said. He was wearing a different tuxedo. A black glove.

"Oh, hi," I said. I brushed past him and kept walking. The dog followed slowly.

"Hold up," he said, "I want to talk to you."

"What," I said. "I'm in a hurry." I hadn't heard his car. But I hadn't really been listening.

"I want to make sure you're okay," he said. "That you don't have, like, a concussion or anything."

"I'm okay."

"Because you just left like that, we thought you might have amnesia or something. Is that your dog? That's a mangy-looking dog."

"I'm okay."

"We just wanted to make sure you wouldn't forget how you promised to give my dad the book back." The dog wasn't keeping up. I had to slow my pace.

"Listen, Stella," I said, "I don't have amnesia and I never promised to give your dad the book. I don't even have the book anymore. And I've got to go meet my mother at the airport." I stopped and picked up the dog. He was heavy. I hoisted him half over my shoulder. With the dog food and carrots, I was uncomfortably weighted down.

We were on the sidewalk now. The street completely deserted. The stoplight on the corner changed from red to green and no one gave a damn. I walked as fast as I could, clutching my possessions like a refugee.

199

"Wait up," said Seth. "C'mon. Wait up. Let me talk to you."

"I'm late," I said. I was half running now. The dog bounced against my shoulder, digging its nails in to keep from slipping. I heard Seth's shoes behind me.

"But he put you in his movie," he said. "Doesn't that mean something to you?"

"Okay, you're right. He can have it. I'll call you about it later," I said. "I'll bring it by your dad's house or something." My arms ached but I kept going. If I had to, I could lose the dog food and carrots.

"If you've got it," he said, "I want it now."

"No, no, I don't have it now. I've got to go pick up my mother."

"Slow down," he said. I felt a tug and the dog yelped. He was pulling on its paws to stop me. I turned around.

"Don't hurt the dog!" I said. Seth was standing with his knees slightly bent, like a tennis player ready to return. I shifted all the dog's weight to one arm.

"Oh yeah?" Seth said. "Then listen up, you bitch —" I swung the bag of dog food and carrots once around the top of my head and hit Seth broadside. He stumbled sideways and banged his head on a parking meter. He said, "Auoof," and slid to the ground. I put the dog down behind me and turned back to face him. He was shakily getting to his feet, using the parking meter as a crutch. I started swinging the bag over my head again. "You'll be looking for your teeth under every parked car for miles," I said, "unless you understand that I want to be alone with my dog."

"Oh," he said, "oh, you're pissing me off." He held on to the parking meter with both hands, like he was trying to rip it from the ground.

"And you, me," I said. The bag made an enginelike noise as it cut though the air. I hoped the handles wouldn't break.

"You'll wish later that you hadn't been such a baby about all this," he said.

"ZZZzzz, ZZZzzz, ZZZzzz," went the bag. He looked at it while he spoke. "But I'm going to get in my car now." He walked drunkenly toward the only car parked on the street. He walked all the way around it before getting in. I kept swinging the bag over my head. When he was starting the engine, the bag broke and the cans and carrots flew out of it like factory-made hail, spinning through the air and landing with heavy thwunking sounds on the street and sidewalk.

One can hit Seth's car and he craned his head out the window to look at it and me before driving away.

"That wasn't on purpose," I yelled.

The vet had almost finished his chicken. I set the dog down on the counter.

"This dog just got in a fight with a maniac cat," I said.

"What did you do to this dog?" he said. "Did you hurt this dog?"

"No," I said. "I'm telling you, it was some psycho cat. It got me, too." I showed him the scratch on my hand.

"Oh dear," he said. He looked closely at my hand. "Was it demonstrating signs of rabies?"

"No," I said. "I'm certain it wasn't rabid."

201

He put aside his chicken and wiped his hands on his smock. He said, "I would like you to write down your correct name and telephone number and address on this piece of paper." He slid a piece of scrap paper across the counter and slapped down a nub pencil. The kind you use miniature golfing.

"Why?"

"Never mind," said the vet. "Just do it." I jotted a little fiction onto the paper. He looked at it. "Very good, Lou Ellen. I'm going to need to sew up the cut." The dog shook himself as though he had just had a bath. Blood from his cut sprayed across the vet's smock and the rabbit fur coat and the chicken. "Oh my chicken," said the vet. He looked sadly at his chicken and put what was left of it into a bag and put the bag in a garbage can. "I will need you to hold him for me."

"I'm not very good with blood," I said.

"You can keep your eyes closed."

"Uh huh," I said. "Well, are you going to sew him up right here?"

"No, no. We'll bring him into one of the rooms," said the vet. "Follow me, please."

I picked up the dog as gently as I could. Walked around the counter and through a door the vet held open. I put the dog on a stainless-steel table and he began to squirm. I had intended to bolt at that point and head for Mike's place, but I figured the vet couldn't handle the dog alone. I held on to the dog. Said, "Be a good dog."

But he wasn't good. He fought like a dervish. Scrabbled around the steel table with me trying to pin him down. Eventually, the vet had to give him a shot that made him slow and sloppy. Drool eased out the side of his mouth and his tail worked its way up and down like the handle of a water-pump.

The vet finished with the dog, then turned to me. He cleaned the cut on my hand and bandaged it. He used plenty of bandage. While he was working, he got a look at the bruise on my head.

"Lou Ellen," he said, "how did you get that bruise?"

"That was also the cat."

"You know," he said, "I shouldn't ask questions. If I decide to do a good deed for someone, I should not allow my curiosity to sully it."

"That's true," I said. "I have to go now."

"Lou Ellen, due to a scheduling problem, I shall be working here straight through until tomorrow evening. It is unsafe for me to work for such a long period of time. But the owner of this establishment does not seem bothered that . . . well, we don't need to talk about it. I will keep your dog here until tomorrow."

"Okay," I said.

"Maybe the next day. If you do not return, I will be forced to call the humane society. They will keep the dog as long as they can, try to find a home for it, but if they cannot, they will destroy it."

"I'll be here tomorrow. Do you have a back door?" The vet sighed.

"Why do you need a back door I don't want to know." He directed me to the back door.

"I'll be back tomorrow," I said again. For a second, I almost believed it myself.

203

15.

It took me almost an hour to get to Mike's place. I walked on lawns. My head down, my hands in my pockets. The dewy grass froze my feet but I preferred it to the sidewalk. I think I ranted a bit. More after I stubbed my toe on a sprinkler. Dogs barked at me, cats ran from my path.

I walked past a house where an old couple was already up and about. Eating breakfast in the nook and reading the paper. The old guy poured both of them some tea from a china teapot. The woman smiled at him. I was full of self-pity all right. Seeing a life I would never have, wishing I could scrape myself out onto the lawn and replace all the old stinking crap inside with something, well, a little less fetid. I made myself sick and I thought it was all useless. Except maybe the bookstore. That was why I had to get things straightened out. So I could get back to the bookstore and try to settle myself. Try to pull it all together again. I would never be normal, but it was as good an imitation as I could find. I picked a purple flower from their lawn and ripped at it while I walked.

It was still dark but I could see clouds against the blue-black sky. And the tops of palm trees swaying against the clouds like storybook monsters. One tree had no top. Just a long bare trunk leading to nothing.

Mike lived in a tiny apartment in Hollywood. The apartment was in the house he grew up in. His dad had busted the place up into rental units when he and Mike's mom moved to Palm Springs. His dad was a Russian immigrant. He and Mike fought all the time. Mike was supposed to manage the building but he really fell down on the job. His dad came to L.A. unannounced to check up on things and to tinker. Whenever I saw him, he was putting in a new plug or moving a door. He said, "I am licensed contractor. I fix **205** everything!"

The house was in a borderline neighborhood. A block away from his place, a car slowed and the driver waved me over. I kept walking. "Want a ride?" the guy asked.

"Naw," I said. "I'm done for the night."

"C'mon, baby," said the guy. "Just one short ride around the block."

"Look, numbnuts," I said, "do yourself a favor and go home. I'm undercover and a cop in that van over there"—I pointed to a saggy VW bus on blocks —"is getting this all on tape. Shit, I'm not even a woman, you moron." The driver tucked his head under his sleeve and accelerated fast. "And don't speed!" I called after him. He actually slowed down.

Mike's apartment had its own entrance at the back of the house. I walked up the steps and pounded on his door. The dog barked. But Mike didn't answer the door. There was an open window to the left that looked onto his bedroom. It was above the lower steps so I couldn't see in. The window had bars but no screen. I walked down the steps and around to the front yard, where there was a lemon tree. There were lemons all over the ground and I filled my pockets. On my way back to Mike's apartment, I noticed two teenagers on the front stoop of the house. They were kissing and one of them, the boy, was crying quietly. "I have to go now," he was saying. "I have to go." The girl looked at me briefly. Accusingly.

I got back to the window and began lobbing lemons through the bars. If Mike was in his bed, a couple of them were bound to hit home. If he had passed out in the living room, I was out of luck. After a dozen lemons, I saw two hands grab the bars. Then Mike's face pressed up between them. His lidded eyes darted around. I tossed another lemon and hit him square on the forehead.

"Open the door," I said. "It's Jill. It's important." His head tipped down to get a look at me but the angle was too sharp.

"What sort of thing is that to throw balls at me, throw them at my head? In the middle of the night."

"Mike. It's important. Come open up. C'mon. Go open your front door."

"Oh boy," said Mike. His head disappeared. I walked up to his door and waited. Just when I thought he had gone back to sleep, I heard him working the latches. He peered out the door with the chain on.

"Are you alone?" he asked.

"Open the door," I said. His bloodshot eyes rolled over me, over the landing and steps behind.

"I can't see shit," he said. He opened the door. He was wearing pajamas with a note pinned to them. *WORK AT BOOKSTORE TODAY,* it said. *CALL FISH.* "I thought you might be here for the dog. Like a repo guy. I should smoke more pot. It increases, increases your night vision." The dog darted past both of us, ran down the steps, and squatted in the yard.

"Oh why'd you . . . she doesn't come back in. Now I have to give her something to make her come back in." I followed him into his apartment. He turned on the light and winced. Mike's friend from the store was passed out on the couch. A cheese sandwich was sticking partway out of his mouth. Mike walked over to him and extracted the sandwich and went outside with it. I heard him say, "Who wants a sandwich? Who wants a sandwich?"

207

His place was a mess. Burns in the carpet, empty bottles, magazines everywhere. Mike read a lot of magazines. All kinds of magazines. Magazines about skiing, about tattoos, old cars, needlepoint, how to make homemade bombs. They lay open-faced around the room. He loved trivia. Unconnected bits of information. Every day he learned something new and every night he forgot it again.

I stepped back out onto the landing.

"Do you have my backpack?" I asked. Easy questions first.

"Sandwich!" he said to the dog. "Who loves cheese! Who's a Lassie that loves cheese!" The dog stood very still with its head cocked, looking toward Mike. "Yes!" said

Mike. "That's right!" The dog sniffed the ground and began to walk away. Mike ran for it with the sandwich. It skittered off with its tail between its legs.

I went back inside and poked around the apartment. I found my backpack in the kitchen. The gun was gone. I wasn't surprised.

I went into the bathroom. Only *Bon Appetit* magazines were allowed in there. And soap scum and dirty tissues and short tough hairs. I used the toilet and looked through the medicine chest for some aspirin. He had a big generic bottle of it. It was unusual for him to be that well stocked. I had noticed some supplies in his kitchen, too. It probably meant that his mom had been in town and gone shopping for him. She had an idea that having food around would keep him from drinking.

208

In his bedroom, I found a pair of jeans that looked clean. They were huge on me. I used a woven belt to keep them from sliding off. I rolled the bottoms and put on a white T-shirt and a V-neck sweater that I discovered on a top shelf in the closet. The sweater still had a tag on it, which I ripped off. Another present from his mom. I hung the flapper dress in his closet along with the rabbit fur jacket.

I checked under the pillow and under the mattress but no gun. I went back into the kitchen and put some water on to boil. The only clean pot was a frying pan so I used that. The gun wasn't in the kitchen either. I opened a new jar of instant coffee and put some in a mug. When the water boiled, I added it. There was some unspoiled cream in the fridge and a Tupperware container filled with some sort of Russian dumplings. I ate a couple. They were good.

Mike came in without the dog.

"Because now he's *gone* now. So I hope you're happy."

I slurped my coffee. "Where's the gun, Mike?"

"This is a dangerous neighborhood for a dog. A dog alone. They *steal* dogs is what they do. They use them to train the PIT BULLS, is what they do. But if she thinks I'm just going to run around. . . ." Mike was still holding the cheese sandwich. He took a bite of it. "Oh," he said. "It's wet."

"So where's the gun?"

"What gun?"

"The one that was in my backpack." I held up the backpack for his inspection.

"That's your backpack?" he said. "Somebody left that backpack at the bookstore."

"Yes," I said. "I did. Give me the gun."

"Um, sold it," he said.

"Oh Christ. You can't have sold it." I slumped and turned a full circle before addressing him again. "Who'd you sell it to?"

"I sold it to Pete."

"Who's Pete?"

"You know, my friend Pete. Haven't you ever met Pete?"

"No, Mike" I said. "I've never met Pete. Jesus. It's not my gun."

"I thought maybe that backpack had been there forever. I thought the owner had forgotten it was ever there, you know? Because it's old."

"All right," I said. "Let's leave the gun for a minute. I have to ask you something else. Okay. Do you remember selling a book by Jack London? It wouldn't have had a price in it. You would have had to make one up. *The Cruise of the Snark* by Jack London."

Mike snorted once at the name. "No," said Mike. "Um. Hold on. No."

"An old book. But in good shape."

"Nope." He was shaking his head. "It's funny, I really don't want to be awake right now."

"Think, Mike. After I left in the evening. There were only a couple store hours left."

"Nope," said Mike. "Although, you know . . ." He yawned his way over the rest of the sentence.

"What?"

"I was gone part of that time," he said. "I had to meet Krista for a drink." He walked out of the kitchen and I followed. "I've had enough," he said. "I'm going back to bed."

"Mike —"

210   He whipped around. "Aw you're jawing jawing jawing at me, you're getting me down!" He waded through the magazines in the living room, kicking at them like a kid in new snow. In front of the sofa, he stopped. "Hey, it's Pete!" he said. "Pete was looking after the store. Hey, Pete!"

"That's Pete," I said.

Mike nudged him with his foot. Then he tickled him until Pete groaned and sat up. Pete said, "Oooh, I gotta piss." Stumbled toward the bathroom. He had been sleeping on the gun. Mike started to go to his bedroom.

"Where are you going?"

"Back to bed, I told ya."

"Ask Pete about the book."

"You ask Pete about the book and then both of you numbchucks find my dog." Mike could get pretty ornery when the booze was wearing off. He scooped an issue of *Dog Fancy* off the coffee table and strode into his room.

While Pete was in the bathroom, I put the gun into my backpack and ate a couple more dumplings. Pete was in there a long time. I knocked on the door. "Pete," I said. "Pete." I cracked open the door. Pete was asleep on the toilet. Pants around his thighs. I threw a magazine at him and closed the door after it. A second later, he came out of the bathroom, pants up, eyes unfocused. He rocketed forward and belly-flopped onto the sofa. Then he rolled over and unbuttoned his shirt. His belly hung like a loose lip over the front of his pants. He was wearing a long gold chain with a cross around his neck and he fumbled for the cross and brought it to his mouth and kissed it.

"Pete," I said, "want some of my coffee?" I had only drunk half the cup but the rest was cold.

"Time is it?" he said. He had a fake Rolex on his wrist. At least, I assumed it was fake. I screwed my head around to get a look at it.

"Six-forty," I said.

"Oh," he said. "Yeah, gimme. I gotta goda work soon." I gave him my cup. He blew on it before taking a sip.

"Pete, when you were looking after the store yesterday, did you sell a book that didn't have a price in it? A book by Jack London?"

Pete gently stroked his belly. "What was yesterday?"

"You were looking after the bookstore? When Mike left to drink with Krista?"

"Yeah, that's right," he said. "I sold some of those books."

"An old book called *Cruise of the Snark?* Remember that?"

Pete shook his head back and forth. "That bastid. He told me he was going to talk to the loan officer there. He didn't say dime one about Krista. Ah, I'll yell at him." He threw back the rest of the coffee as though it was a shot of tequila.

"What about the book?" I said. "Do you remember a book without a price?"

"Got the guy to pay six bucks for it. Most of those hard-covers at the store, they go for around five bucks. I took a look in a couple. I told the guy six bucks because the book looked old."

"So you definitely sold it?"

"Yeah. Some black guy." He paused a second. "But smart. Nice guy."

"What did he look like?"

"You know, dark. And he had a scar like he had been fucked up in a fire."

"Was it Greg? Or Charles? The water delivery guy?" Oh *please*, I thought. Oh please.

"He had on a shirt like that but he didn't deliver any water that I was aware of."

"Beautiful," I said.

16

The only number I could find for Aqua Mountain was an 800 number. The recording told me all about the fresh clean taste I could expect if I had Aqua Mountain delivered to my office or home. It also said that no one would be there to take my call until 9:00 A.M. I couldn't find a number for the regional office. And I didn't know Greg's last name. I was going to have to wait until nine.

Pete was making some sort of frittata in the kitchen. He put cheese in it and some dumplings. He said, "I gotta eat eggs when I'm all fucked up like this. My mom made eggs good. Oh yeah. Forget about it." He kissed his cross again.

I took a shower in Mike's bathroom. The water didn't drain, so I made it quick. When I got out, I put Mike's clothes back on. What I really needed was shoes. I took another inventory of my pack and realized that the key to Scott's motorcycle was gone. Then I remembered that it was in the front right pocket of Debi's jeans. The jeans I had left in the wardrobe truck when they dolled me up for the movie shoot. The jeans I would probably never see again.

"Hey Pete," I said. "Where do you work?"

"Aw, I got a warehouse but I'm not going there. I gotta make some pickups."

Pete drove a cargo van. "Betty's Flower Boutique" was painted on the side of it. And a picture of a smiling guy holding out a bouquet of roses. It was a bad picture. The guy's smile had a very evil look to it. A "take these flowers because I need both hands free to kill you" look.

"You deliver flowers?"

"Naw," said Pete. "Place went out of business an' I got this cheap. I keep meaning to paint over that fucking sign but . . . who gets around to things?"

The van was empty except for a Flexible Flyer sled tied down near the back. When we went over bumps, the back moaned and groaned. Like the thunder sound in a high school production of *The Tempest*. Some drama nerd waving a sheet of metal up and down and making *whaampa whaampa* noises.

It was a quick trip to Scott's place. Though there were times I didn't think the van would make the hill. Pete said, "This fucking thing. Well, you get what you pay for."

He dropped me off. I tried to get him to stick around and give me a ride over to Scott's bike, but he was going to the Valley. Wrong direction. He asked me if I wanted to go out with him sometime to see a movie. Eat some nice food. Something. I said I liked him but I already had a fella.

214

Scott's front door was locked, which was unusual. I rang the bell and pounded. Debi answered the door wearing a silk kimono. Her hair in fat rollers. When she saw me, she said, "Oh," and stepped aside to let me in. "He can't come back," she said. "I don't want him back. I'm still too pissed. Or are you here for his clothes."

"Huh?" I said.

"Did he send you for me or for his clothes? He's not out there, is he?" She pushed aside a curtain and looked sideways at her front yard.

"What's going on, Debi?" I asked.

"Isn't he at your place? You haven't talked to him?"

"MOM!" It was Nellie screaming from the kitchen. "Momomomomom MOM!"

"Okay, honey," said Debi. To me she said, "C'mon."

I followed her to the kitchen. In the dining area, we stepped over a broken dish. "Oh," I said. I walked carefully in my bare feet. Debi scooped a couple wooden mixing spoons off the floor. The window in the kitchen door had a neat round hole through the middle.

I said, "I haven't talked to him for . . . well it seems like a long time but I don't know."

Nellie was sitting on the kitchen counter, drawing faces on toast with squeeze margarine. She hardly gave me a look. When Debi was around, Nellie got a little cold toward everyone else. She held up a piece of toast for us to see.

"It's a troll!" she said.

"Ooh, I see," said Debi. "Are you going to eat him?"

Nellie giggled. "Yc-cs! First I eat his ears!" She bit the toast. "Umm! Yummy ears."

"So . . . I threw him out," Debi said. "And really, honestly, he can stay out. I mean, he's such a fuckup. I went through all that with Jan, I'm not going through that again, you know? It's too self-destructive." Jan was her Icelandic ex-husband.

"Mmm," I said.

"I mean, that guy. That guy. He's got me smoking again. For that alone, I just want to kill him. I forget, do you smoke?"

"No," I said. "Well, sometimes."

"But you don't have any on you?"

I shook my head. Though there were a couple stale cigarettes floating around my backpack somewhere. I just didn't want to contribute to her habit. I said, "Hey, you got a nose ring."

"Oh yeah," she said. "Yeah, I don't know." She walked over to a small wood-framed mirror hanging on the wall by the door of the kitchen. Looked at herself. "I was worried that if I ever decided to stop wearing it, I'd have, like, a permanent hole in my nose. But it's a thin earring and the girl that did it said that you won't see the hole. Or you just put some makeup over it."

"Did Cox come . . . where's Cox?" I asked. If Debi didn't know about his running away, I didn't want to be the one to tell her.

"Malibu."

Nellie said, "Now your eyes and then you're aaaalllllll gone." She chewed noisily. "Mmmm, eyes," she said.

"I haven't been to my place," I said, "but he has a key."

"He has a key?" said Debi. "Really. Huh." I felt like

Debi always assumed that Scott and I had something going on. Maybe because I wasn't very nice to her.

"Oh, shit," I said. "He went to my place? Shit." It suddenly occurred to me that my place was not a very good place to be.

"Hem, we don't do that in front of N-e-l-l-i-e," she said. "She gets enough of that language off the other kids. And the movies." I was always forgetting not to curse in front of the kids. A bad influence.

"I've got to use the phone," I said. I picked up the kitchen phone. It smelled like perfume.

"Well are you calling *him?* Because I don't want to be in the same room when he's on the phone."

"I'm calling my place," I said. I hit the buttons.

"Keep an eye on Nellie," Debi said. "I'm getting dressed." **217**

My phone rang four times. Then the machine picked up. I said, "Scott, pick up the phone. Pick up the phone!" I yelled it a couple times but he didn't pick up.

"Down," Nellie said. She sat at the edge of the counter with her arms stretched toward me. I racked the phone and helped her down. Her greasy fingers lightly mashed my face. She left the room, shimmying around like a circus chimp. Then she came back in, put the bottle of squeeze margarine under her shirt, and ran away again.

I called my place and this time when the machine picked up, I punched in the code that allowed me to check my messages. The first was from my sister. She and her boyfriend had taken a trip to Martha's Vineyard. They went for a bike ride. Ate some ice cream. The couple in the room next to theirs had noisy sex. She almost bought a T-shirt for me but decided I wouldn't like it. She saw a boy on the ferryboat who looked like Larry Liebowitz, the kid we grew up with who tried to tongue-kiss everyone, including the teachers. She stepped on a bee and it hurt like crazy.

The next message was from Paul. Yesterday's call. It said, "Hello, Jill, this is Paul. It's six-fifty and I can't seem to reach you at the store. It seems a little early to have closed. Perhaps you are very busy selling books. Oodles of books. Well, we'll see. You can page me to let me know where you are. I'd like to get that concert information from you. Good-bye." The message after that was also from Paul. "Hello, Jill, this is Paul. Well, I never got paged. Hmm. It makes me a little worried about things. I'm not quite sure what to do. Hmm. Perhaps there is a problem with the phone. I hope so. Please get in touch with me."

The last message was from the Joke Man. It said, "Hello, it's me. Your friend dropped by your place so we invited him to come and hang out with us for a while. Just so you understand. That book's gonna be returned to us. I did, in fact, ask you not to dick around." Somehow the message didn't surprise me. Didn't surprise me at all.

I dialed the Joke Man number. The dwarf picked up. I said, "Put him on the phone." He said, "Well hello to you too." Then I heard him pass the phone.

"Good morning," said the Joke Man.

"I've almost got it," I said. "You didn't have to take him. He's just my friend." I was angry more than anything else. Angry that things had a way of becoming more and more complicated. That my own problems had a tendency to bleed into other people's lives.

"I had an interest in some sort of collateral. He happened to come by while we were visiting your place. The fly and the spider."

"Put him on," I said. There was some background talk. A laugh like a howitzer. Then Scott got on the phone.

"Hey," I said. "How are you?"

"Good, I guess. I don't know. This is weird. I don't know how you got into something so weird. It's all fucked up." He sounded small.

"What are you doing?"

"You know. Just hanging out. Watching TV. They made me this big breakfast but I think I'm a little too freaked out to eat it."

"Look, I just have to give them this book."

"Yeah, that's what they said."

219

"It's going to take a few hours. It's no big deal. I know exactly where it is."

"You know where it is?"

"Yeah."

"Oh. Okay. Because I was going to say, otherwise you should maybe, you know . . ."

"What?"

"You know . . ."

"What?"

"Forget it."

"It'll just be a few hours."

"They put a bag over my head. To drive here."

"They just didn't want you to see where it is."

"Yeah but . . . a bag over your head . . ."

"Where's the extra key to your motorcycle?"

"Aw shit. There's a drawer in my kitchen with a whole bunch of keys. One of those should be for the Honda."

"I'll be fast."

"All right," he said. "So, you won't decide to skip the whole thing, will you?"

"What do you mean?"

"You know . . ." His voice became muffled, as though he was cupping his hand around the mouthpiece of the phone. "Because sometimes I'm not sure you care about me all that much."

I heard the dwarf say, "No private conversing!"

Scott replying to him: "It was private!"

"Oh, Scott," I said, "don't piss me off. I've got to go. I'll be there in a few hours. I will *be there*."

Debi let me borrow a pair of old sneakers. While she was looking for them, I stuffed one of her wigs in my backpack. She had a couple lying around that she used for practicing new hairstyles. I also took a pair of Scott's sunglasses. Big, funky mirrored ones. He was very proud of them and wore them as a goof when his band played at clubs. Debi said, "What did he say?"

"Not much. He was eating breakfast."

"Breakfast!" said Nellie. "WE should eat some breakfast."

"You already had your breakfast, nubbin." Debi pretended to steal Nellie's nose. "What did he say about me?" Debi asked.

"Nothing," I said.

"Well," she said, "that's just effing typical."

Debi didn't want to give me a ride to the bookstore and

I didn't want to ask more than twice so I walked down the hill to the market where my bicycle was still locked to the handicapped parking sign. I got on and rode to the bookstore. It was mostly downhill and the morning air on my face felt good. I suddenly had the hope that, in just an hour or so, the whole thing could be put to rest. That Scott and I could sit in a bar that night and giggle over the goddamn looniness of it. That I had not been so shaken that I would have to start my life from scratch again.

On the side streets, I rode no-handed and flapped my arms like I was a bird. Trying to shake my feelings of dread. I rode past some kids waiting for their bus. One of them said, "Hey, coo coo!"

221

Around the corner from the bookstore, I put the wig and glasses on. They wouldn't fool anyone for long, but they might buy me a couple minutes. I caught a look at myself in a store window. The crazy thing was, the wig looked a lot like my own hair. Straight and blondish. Oh well.

I rode past the store and locked my bike to a meter in front of the Thai restaurant. In my backpack were a dozen keys from Scott's key drawer. Any one of them could be the spare motorcycle key. I palmed them all and walked casually over to the Honda. Straddled it. Began trying the keys one by one. I sang softly, "Get your motor running. . . . Head out on the HIGH! WAY!" I hated that song but I had no choice.

A cop car drove past me, made a U-turn, and came to a stop nose-to-nose with the motorcycle. A young, good-looking cop got out. So did his partner.

"Hi!" I said. "Are either of you guys any good with keys?"

"Hello there, miss," said Good-looking Cop. "Do you work in that establishment?" He nodded at Bitter Muse.

"What's up?" I asked.

"You work there?"

"Why, what's the problem?"

"Now don't ask me a question, answer my question. Do you work there?" He stood with one foot in front of the other, his weight back. John Wayne casual. He spoke a little like the Duke, too. But he looked more like Tony Curtis. Smooth and twinkly.

"Yes," I said.

"Your name Jill?"

"Jill what?"

"Is your name Jill?"

"Part of it is."

"Well, Jill, you're going to need to take a little trip with us downtown." He touched his cap.

"Uh huh. Why?"

"We'll talk about that later."

"Okay. Why?"

"Because."

"Right. Because why?"

"Because I said so. And I'm the law." He gave me a wind-up smile. "Now if you'd come with me . . ."

"Hmm. It's just that, you know, I think the law says — not *you* the law but the other law — says that I get to know what this is about." I sat and looked at him as winningly as I could to make up for being fresh. The other cop, a big ugly guy, had been half sitting on the hood of the car. His arms crossed in front of his chest. Now he piped up.

"You know a Tim Harris?"

"Oh," I said. I got off the bike. What was I going to do, run from some cops? They walked me over to the car.

"We better cuff her," said Ugly Cop. "And take her backpack."

"I was going to do that," said Good-looking Cop. He took my backpack from me.

"It's not my backpack," I said, "I'm holding it for a friend. I don't even have *a* clue what's in it." Good-looking Cop felt around his uniform for his cuffs. He had a little trouble locating them. He pivoted one way, then the other.

"They're right there on your left side," said Ugly Cop. His nose was a size too small for the rest of his face. "Button Nose" his mother probably called him.

"I know, I know," growled Good-looking Cop.

"You don't need to cuff me," I said.

"It's just as a precaution, ma'am," said Good-looking Cop. He had gotten ahold of the cuffs and was working them on me. Ugly Cop chuckled a little with his hand over his mouth. "Ma'am," he repeated. Made it like he was clearing his throat.

"Looks like you hurt your hand there, ma'am," said Good-looking Cop, eyeing the bandage.

"What do you mean?"

"Your hand?"

"Oh," I said, "that's just to remind me to do something."

A couple cars slowed as they passed, but all and all the street was pretty deserted. I heard the phone ringing inside the bookstore.

"Can I get that?" I asked. "It might be for me."

223

"No." They said it in unison. Tweedledee and Tweedledum. Ugly Cop opened the back door of the cop car. Good-looking Cop got ready to guide me in.

Ugly Cop said, "Don't forget there, you put your hand on top of her head and ease it on in."

"I was going to do that," growled Good-looking Cop. And he did.

I saw the owner of the mini-market watching from down the street. He was holding two buckets full of cut carnations and frowning. I hauled my hands around enough to give him a finger wave through the glass. He didn't wave back. My vet friend was nowhere around.

Ugly Cop drove. Good-looking Cop unzipped my backpack.

224

"Don't do that," said Ugly Cop. "Let him do that." Good-looking Cop shrugged and put the pack on the floor by his feet. They sat in silence. Scott's sunglasses had fallen down the bridge of my nose and I leaned my face against the door to push them up. Then I sat back against the seat as much as I could with the cuffs on.

I couldn't believe Timmy had dropped the dime that way. He had to realize that the truth would put him in deeper dutch with the cops than me. Maybe he wanted me out of the picture long enough to get a lead on the book. Then he'd drop the charges. But at this point, with Scott at the Joke Man's place, I wasn't too far away from spilling the whole story to the cops myself. Let them join in the fun. Yeah, what the hell. I'd talk to the guys downtown. Talk plenty. The problem was, I had more faith in the Joke Man's abilities than in the cops'. I hunkered down lower onto the seat. The upholstery smelled new.

"Why are you taking Melrose?" said Good-looking Cop. "Isn't it on Beverly?"

"You said Melrose around Western," said Ugly Cop.

"No, I said Beverly around Western."

"I could swear you said Melrose."

"Aren't we going downtown?" I asked.

"Well, the captain's on assignment. We're taking you there." Ugly Cop slowed the car in his uncertainty. Other cars backed up behind us. You don't honk at a cop car.

"You know I didn't think cops actually said, 'We're taking you downtown,'" I said.

"Oh yeah, we say it."

Ugly Cop spoke under his breath. "Don't you have it written down somewhere?" I sat up again to be closer to the action. Good-looking Cop swerved around to try and get at his back pants pockets. Then he realized he had no back pants pockets.

225

"Damn!" he said. "It's in my other pants. My, uh, civilian clothes." His John Wayne bravado slipped a couple notches.

"Use the radio," I said.

"What are we going to do, call him?"

"Why don't you just use the radio," I said.

"Because I'm not going to call him if we have to call him," said Ugly Cop. "If we have to call him, you're doing the calling, my friend."

It occurred to me that the radio hadn't squawked since we had been in the car. Hadn't made a peep. "What's wrong with the radio?" I asked.

Good-looking Cop turned to face me. "Shut up! It's broken! Achoo!" He sneezed unexpectedly. A loud exclamation mark. It seemed to scare him.

"Yeah, shut up," said Ugly Cop.

Suddenly it was so clear to me. I couldn't believe I was such a chump. Duped by a couple of half-wits from the Acme Extras Corporation. "Oh you fuckers," I said. "You lame, lame Starsky and Hutch pieces of shit."

"Shut up!" In unison.

"Did you have to audition for this or did you get cast purely on the basis of your asshole looks?" Good-looking Cop smacked the mesh that separated the front and back seats. It made a feeble pinging sound.

"We're getting close to Western." Ugly Cop.

"Pull over by a phone."

"You have his cellular number?"

"Pull over up here."

"You remember his number?"

"I can get it."

"Great. First-class operation."

I looked around the back of the car. It was enough like a cop car that it had no door handles. We pulled to a stop in front of a donut place. Good-looking Cop got out and trotted over to a pay phone. Ugly Cop watched him intently. Kept the motor running.

The cuffs were on tight. I tried wriggling my ass through my arms to get my hands in front of me. No dice.

Out in the parking lot, a middle-aged Hispanic woman ran over to where Good-looking Cop was talking on the phone and she tugged on his arm and gestured wildly down the block. He shook his head and yelled at her with his hand over the mouthpiece. She kept gesturing and tugging. He kicked out at her. She started yelling angrily. Ugly Cop watched all of this intently. He said, "Oh, what *the* . . ." but he didn't get out of the car.

I lay down on the seat, pulled back my knees, and pistoned my feet at the window, hard. The glass gave a bit but didn't shatter, didn't even crack. My clogs would have done a better job.

"Hey!" Ugly Cop turned around. I gave the window a few more quick shots with no result. "Hey! Knock it off there!" He had his fingers in the mesh divider and he rattled it. "Quit it! Quit it!" I kicked out as hard as I could and the glass cracked. Not a genuine cop-car window after all. "Quit it!" Another shot and it gave way. Ugly Cop jumped out of the car and blocked the gap where the window had been with his big belly.

I heard the woman in the parking lot screaming in Spanish and Good-looking Cop screaming back. "Shut the fuck up!" he screamed. "I am a cop! I will DEPORT you!"

I got up on my knees and head-butted Ugly Cop in the gut. He staggered back a couple of steps and I tried to project myself through the window. With my torso pretty far out, I joined in the screaming. "Help me!" I screamed. "Help ME!" Ugly Cop recovered his balance, grabbed me by the top of the head, and started stuffing me back into the car. My wig came off in his hands. He looked at it for a second, his face twisted in confusion. Then he whipped it onto the ground. He grabbed my head again and I shook it crazily to get him off. Scott's sunglasses flew beneath the car. He got a firm grip on my ears and slammed my forehead against the window frame. I guess he did it a couple more times, but by then I was out cold.

17

Someone threw cold liquid in my face. A piece of ice bounced off my cheek. I gasped and got a mouthful of Coca-Cola. Sweet and fizzy. I licked my upper lip. Blew some soda out of my nose. In front of me, a hand held a jumbo-size drink cup from Taco Bell. The hand jerked and soda hit me in the face again. A straw hit my eyebrow and landed in my lap. I tossed my head to shake off the Coke. "I GET THE PICTURE!" I screamed it to wake myself up. And to give myself a little confidence.

"Man!" said a voice, "she wakes up grumpy!" Some laughs.

My head felt like it had been kicked around a field by the entire gym class. A bright light shone in my eyes. I couldn't see much because of it. My hands were cuffed behind me. I moved them a little and discovered that the cuffs laced around the back of the chair I was sitting on. My legs were free, though. I kicked out and nailed the guy holding the cup in the knee.

"Wha-OW, shit!" The cup fell to the floor.

"I warned you." That was Seth.

"Ow! Jesus! That's the knee I fucked up skiing. Jesus, that bitch."

Seth laughed. "I warned you." The guy swore under his breath awhile. "You all right?"

"No."

Seth laughed. "Sorry, man, but it's funny."

"It's not funny. Shit. I just started playing tennis again." The guy I had kicked edged back into the light. He was wearing a kid's Halloween mask. Wonder Woman. He slapped me hard across the face. For a second my head went numb. Then the pain flowed back into the dead empty spaces.

"C'mon, man, the camera's not on yet."

"Well I had to."

I said, "Hey you guys . . ."

"What! Shut up! Don't talk unless you're talked to!" said Wonder Woman. He ducked his masked face close to mine. The big, grinning hole of a mouth had an extra plastic drip in the corner. Sloppy workmanship. His breath smelled like onions.

"What's up with that?" said Seth. "'Don't talk unless you're talked to?'"

"It's a good idea."

"No it's not."

I closed my eyes against the hot light. "Do either of you neat guys have any aspirin?" I asked. My voice came out in a ragged whisper. I cleared my throat as if it would help.

229

After a second. "No," said Seth. Sarcastically: "Sorry, no."

"*I* could use some aspirin," said the guy I kicked. "You don't have any aspirin on you?"

"No," said Seth.

"Was there any in her bag?"

"Nah."

"What about in your car?"

"No, man. Get off it."

Wonder Woman sat down on the floor in front of me and rolled up his pant leg. He had a scar on his knee and he gently pushed at the flesh around it. "You see, this worries me," he said. "Because it hurts the way it used to hurt."

Seth said, "You know what that is?"

"What."

"An identifiable scar. Ha ha!"

Wonder Woman rolled his pant leg back down. "Whatever," he said. "Like a million people don't have knee operations." He pushed himself awkwardly off the floor. Brushed at the seat of his pants with a few quick slaps.

Seth said, "Did you bring the box?"

"Oh, yeah, it's in my trunk."

"Go get it."

"But my knee's killing me."

"You want in on this? I'm the fucking director and I am now directing you to go and get it."

The guy moved away slowly. Exaggerating the limp and grunting every step. The sounds echoed. The way they do in a cavernous space. An airport hangar. A warehouse, maybe. Or an abandoned church. I felt the enormity of the place

230

and it sent my heart into my mouth. "Oh Christ," I said. "Oh God in heaven."

"You believe in God?"

Seth moved into the light. He was wearing a Batman mask and gloves on both hands. But it was him.

"No," I said. "I just believe in throwing his name around." He moved behind me. Looped some rope around my legs to secure them to the chair.

"What's with the mask?" I asked.

"Does it scare you that I have a mask on?" If he was trying to disguise his voice, he was doing a lousy job.

"Yes," I said. "Quite a bit. I just made some sort of trouser treasure."

"I hate to say it, but it should."

"I know," I said. "The dreaded interrogation scene." He **231** pulled the rope tight. I could hear pigeons flapping around in the rafters. Cooing and flapping. Believing they actually had some sort of destination. "Do you know," I said, "— was that Diet or regular Coke he was throwing at me? I'm pretty sure regular Coke stains and Diet doesn't." I was playing it cucumber cool. Like we were a couple of old pals shooting the breeze.

"I'm telling you," he said. "I'm not kidding around. Well . . . you'll see."

"It's that . . . these aren't my clothes."

"You'll see." He moved out of the light. Fiddled with something. Some type of equipment. I didn't have the energy to talk just for the sake of talking. I decided to take his advice. Wait and see. But I knew if I thought too hard about my current situation I would get a little weepy so I hummed instead and thought about humming. I hummed the kind of music they play in the suspenseful parts of movies. Then I tried to make the noise that UFOs make in all the old '50s sci fi flicks. Seth said, "Cute. Very cute."

The other guy limped back in. The sound was like a spastic heartbeat that started with the opening and closing of a door somewhere. After a long time, he reached us and placed a boom box on the floor near me. I could tell by his physique that he wasn't one of the fake cops. He was too small.

"What tunes did you bring?" asked Seth.

The guy ejected the tape that was in the box and looked at the title. "James Taylor," he said.

232

"Wait," said Seth, "all you brought is James fucking Taylor? For this?"

"It's my sister's box. I forgot my tapes. It's no big deal. We can listen to the radio." He turned on the radio. Lousy reception. He flipped the dial, searching for something he liked.

"That was good," said Seth, "go back." He flipped back. "What — this?"

"Yeah," said Seth. "Leave it." The song ended and an ad for beer came on. Telling us to tap the Rockies, whatever that meant. Even the real things felt unreal.

"Did I tell you about that voice-over job I almost got?"

"Yeah, you told me."

As the Coke dried on my face, it felt as though somebody was Saran Wrapping my head. I started nodding out. Swaying forward, jerking back. So tired. For a moment, I thought

I was in an Art History lecture. Facing the wrong way, the light of the slide projector in my eyes. And the professor saying something about loving me all night long. I shook off the sleep. Barry White was on the radio.

"Okay," said Seth, "I'm pretty set up. We gotta figure out exactly what we want to do. I don't want this to be random and all over the place. I want to be proud of it." I heard their footsteps echoing away from me. Falling off into the dark like the remnants of a dream. And out I went again.

My mother was lying on a bed. Her oldest nightgown white against a field of, oh, poppies I guess. She had fallen asleep reading. The book lay open next to her hands. The sun beat down. Hot against her damaged skin. And no shade. It was time to go. I stepped toward her. The plastic bag lay hidden between the sweater I wore on the outside and the one I wore on the inside.

"Don't touch her," my sister said.

"Why?"

"Don't touch her." She held me by the shoulders and I cried out to my mother, her skin more translucent by the second. My sister dug her hands into my flesh. "Be quiet. She has to."

"Moochie," I whispered to my mother. A child's naming. "Moochie, pull away." My mother twisted back and forth. She was breathing. Still breathing. And I was lying beside her on the bed with my face very close. We were alone now in the room. Alone in the house. She opened her eyes slowly. The cricket inside her mouth said, "You promised me . . ."

"I can't!"

". . . that you wouldn't let me wake up." I took a plastic pillowcase off the pillow and began to edge it toward her. My mother's arms flew from her sides and she hit my face with a hand that was heavier than her own. "Don't you stop!" she said. I woke up. Seth's hand was still on the upswing. They were ready for me.

They used things they had seen in movies. First, a toothpick pushed deep under my fingernail. That one I knew. *Lives of a Bengal Lancer*. Before they got started, I said, "Don't you want to ask me about the book?"

"Not yet," said Seth.

234

"I don't have it."

"We'll get to it later. After we have some nice footage."

The guy in the Wonder Woman mask ran the camera. Sometimes he told Seth not to block me. But Seth was really running the show. He said, "Lights, camera, action."

They took a break once in a while to change the radio station. Find one better suited to the work at hand. Wonder Woman liked punk. Seth thought that oldies sounded cooler. I tried keeping quiet until I realized that it was easier to yell. When I could, I formed the screams into words — lyrics to the songs on the radio. A lot of times, I didn't know the exact words and I made up new ones. They didn't like that.

They rubbed steel wool on the inside of my arm, then poured salt on it. I didn't recognize that trick. They cut off Mike's sweater to access my arms more easily. They didn't want to uncuff me. When they first started cutting, I figured

I knew what was coming next. But they left the rest of my clothes on. Wonder Woman said, "Ah, it would be so great if we saw her tits here." And Seth said, "No."

"Don't worry," I said, "they're nothing special."

"I wish we had a rat," said Wonder Woman. "A rat and some peanut butter."

They passed a lighter beneath my chin. Wonder Woman said, "Did you ever do that thing as a kid? What was it, you would put a yellow flower under someone's chin and say, 'Do you like butter?' and if they did, the bottom of their chin would look yellow?"

"I remember that," said Seth. "Do you like butter?"

"Naw, man, it's more like, 'Do you like fire?'" I blew at the flame. It flickered and they held the lighter closer.

"What do you feel?" Seth asked me.

235

I wasn't all right with the pain, but I was closer to all right than I thought I would be. Maybe I realized that I had been waiting a long time for this kind of punishment. Maybe I thought I was paying once and for all. Clearing the books. And for a moment, I let myself see it. The lilac sheets. The melted ice cream in the dish there. Next to the bed. Empty pill bottles. The plastic against her face and the crackling awful crackling it made as she sucked in blew out. As I lay across her so that she couldn't lift her dry twig arms.

"I know why you're here," I said. "I know." But even as I said it, the picture was speeding away. And again I felt nothing but the details of pain.

They tried something with a battery. They fiddled for a while and couldn't rig it right. They gave up. A disgrace to their seventh-grade science teachers. Seth hurled the battery. It broke glass somewhere. A window, perhaps.

"It's all right," said Wonder Woman. "Let's move on."

"Idiots," I said. I was laughing and crying at the same time.

"What?" said Seth.

"You guys are all, all IDIOTS." I filled up the place with my voice. Heard the words crawl into every corner. "Jesus, you are STUPID."

"Idiots?" said Seth. "Really? Then how come you're the one in the chair and we're the ones doing the stuff?"

"Because," I said, "I have to." Softly. It hurt too much to yell. Took too much out of me. "Listen, I'm thinking you should just . . . just bump me, you know, off."

"You think you're so sassy, so smart," said Seth. He stomped on my foot. He was wearing heavy work boots. "So cute and smart and funny." He punctuated the words by jumping up and down on my foot. I screamed, then I changed it to a whisper. I whispered, "Seth." Every time he jumped I said it. Glaring up at him through my Coke-tangled hair. He stopped jumping up and down.

"What did you say? What are you saying?" He leaned in close to hear me. I kept repeating his name. A tiny mumble. My eyes stung and I thought it might be from the hate. "What?" he said. "What?"

"She's saying 'stop,' " said Wonder Woman. "Stop, stop."

"Shut up," said Seth. To me: "Louder. What are you saying?"

I said it louder. "Seth," I said. "Seth Seth."

"Oh shit, man —" said Wonder Woman.

"Seth Seth Seth," I whispered. "Seth Seth Seth Seth."

"Oh yeah?" said Seth. "Oh yeah? All right, fine." He took the Batman mask off. There was a bruise on his temple where I had hit him with the bag of dog food.

"What are you doing, man?" asked Wonder Woman.

Seth took off his right glove and tossed it aside. "It doesn't matter. She knows who I am."

"Yeah but she couldn't say for sure in court if she didn't see your face, man. I asked my dad."

"I don't give a shit. I'm hot," he said. "I don't want that fucking thing on my face anymore."

"Well I'm hot, too. You think I'm not hot?"

"Take it off, then."

"No way. No way. I'm not stupid. Besides, you don't really have to worry. You're covered. But my dad couldn't get me out of a parking ticket."

"Where's that bottle of water?" Seth asked. Wonder Woman threw a plastic Aqua Mountain bottle at him. Seth caught it and took a long pull. "All right," he said, "now do you want to talk about the book?"

"Already?" said Wonder Woman.

I slowly stuck out my tongue. Not the way a kid does, but a corpse. It felt huge outside of my mouth.

"Tell me if you're going to start again," said Wonder Woman, "because I paused the camera." Seth karate-chopped me in the forehead. The spot that the fake cop had smashed against the door frame of the car. Fresh blood trickled down my face. I went limp. Made it look like I had checked out. "I told you to tell me if you were going to do something," said Wonder Woman. I heard the pigeons again. Flapping around. Flapping around up there.

"Fuck it," said Seth. "Toss me the ammonia capsules."

After a moment, Seth opened one of the capsules under my nose. The fumes stung my face. Choked me up. I coughed, tapering off slowly into a dainty "ahem."

"Now stay with me here." He walked away and came back with my backpack. "What about all these keys? Could any of these keys tell us where the book is? What's this locker key?" He held up a small key with a plastic handle. "You want to tell me where this is from?" At first I had no idea where the key was from. Then I remembered that I had left some items in the train station in Rapid City, South Dakota, when I was driving around the country. Just some small personal items I didn't want to have around. But didn't want to throw away either.

238 "That's for a locker in a train station in New Haven, Connecticut," I said. "And there's seven hundred and fifty thousand dollars inside." My voice was a little slurry. "Go get it."

"Uh huh. Seven hundred and fifty thousand dollars."

"Whoa!" said Wonder Woman. And then, "Oh . . . no, I guess not."

"No, I don't think so," said Seth.

"That would be just too lucky. Jesus, she is a bitch. She's horrible."

"Oh, little Wonder Woman," I said. The camera was just within the light. He stood behind it with his eye pressed to the viewfinder. Watching my television image sigh and rage.

"Your aunt's got the book," I said to Seth. "Your aunt's got it. If you want it, you'll have to talk to her."

"You see," said Seth, "she doesn't have it. You're lying. I

know for a fact she doesn't have it. That it's still out there somewhere."

"Tell him where it is," said Wonder Woman. "It's his dad's book."

"Yeah," said Seth. "I *like* my dad." He jabbed at the cut on my head with the sharp end of the locker key. "He's a *good* dad."

I let him waste another ammonia capsule. When I snapped up, Seth said, "You know why this place is so cool?"

I leaned sideways as far as I could and vomited onto the floor beside the chair. A yellow bile. "Excuse me," I said. "What?"

"Oh!" said Wonder Woman. "That was incredible. That was sick. I got it. I was right on her."

"This place," said Seth, "this was just used for an interrogation scene in my dad's movie."

"I don't know where the frigging stupid book is," I said. "You pile of shit." I laughed giddily. Vomiting had made me feel better. "You know," I said. "If shit could shit, it might produce something kind of like you." I laughed a little more wildly. "I just made that up!"

"AND IN THE MOVIE!" said Seth, "it's really SAD because the guy DIES. He doesn't TELL them, AND THEY KILL HIM. In a serious way. How do you feel about that?"

"Uh, nonplussed?"

"You want me to think you don't care if you die. Don't care about any of this."

"I do care. But not much."

"I don't think you want to die."

"Never assume," I said.

Somewhere far away a door opened. Someone took a few tentative steps. Then silence. Seth and Wonder Woman looked at each other for a moment, then at me, then back at each other. Seth said, "Go check that out."

"Why?"

"Because you're a better actor than me."

"Yeah, okay." Wonder Woman turned off the camera. "But lose the mask."

Wonder Woman's sneakers squeaked like tiny birds against the floor. His limp was less pronounced.

"He's not a better actor than me," said Seth. "But he has a huge ego."

I heard voices at the other end of the room. Just the rumble. Sounds could really hustle in this place.

Wonder Woman came back and whispered in Seth's ear.

"Oh, please," Seth said with disgust. He walked away. Yelled out, "You're a pussy, man," to the stranger in the corner. No reply. Then soft voices again. The stranger's no more than air though an open window.

While they talked, Wonder Woman watched me. He drank some water. The top of the bottle was too large for the opening in the mask. Some of the water dribbled down the plastic. A superhero's drool.

He said, "There's not any money in that locker, right?"

"Huh?"

"In New Haven?"

"Fuck you," I said.

Seth jogged back to us. "What a pussy he is," he said. "Is he staying?"

"I don't know. He may hang around awhile but he doesn't want to be too close, you know?"

Wonder Woman stretched his arms, rotated his neck. "I'm getting hungry."

"Yeah," said Seth, "me too."

"I only had those two tacos."

"All right," said Seth, "let's speed things up some."

"Otherwise, maybe we could have something brought in."

"Don't be an asshole." Seth fiddled with the radio dial again until he found something he liked. A Johnny Mathis tune. "I met this dude," he said. "My dad showed him to me once."

"Johnny Mathis," I said. Timmy had had a picture of Johnny Mathis in his house. I guess all famous kids meet Johnny Mathis. "Johnny Mathis," I said again.

241

I was barely there. The pain the only thing keeping me conscious. And I wanted so badly to give up. Let go of it all. But the thought of Scott pulled me back. Scott, watching TV in a strange house. He was in this thing because of me. And I would have to get him out. Then. Then I could find a little peace.

I decided that tough was not the way to go now. I decided to go the opposite direction.

"Don't hurt me anymore. Okay?" I sobbed. Was it real?

Seth moved out of the light, came back smoking a cigarette. "If you let me go," I said, "I can find it and then I'll give it to you. I promise you can have it." Tears and snot ran down my face. I bent my head.

"Let me have a drag," said Wonder Woman. He held out his hand for the cigarette. Seth ignored him.

JEN BANBURY

"You can have it," I said. My voice pleading. "You can have it." I took hiccupy gulps of air. "But you have to let me go for me to find it." I knew I was saying all of this loud enough for the guy in the cheap seats to hear.

"I saw this cool thing on the Discovery channel," said Seth, "about this tribe in Africa or South America. They scar themselves on their face and they think it looks really good. And it does. It's gonna be the next big thing." He reached into his pocket with his left hand and withdrew something small, flat. He unwrapped it, dumped the wrapper. A razor blade.

"Seth, don't," I said. "Don't do it. You'll go to jail for it. If you let me go now, I won't tell anyone about this. And you'll get the book. If you keep going, it'll be bad. A mistake." I was yelling and sobbing the way you do when you're little and you hate the world for the first time.

He shook his head back and forth. "Jail? You gotta understand . . . the way it works is, I don't go to jail. For *anything*. I just don't."

"Yeah," said Wonder Woman, "if you went to jail, you'd already be there."

"Where's the book?" said Seth.

"Don't, Seth."

"Where?" He made a gesture with the hand that held the razor blade. A question mark in the air.

"Don't do it. You know I don't know."

He made another question mark, moving his arm with the slow grace of an aging ballet dancer. I shook my head. "No," I said. "No I don't." Seth repeated the gesture one more time. Then he stepped in toward me. He sat down on my lap. A toddler posing with a department store Santa. He wrapped his right arm around my head and held tight. The cigarette dangled in the corner of his mouth. With his left hand, his gloved hand, he moved the blade toward my cheek. I remained still until his hand was a few inches from my mouth. Then I jerked my head and got my teeth on it, just missing the blade. He yelled and sprung away. "Ah, FAAACK!" The cigarette dropped from his mouth, rolled across the floor.

"What happened?" asked Wonder Woman.

"Ah, fuck. She bit Priscilla!"

"Ouch."

"Hold her head, c'mon."

"What about the camera?"

"Just put it on a wide shot." Wonder Woman fiddled with the camera for a moment, then came over and stood behind me. He pressed the back of my head against his stomach. His hot wet hands on my hot wet face.

"Got her?"

"I got her." Yeah, like my head was a balloon and he was trying to pop it.

"It's in the bookstore," I said.

"No shit?" said Seth. He picked the cigarette up off the floor and put it back in his mouth. It was down to a nub.

"Hidden in the books."

"Oh really?" He straddled my lap. Kept his hand away from my mouth. I didn't feel the cut. I felt the blood. Like a couple harmless bugs racing down my face. He took the cigarette from his mouth and pressed it into my cheek. I screamed. "That's one," he said.

"YOU JERK!" The words exploded in the space. So loud they were almost unintelligible. But for once, it wasn't me screaming.

Seth turned around. I looked up. For a second, my bashed-up brain had me thinking it was Luis. But it wasn't Luis. It was Timmy. Standing behind Seth with a chair in his hands.

"What are you —" Timmy swung and knocked Seth off my lap. Hitting me in the bargain. I got over it and pushed off the floor as hard as I could, rocketing myself and my chair backward. It took Wonder Woman by surprise. I had pushed hard enough to topple him over with me and I landed on him. When he hit the floor, his head cracked against the cement and he let out a small sigh. Like he was bored. Then he didn't make any noise at all.

"What the fuck, man, what do you think you're doing?" Seth said. I heard him scrabble up off the ground.

"You went too far."

"Fuck you."

"You went too far, Seth. You're a sick fuck."

"It's not even . . . it's none of your business!" Seth's voice broke.

"John didn't want all this."

"John just said lay off the sex stuff."

"I'm going to take her with me."

"You really are a pussy."

I had projected myself out of the light. As my eyes adjusted, I saw the ceiling high above me. The pigeons flapping around. Unsettled by the commotion. Waiting for things to end. I couldn't see Seth or Timmy. My hands were pressing hard against Wonder Woman's belly. He had sweated through his T-shirt. I wiggled down his body so that I could feel the outside of his pants pockets. The right side bulged up with the outline of some keys and I began furiously digging my hand in to reach them. Seth and Timmy were yelling at each other. Their shouts overlapping and echoing into a single white din. Then, for a moment, silence. I almost had the keys.

"Oh great," said Timmy. "What are you going to do, like, shoot me?" I jerked my head around, trying to see what was going on. Useless. "Put it down, Seth. You're not going to shoot me. You put down the gun, then I'll put down the chair. An even-Steven." Nothing. "All right, look, I'll put down the chair. . . ." A sudden rush of movement, a charge. A blow. The gun went off. Someone stumbled backward. Landed on the ground next to me.

245

"Tim!" I said. "Timmy!" It wasn't Timmy, it was Seth. Flat on his back with a gash on his forehead. I saw his chest heave up and down. He wasn't dead. "Timmy!" I heard panic in my voice. "Tim!" No answer. There was blood all over my face and I was light-headed as hell. I realized I had better move or pass out. "Oh, GOD oh GOD!" I yelled. I worked the keys out of Wonder Woman's pocket but I could feel they were too big to be handcuff keys. I moved my fingers over his pants again. This time I felt two small outlines. Deeper in the same pocket. I got my hand in and wiggled my whole body down toward those keys.

"Come on!" I yelled. "Come on you goddamn keys . . . come on!" My hand wouldn't go any farther. I pinched the fabric of the pocket in my fingers and pulled on it, turning the pocket slowly inside out. The keys jumped away, pinging onto the floor. I rocked sideways off Wonder Woman and felt around until I found them. They were handcuff keys all right. I pinched one between my fingers and used my thumb to feel around for the keyhole. I took a deep breath and tried not to rush the job, not to fumble. I guess origami makes you dexterous. I eased the key in without much trouble. And I was free.

Timmy was lying on his side. His legs bent in a running pose. His face mostly missing. A large pool of blood haloed his head, spreading. Growing enormous. I cried and kicked at one of his feet. I knelt beside him and pressed my head into his stomach as though I could find a place to rest there. Filled my mouth with his T-shirt to block the noises I was making. Then, soon enough, I forced myself away and stood up, breathing hard.

I turned around a few times, trying to figure out what to do. Seth or Timmy had knocked over the light and it lay pointing sideways on the ground, making a small white puddle. I was in a warehouse. I could see around, but the natural light had a dirty quality to it. Unfocused. I walked over to the camera and picked it up by the tripod and smashed it against the ground. I smashed it until shards of plastic jumped away from it like grasshoppers and the tape popped out and I smashed that too.

I saw Wonder Woman's car keys lying on his belly where I had pulled them from his pocket and I stooped to pick them up. His head rested on the corner of a cinder block and blood rushed from that unnatural pillowing. While I was down getting his keys, I lifted the Wonder Woman mask. His eyes were wide open, glassy. Even dead I recognized him.

246

The guy in the John-O Burger commercials. Very popular. He had a flannel shirt tied around his waist and I rolled him off it and used it to wipe the blood off my face. I didn't care that it was a dead man's shirt.

Seth took a deep breath, kept breathing. I pulled him, unconscious, into a sitting position and wound up to hit him in the face. But I let him go without hitting him and he fell heavily back against the concrete floor. Instead, I retrieved the handcuffs and cuffed Seth's and Wonder Woman's wrists together, then pocketed the keys. I found Debi's gun a couple feet away. Next to it, the Rapid City locker key. I put the key in my backpack and held on to the gun. I shouldered the pack, pressed the flannel shirt to my face, and limped toward the door.

18.

Wonder Woman owned a convertible BMW. It was parked right outside the door. Timmy's car was there too, and Seth's. I lifted up the hood of Seth's car and looked around, but I couldn't remember any of the ways to disable it. The parking lot was behind the warehouse and it was empty. I pointed the gun at one of the tires and fired. Again, I coughed to mask the sound. I don't know why. The bullet ripped a large gash through the rubber.

When I opened the door to Wonder Woman's car, the alarm went off. Fiddling with the gadget on his key chain made it stop. I wrapped the flannel shirt around my head and tied the sleeves beneath my chin so that the cuts on my head and cheek were mostly covered. Then I eased myself into the car, put the gun in my backpack, and placed the backpack, unzipped, on the passenger seat beside me.

The fake good-looking cop had been right — the warehouse was near Beverly and Western. I started driving without knowing where to go. I felt so dizzy. Like I had been spun around a couple minutes and it was my turn to pin the tail on the donkey. The blood soaked through the flannel shirt. I thought about stopping at a pharmacy. Getting some bandages. A first aid kit. I couldn't remember if there were any pharmacies nearby. Without thinking about it, I was driving in the direction of the bookstore. It wasn't all that far. But I didn't want to go to the bookstore. I wanted some bandages and a telephone to call Scott. The clock on the dashboard told me it was 3:38 P.M. I kept driving. When I stopped for a red light, a Mustang pulled up beside me and the woman driving gave me a crazy look. "I had a bad day," I said.

249

I drove past the bookstore. It was closed. I hadn't asked Mike to cover for me. At the end of the block, I made a right, then another right into the alley behind the twenty-four-hour vet. I had an idea.

I pounded on the back door for a couple minutes before someone came to open it. A young woman, an assistant. When she saw me, she said "Uh, ye-es?"

"Is the vet that was on duty last night still here?" I asked.

"Uh, yes, if, do you mean — Dr. Prusty?"

"I need to see him please."

"He's with someone, uh, a dog."

"Can I wait?" She nodded slowly and let me in. Dogs yelped. Cats meowed. She was ushering me to the waiting room.

"Can I wait in an exam room?"

"Uh, sure," she said. "Yes." She pushed open a door for me. I went in. "I'll tell him," she said.

I sat on the examining table. Then I lay down. I had to curl myself up into a ball to fit. That was okay. It seemed like I shouldn't allow myself to fall asleep. But I did.

The smell of ammonia woke me up and I jumped. Thinking I was still in the warehouse. I knocked the capful of the stuff that the vet was holding right out of his hands.

"Calm," he said. "Calm." I sat up. He looked at me so sadly. "What has happened to you, Lou Ellen? What is this?"

250

"That cat," I said, halfheartedly.

"No," he said. "No. This is something serious."

"Just a little trouble. Just a little accident. Will you fix me up?" I tried to smile, but my voice had a desperate catch to it. I wiped my nose with my sleeve.

"You should go to the hospital," he said. "This is not for me."

"I just need some bandages. I don't need the hospital. Please. I'm your —" I laughed and sucked in a sob — "your good deed."

"I'm very tired," he said. "I have animals to see."

"Please," I said. "Just bandage up my face." He sighed and looked at his watch.

"I'll be back in a minute."

He came back ten minutes later holding a large glass of orange juice. "Drink it," he said. "You have lost some blood, it seems."

"Is there anything in it?"

"Just a little dog urine." I looked at him.

"I'm sorry," he said. "This incident has put me in a very odd mood. And with no sleep, you know. It's just juice, I promise you." I drank it and felt much stronger. He removed the flannel shirt from my head and began to clean me up. When he had wiped away a good portion of the blood, he said, "My God. Is that a question mark?"

As it turned out, Seth hadn't cut very deeply. The vet used butterfly bandages instead of stitches. Put some salve on the burn. Then he wrapped my head in gauze. Covered the whole right side of my face, my forehead, under my chin.

"I have to use your phone," I said.

251

"I need to fix the rest of you," he said.

"Let me use the phone first," I said. "I won't go anywhere." He agreed to let me use the phone while he took care of his next appointment. He showed me to a large closet that he used as an office. He closed the door on his way out.

I called the Joke Man. The dwarf answered.

"Let me talk to him."

"Where have you been?"

"Let me talk to him."

"He's not here."

"I got held up," I said. "But I've almost got it. Let me talk to my friend, then."

"Oh. He can't talk right now."

"What do you mean?"

"He's doing stuff. He's out doing — la la — an errand."

"What's wrong?"

"Nothing. Nothing. I swear. He's out on an errand with Barry. Picking up food, I think."

"Ah Jesus," I said. "Ah, Jesus. All right, listen. I'm going to call back in half an hour and they both better be there. Or no book, just lots of cops."

"Ooh, don't tell me that. Don't even say that." I hung up. Called the Aqua Mountain 800 number. While I waited on hold, I rifled through the vet's drawers, looking for pills. He didn't want to give me anything stronger than Tylenol because he thought I might have a concussion. But I wanted something that would really put a lid on the pain. All I found was more Tylenol. And some pictures of people seated around a table at a restaurant. His family, maybe. In one, a young girl held a glass of water above a woman's head like she was about to pour it on her. Like she was having fun. I put the picture in the pocket of my jeans.

The Aqua Mountain operator gave me the number for the L.A. distribution center. I told her it was an emergency.

I called the local number and asked the woman who answered if there was a Charles around. She transferred me.

"This is Charles." A Southern accent. The wrong Charles. And the wrong name. They knew him as Greg.

"Shit," I said. I hung up and dialed again. This time, I told the woman I was looking for a guy named Greg — a delivery guy. I described him. She knew who I meant. I asked if she could patch me in to his truck. She couldn't.

"Listen," I said. "He delivers water to the veterinary clinic where I work. I don't think we're supposed to get a delivery today, but we're out of water and they turned off the faucet water because they're doing some construction somewhere and the animals here are very thirsty. They're going nuts. So if he could swing by . . . do an emergency delivery . . . we'll pay for the inconvenience."

"Sure, sure," said the woman. "We do emergency deliveries."

"Oh good," I said. "Okay. Although, it will definitely be Greg, right?"

"I don't know. It might not be."

"No," I said, "it has to be. He knows how we like the water delivered. He . . . please ask him to do it. He's good with the animals." I told her we bought a lot of water and would be very disappointed if they sent anyone else.

"I'll see what I can do," said the woman. "Why don't you give me your account number." I explained that our new accountant took all that information home with him to familiarize himself. I gave her the name and address of the clinic, told her to look it up in the records. Thanked her profusely. Said, "Time is of the essence."

253

I sat for a minute, rocking back and forth in the desk chair. Looking at the stuff on the walls. Dog and cat anatomy posters. And a kid's drawing of a poodle with the words, "ThaNK You FOR SAveing Missy." There were a bunch of seashells on one corner of the desk. None of them seemed very unusual.

I picked up the phone again and I dialed my sister's number in Boston. She answered.

"Hi!" she said. "We're having a barbecue. Oh! You know who's here? Oh, wait, you don't know him. I'm kind of drunk. I made this disgusting potato salad. It's repulsive." To someone else: "Yes it *is!* It's *foul!*" To me: "So what's going on?"

"Oh . . . I think I might have killed a guy," I said. I choked a little.

"Aaahhh shut up. Listen, Uncle Jay's birthday was yesterday, did you call? You've got to call, you know how he is about stuff like that, you're already sort of on his list — hold on, Andrew's trying to get the phone." Andrew, her boyfriend, got on.

"Hey there, Sucker Punch!" I hung up the phone. Then I called back. Andrew answered.

"Hey," I said. "It's me. Sorry about that. I'm at a party, too, and they keep playing with the phone. I can't talk. I just wanted to say 'hi' but — okay, I'm coming! — yeah, I have to go. It's my turn to, um, I'll talk to you guys later. Bye!"

The thing was, my sister didn't know about my mother and me — about our little deal. My mother thought that my sister wouldn't go for any of it. That she'd want her to tough it out. The biggest problem was that my sister was a little bit of a Catholic, though none of us knew where she got it from. That left only me. And I did a good job. A clean killing with no suspicion of foul play. Only after, I started to tumble. And I never really stopped.

I found the bathroom down the hall. Looked at myself in the mirror and laughed. The vet had been generous with the bandages again. Only a quarter of my face showed. "Invisible man," I said. I touched the small area of exposed flesh. "Almost." I washed my hands gently.

The vet examined my foot and decided it wasn't broken, just bruised. He salved and wrapped my inner arm where they had used the steel wool. Once in a while he said, "This,

I don't understand. I do not understand." He squeezed some disinfectant into the cuts under my nails and bandaged my fingertips. He recleaned the cat scratch on the other hand. Sometimes he left for a while to see an animal patient. He drank coffee from a cup with a *Far Side* cartoon on it. "What a dog hears: 'Blah blah blah blah blah Ginger blah blah blah.'"

At one point, he came back into the room, leading the black dog. It had one of those lampshade collars around its neck to prevent it from scratching the bandage off its face. It looked pathetic. Like some circus trick gone wrong.

"Look who it is!" he said.

"Oh." I said. "Yeah. I forgot about him."

"Her."

"Oh." The dog wiggled around. Wagged her whole body.

"You can take her with you," said the vet.

"Look. She's not my dog. I can't take her."

"You should have her. I think you need this dog."

"She belongs to someone else. She's not my dog. I just found her."

"She has neither collar nor tags."

"My building doesn't allow pets." The dog made an attempt to lick the vet's hand. "She likes you," I said.

"No, no, it's just the lunch on my hands."

"Oh."

"But if we send this dog to the pound . . . I don't need to tell you they destroy dogs at the pound."

"I'm not taking the dog! All right? Stuff is happening all around me. All the time. I'm not going to be able to have a dog with me. Understand? Now will you leave me alone?"

255

"I do not understand," he said. "I do not understand anything." We stood in silence for a while. I could tell he was looking at me. I thwacked my bandaged fingers idly against my bandaged hand. The silence kept up. Even the dog observed it.

"I'm going to the bathroom," I said. I got up and went to the reception area. A man sat waiting with a cat in his lap. He whispered to the cat. "Oh you're so good. Soooo good. My good girl."

The receptionist looked up from her work. The same woman who had opened the back door for me. She gave me a funny smile.

"When the guy shows up to deliver the water, please send him to talk to me."

"Oh, uh, okay. I don't know if we're due for a delivery."

"Well, he's coming."

"Oh."

"So just send him my way."

"All right."

"Thanks a lot," I said.

"It's all right," she said. She leaned across the counter to speak more intimately. "I hope . . . is everything okay?"

"Sure," I said. "Thanks."

"And I hope . . . do you know, it's true you have a friend in Jesus?"

"Right," I said. "I tend to forget."

I called the Joke Man number again. This time, the machine picked up. I said I would call back soon and I wanted to speak to Scott. I said I wasn't kidding around.

I waited for Charles in the vet's little office. It was 5:00 P.M. I sat in the vet's chair and pointed his fan at my face. The vet came in and sat on the edge of the desk. I told him a friend was coming to pick me up. I'd be out of his hair soon. He said he was going home. Finally. After almost twenty-four hours. He said I should stay in his office and wait for my friend. He said the dog could stay a few days until I could come pick her up. I shrugged. He advised me to get away from the trouble I was in. He asked if I had any family who might help me. I said, "Sure." He offered to drive me and the dog to another town. I said thanks but no thanks. He said he would let me stay with him for a day or two, but his mother was visiting and she was very traditional and there was no space. I told him he'd already done plenty. Then he said he was lying, his mother wasn't visiting, he just didn't want to get involved in trouble. He was weak that way, he said. I told him not to worry. He said that he would **257** expect me in a day or two to get the dog. I complimented him on his shell collection. With a long sigh he left, closing the door behind him.

I dozed a little while. Dreamlessly for once. A light knocking woke me up.

"Hold on." I sat up. Got my hand on the gun inside the backpack. Put the pack in my lap and pointed it toward the door. "Come in." The door pushed open and Charles poked his head tentatively around the corner. "Oh finally," I said. "Hi."

"You wanted to see me?" He looked confused. Didn't recognize me with all the gauze on my face.

"It's Jill from the bookstore," I said.

"Are you serious?"

"It's me."

"Well what in the name of all things holy . . . ?"

"I was in a car crash," I said. "It doesn't matter. But, listen, you know that book you bought yesterday? That Jack London book?"

"Hold on a minute. Let me digest. Um, car crash. Jack London book? Yesss."

"Where is it?"

"I'm giving it to my nephew. I already wrapped it. It's, let me think . . ." He closed his eyes. "It's on my mail table." He was standing sideways in the doorway. One arm looped around his neck. Maybe the bandages triggered something.

"At your place?"

"That's right."

"Good. Good. Okay. I need that book very badly. It belongs to someone. It shouldn't have been sold. So we've got to go get it so I can give it back."

"What have you gotten into? What's all this drama now?"

"We've got to do it right away. It's uh, it's, it's rather important."

"I've got a couple deliveries yet."

"Look at me. We've got to get it now. Okay? Can't you tell it's important? I've got to give it back to these people now. You can't give it to your nephew. And you've got to just tell them at work that you have to do something, some errand — something essential — and you'll finish your route a little late."

"Right now, is what you're saying?"

"Now! Now! Please! Let's go, let's go, let's do it!" I got out of the chair and put on my backpack.

He nodded his head slowly. "I can see that this is something of substance we're dealing with here. And you don't strike me as the practical joke kind. Yes. All right."

"We can go right now?"

He gave another slow nod. "Let's proceed."

His truck was parked out front. I waved to the receptionist as I left. She smiled and gave me the peace sign. I glanced across the street at the bookstore. There was a bum taking a nap against the door.

"It's against company policy to give anyone a ride in the truck," Charles said. I took another look at the bum by the store. Then I ran toward him. A car screeched to a halt to avoid hitting me. I was at the store in seconds. It was Scott. **259** I knelt down beside him. He was wearing his old gas station jacket and there was some blood on it.

"Scott," I said. "Scott!" His eyes were closed. I shook him and he moaned. I slapped his face lightly.

"Don't, don't," he said.

"It's Jill. It's all right." I unzipped his jacket to try and tell where the blood was coming from. My hands shook as I tugged on the zipper. His chest and stomach were clean.

"Oh my arm," he said. That answered the question.

"Scott, what happened?" Charles had crossed the street by now. A couple people walking by slowed down to see what was going on.

Scott shook his head back and forth. "Shot. I can't fucking believe it. I'm shot."

"Do you know him?" asked Charles. He knelt down to get in on the action.

"I can't believe it," said Scott. "It's so weird, I just can't believe it." He made a delirious half-laugh. "I'm fucking shot." He opened his eyes. "Aah! You're scary looking!"

"I'm okay," I said.

"Is this part of everything else?" asked Charles.

"Yeah."

"I want Debi," said Scott. "I want Debi and I don't want to die."

"Don't worry. It's just your arm. I'll take care of it." Looking closely, I saw the jagged rip in the sleeve of the jacket. "Was it the tall guy that did it?" I asked. "Barry?"

"I don't know," said Scott. "I was running. . . ."

A cop car pulled up right in front of us. One cop got out. He was alone. He hitched up his pants.

"Oh, shit," I said.

"Need some help?" he said. "What's going on? Did he faint?"

"This man's been shot in the arm," said Charles.

"Charles, no," I said.

"Really?" said the cop. He sauntered toward us. Middle-aged, soft looking. Looked even less like a cop than the other guys. I positioned my body so that I was blocking Scott from him. Squatting over the hot cement like a kid on a potty. At the same time, I got my hand inside my backpack.

"Back off," I said.

"Excuse me?"

"Stay away from him."

"Uh, miss, it looks like this man needs a hospital. And it looks like you may need one, too."

"Yeah," said Scott, "what are you doing?" He moaned. "I want a hospital. My arm is numb."

I ignored Scott. "Just get the fuck away," I said. "You're not getting him."

"He should go to the hospital," said Charles.

"He's a fake cop." I whispered it between clenched teeth.

"What?"

"Now, whoa, let's be smart, miss," said the guy in the cop suit. "I'm going to take the two of you, you and your friend, to the hospital."

"In your car, right?" I was having a hard time getting my index finger on the gun trigger with my hand all bandaged up. I glared at the cop, with my hand jumping around inside the bag like I was searching out a lipstick.

"Sure. In my car. But first you've got to let me take a look at him. Now c'mon now."

"Get the fuck away. I mean it. Get out of here." God, I hated actors. All actors.

"Um, are you positive he's fake?" Charles whispered. I nodded. "Because he's a pretty convincing facsimile of all cops I've had the privilege of dealing with."

"Fake."

Scott moaned some more.

"C'mon, miss, I'm not fooling around. I'd like you to put your bag aside and stand away from that man." I was still working my fingers inside the bag. Waiting for the guy to chicken out. To realize that the role was more than he had bargained for, get in the car, and drive right back to the costume shop. Strip off the cop uniform and put on his chinos. Call his agent up and jaw him out for setting up such a ridiculous gig, never mind the money. Drive home to his apartment in Los Feliz, kiss his wife and kids, and get ready to spend another night with a stupid grin on his face, hauling pasta around for tips. "Okay now," said the fake cop, "I am telling you for the last time . . . I *will* be taking you and that man with me. Now we can go easy, or we can go hard." He stepped closer and made a move with his hand. Going for his piece or maybe his nightstick. I guess the money was that good. I tried one more time to get a better grip on the gun and I pressed too hard. The bullet exploded through the backpack, hitting the fake cop in the foot. He cried out and fell to the ground.

"Oops, shit!" I said. Bystanders screamed and fled. Scott said, "Aah!"

"What the hell are you doing?" said Charles. I raised my arm, pointing the backpack with its big hole right at the cop suit.

"I'm sorry," I said. "But you should have listened to me. You should have gone home to your wife and kids and your tips." He clutched at his foot. Looked at me with hate. "Now please toss me your gun very slowly," I said. He rocked back and forth over his foot.

"Stupid," he said. I don't know if he was referring to him or me.

"Your gun. Slowly but expeditiously," I said. I shook the backpack. "Now, dumbass!" He unsnapped his holster, removed his gun, and slid it toward me. I picked it up, held it with my free hand. "The problem is, you're a shitty-ass actor," I said. "You suck!" Then I heard a noise. A noise that bugged me. What was it? The sound of the police radio in his car. I hadn't heard it before. But it was squawking like crazy. Genuine cop squawk. I looked over at it, then quickly back at the cop. "Oh shit," I said. "Oh shit." The cop looked at me, gritting his teeth. A real cop. "Um . . . ," I said, "uh . . . hold on a second here."

"You're in a lot of trouble," said the cop, "and I suggest you surrender yourself to me." He spat out the words, spat around the pain.

"Um, please shut up," I said. "Shit!" I looked at Charles and Scott. They looked back at me. Waiting for my next move. "Okay . . . you!" I pointed the cop's gun at Charles. "You help me get this guy in your truck." Meaning Scott.

"What the hell?" said Charles. "Don't point that thing at me."

"Just do it!" I said. I gave him one of those meaningful looks. I kept one gun on the cop, one on Charles. The fire-play had animated Scott. He stood up with just a little help from Charles. "Let's go!" I said. "Let's go! Into the truck!" My backpack over my hand like a giant boxing glove. The cop's gun was heavy.

"I don't know what on the earth you think you're doing," said Charles.

"Let's move it, delivery man," I said. Scott and Charles started across the street. I followed them, pointing the guns everywhere, but mostly at the cop on the sidewalk. There was a hole in his boot. It looked enormous.

"You can't get away," he spat out. "Arg! It's a bad idea to try." I ignored him. Some pens fell out of the backpack but I didn't stop to pick them up.

The three of us got into the high cab of the truck. "Get out of here fast," I said.

"Fast?" said Charles. "In this? I doubt it." Still, we peeled away from the scene. I saw the cop get up and hop toward his radio.

263

"We'll go to your place," I said to Charles.

"We're not going to my place," said Charles. "I don't know what all this is, but I *know* I'm not taking you to my place."

"All right," I said, "go north. Make a bunch of turns but head toward Laurel Canyon. I'm sorry about the gun and everything but I wanted it to seem like you were an unwilling participant." I jerked the gun free of the backpack. Then I put it back in and just held on to the cop's gun.

"So once again, was that a real cop or a fake cop?"

"Um, let's say fake for now." I looked behind us and saw a station wagon speeding furiously to catch up. "Make some more turns," I said. Charles made a turn. The truck hiked up onto two wheels, then crashed back down. Scott groaned. The station wagon followed. "That station wagon," I said. "I think that station wagon is following us."

"Station wagon?" said Charles. I could see the driver pretty clearly. It wasn't anyone I recognized. "Is that guy part of this?"

"I don't know," I said. "I don't think so. Oh! Who is that?"

"It's not good to have someone following us," said Charles.

"No shit," I said. "At least he's alone." We were approaching a stop sign. "Stop at this stop sign," I said. Before the truck had come to a full halt, I jumped out and ran over to the guy in the station wagon. Pointing the gun. This time, I was sure that the safety was on.

"Get your hands on the dashboard!" I yelled. The guy obeyed. He had dark, kinky hair, a pasty face. "Who are you? Why are you following us?"

"Citizen's arrest," said the guy.

"Don't fuck around," I said. "Who are you working for?"

"Really," said the guy. "I want to make a citizen's arrest. Or just, you know, follow the action."

"You are an idiot," I said. "Not smart." I opened his door with my free hand. "Get out." He got out. "Now start walking," I said. The gun was still trained on him. He didn't move. "Move!" I said.

He laughed nervously. "I really don't think you're going to shoot me," he said. "My name is Ted and I have three children." He lowered his hands so they were resting on his shoulders. His arms bent to look like little wings.

"Ted, huh?"

"That's right," he said. "My kids' names are Sara —" I switched my grip on the gun and hit him with it. Hard in the face. He stumbled backward.

"Maybe you're right," I said. "Maybe I wouldn't shoot you. But you better run like you're a fucking track star to be on the safe side." He turned and ran. I hurried back to the truck cab. "C'mon," I said. "We're making a switch."

265

19

When we got to Scott and Debi's place, I moved Scott's truck out of the garage and Charles parked the station wagon inside and closed the garage door. Debi and the kids weren't home. Scott walked the house, sobbing and calling Debi's name and kicking stuff around. I got him to sit down and have a drink.

Charles said, "You know, I truly am curious. Was that a real cop?"

"Does it make a difference?" I said.

"Does it make a difference? Does it make a difference?"

"I'm saying that it doesn't matter as far as you are concerned. That I made you an unwilling participant. An innocent bystander caught up in the mess." Scott was drinking from a bottle of Jim Beam. I took it from him, took a swig myself, and handed it to Charles. Charles took a sip and then spat it out.

"What am I doing? I've been sober for eight years. I'm not doing this."

"Sorry," I said. "About all this."

"You tell *him* you're sorry," said Scott.

"I told you I was sorry."

"No you didn't."

"Yes I did."

"Not that I heard."

"I'M SORRY!" I roared in Scott's face. He slumped back in his chair. Looked away. Bit his lower lip and jiggled his foot. "I'm sorry," I said. "I'm sorry."

"I'm shot."

"I'm sorry. Drink more." I handed him the bottle.

"I don't want more," he said. He took a long sullen drink. I got up and looked through a few kitchen drawers until I found a clean dish towel. I tugged Scott's coat off and tied the towel around his arm as a temporary bandage.

267

"I'll take a look at it in a minute," I said.

"What's happening?" he said. "What's going on now? Why don't we call the cops?"

"Why don't we call the cops?" I said. "Because I shot one of them."

"That guy was a real cop?"

"Oh," said Charles. "Interesting."

"I shot half of his goddamned foot off," I said.

"But it was sort of a mistake, right?" said Scott.

"It doesn't matter," I said.

"So . . . what? I'm not going to the hospital?"

"No. You're not going to the hospital. It doesn't look that bad. And for another thing, you don't have insurance. You can't afford to go to the hospital."

"Well that's not exactly the kind of thing I'm worried about right now. Huh? I mean, I don't see any reason for you to be so calm about everything."

"Now hey there," said Charles. "Calm is all right. Calm is very good."

I felt more than calm. I felt a blankness. "Anyway, I'm going to fix this," I said. "I'm going to clean this up. Settle things fast." I turned to Charles. "I need to ask you to do me one more favor," I said.

Charles agreed to drive Scott's truck to his place, get the book, and come back. I was hoping the cops wouldn't figure out who he was for another hour or so. They'd get it soon enough — there weren't too many black, scarred Aqua Mountain delivery men. But if he could get to his place before the cops got there, get the book without his neighbors seeing . . . then he could come back with the book, take the station wagon somewhere, ditch it, and walk to a phone. Tell the cops we had dumped him in the middle of nowhere. I said, "Remind me to remind you to wipe down the inside of the station wagon."

"Oh yes," he said, "I'm good that way." He said he didn't know how I would get out of the mess, but he wouldn't be the one to turn me in. He knew what it was like to be in trouble with the law. He said, "My God, the way things work. You wake up a normal human being trying to get by. And then Lady Fate. Aah, Lady Fate."

"All that philosophy you read," I said, "and you're a fatalist?"

"It varies," he said. "Today, after all this business, I'm a fatalist."

Charles left in Scott's pickup. Scott said, "I hope there's enough gas."

"Jesus Christ," I said.

I cut Scott's shirt off and took a closer look at his arm. The bullet had gone right through the flesh, missing the bone. Lucky. But I had to take another couple shots of Jim Beam before I didn't mind the blood.

"What happened?" I asked. Mostly I wanted to get him talking instead of moaning. Moaning is a sound I can't stand. It eats away inside my head. Her last few weeks, my mother hadn't been able to help it. She made a noise like a drunk blowing over the mouth of an empty bottle. All day and all night. It destroyed her — she needed to put an end to everything. "It's gone on too long," she whispered. "It's time for peace."

"What happened?" said Scott. "They shot me. Couldn't fucking believe it."

"What were you doing when they shot you?" Scott was a little looped already. He sucked on a double Popsicle and licked the drips from his knuckles. I had closed all the windows and the house was hot as hell. I cleaned the wound with alcohol. First I turned the TV on at top volume. I figured the neighbors were used to the TV being too loud. They weren't used to Scott screaming.

"Well, you know, I was just sitting around watching TV — some old AAAHHHHEEEEK!"

269

"I know," I said. "I know."

"You don't know. You've never been shot." He looked me right in the heavily bandaged face.

"You're right," I said. "I have no idea. What movie were you watching?"

"Huh? Oh, some old movie on TV. Before that we watched *The Major and the Minor* and you know, it was so good, I would forget what a weird situation I was in. So we were watching this other movie that wasn't that good and that tall guy was there and the — OW Jesus!"

"Bite down on the Popsicle stick."

Scott bit the stick and talked at the same time. It made him difficult to understand. "— eh a igit az air."

"Stop," I said. "Don't bite the stick. Just talk."

"The midget was there and . . . boy, that was weird too. I think that's the first time I've hung out with a midget. You forget that they exist in real life. That they're not just some movie-made thing, you know?"

"And then . . ." I wiped the blood and alcohol from his arm and started in with the antibacterial cream.

"Then the tall guy left to do something and then the midget was like, 'I'll be right back,' and he left. And the TV room was near the front door and I just figured 'What the fuck, I'll leave too.' So I just sort of edged out the door and I didn't see anyone so I started down the driveway and then I heard someone yell so I started running and the next thing I knew, I felt this wicked sting in my arm and I ran faster and cut through some yards and alleys and shit and hid awhile and then realized I was right near Bitter Muse, so I ran there. But it was locked. And then I guess I sort of passed out."

270

"I told you I would be there soon," I said. I had the wound all cleaned up. The Jim Beam made it easier, all right. I didn't mind the blood. I could even touch the hole. It must have been a small gun. It was a small hole.

"Hey! I was waiting all day for you! I didn't know if you were coming or what! I saw an opportunity."

"I got delayed." I looked around for some gauze and came up empty. Instead, I cut a white cotton tank top of Debi's into strips. It still had the tags on. Calvin Klein. Thirty-two bucks. Scott didn't seem to notice.

"Did you see the woman that owns the house?"

"I don't think so. I met the cook. . . . Oh yeah, once some lady yelled down from upstairs. She yelled, 'Where are the pinking shears! The pinking shears!' And I gotta tell you, that scared me more than anything else." Blood seeped through the tank top as I tied it around Scott's arm. First a tiny point, then a sloppy bloom. I tied on another layer. "And all this is over what? A book? Yeah, I don't think I buy that," he said.

"It's a rare book," I said. "A very rare book. But I'm not sure I buy it either."

"I mean look at you. What happened to you?"

"Oh I just fell down a little." I got up and looked through the refrigerator. I found a juice box. Cranapple. "Got any cookies?" I looked in the cookie drawer. It was empty.

"There's usually some dough in the freezer," said Scott.

"What, to bake cookies? All this is going on and I'm going to bake some cookies?"

"I was just answering the question. Oh *where* is Debi? Christ, where is she? What's today, Sunday? Did she say something about taking the kids to Magic Mountain? Maybe she's wearing her beeper."

271

"It is Sunday," I said. That meant it didn't matter that the bookstore was closed. It was supposed to be closed. That was something.

Scott got up and went to the phone.

"What are you doing?" I said.

"I'm going to try paging her," said Scott.

"No. No. It's better that she's not around. Wait until I get the book and I can get out of here."

He wasn't happy about it, but he agreed. I gave him a handful of children's aspirin. "You have to get some better painkillers," I said. He rolled a joint.

"This is a better painkiller." He offered me a hit, but I declined. "So what happens now?"

"I'm going to be leaving," I said. I sucked on the tiny straw from the juice box. It was like sucking on a syringe. "As soon as Charles gets back with the book."

"*Leave* leaving?"

"Yeah." I hadn't really thought about it until I said it. But as soon as I said it, I knew it was true. I would have to run. Start again. Give up Bitter Muse. Christ, it was hard to live a life. I didn't want to be on the road again. But if I stuck around, I risked landing myself in prison. I was beginning to think that maybe this trip would be a short one. Maybe it would end in just a day or two. A week or a month. End with the muzzle of Debi's gun tickling the roof of my mouth. It was an idea that had been prowling the corners of my head since the night with my mother. And now I was getting so tired. . . . "I'm going to need to borrow some of Debi's stuff," I said.

"Oh here we go," said Scott. I took my shot-up backpack

272

into Scott and Debi's bedroom. Debi had a lot of bags, purses, but no backpacks. I found one in Cox's room and transferred everything from mine into it. Plus Debi's gun. I wiped down the cop's gun and wrapped it in a hand towel, which I added to the backpack also. To be disposed of later. I took off Mike's jeans and sweater and put on a tailored dark gray pantsuit from Debi's closet. Expensive looking. With it, some clunky oxford-type shoes.

"I'm not even going to . . ." Scott took another hit off the joint he had rolled. "I mean, anything I say at this point doesn't matter I guess," he said.

"That's right. Nothing matters."

In the bathroom, I slowly cut the gauze off my face. I said, "It's a miracle! Thank you doctor!" I put a couple of Band-Aids over the gash on my forehead. I left the small butterfly bandages covering the question mark on my cheek. I didn't want to look at it now. I'd look at it later. Or never at all.

273

I was lucky the vet had been so wrap-happy. The cop would have a hard time trying to identify me. If it came to that.

"Where are you going to go?" Scott watched me from the doorway. Slumped. Smoking.

"Doesn't matter."

I added a few other items of clothing to my new backpack. Scott trailed me around the house like a store-bought puppy.

"So now you really hate everything, is that it?"

"I don't hate everything."

"Everybody?"

"Whatever."

Debi didn't have any hats, so I put on one of Cox's baseball caps. A Raiders' cap. It covered the Band-Aids on my forehead.

"What about good people?"

"I hate them the most." I remembered the picture of the vet's family in the jeans I had been wearing. I transferred it to the inside pocket of the suit jacket.

"You know," said Scott, "I'm not kidding when I say this. And I'm saying this for your benefit. And as a psychology major. Jill, your soul is dying. And you better do something."

"I'm going to. Didn't I tell you? I'm going to Disneyland. And Mickey's going to touch me right here." I pressed my fingers against my heart.

274

"I mean it."

"There's nothing to be done. All right? Nothing." I sighed and then I rubbed my hand against Scott's shirt because, really, he was my friend.

"You can't live this way. You'll end up dead or involved in crime."

"Where have you been?"

"I mean, by your own doing." He placed his hand on top of mine and squeezed too hard. "What is it you want?"

"Don't do this now."

"But what?"

I moved away and positioned the backpack by the front door. Ready to go. "I'm going to make a peanut butter sandwich. You should have one too. For the protein." I went into the kitchen and Scott followed. While I was looking for the bread, I noticed one of Cox's report cards tacked to the fridge. All A's and B's.

"Cox is smart?" I said.

"Yeah. You didn't know that?" I shook my head. Good for him. Good for Cox.

"So, do you not want to be happy? Is that it?"

"Scott."

"I'm just trying to understand."

I turned on Scott with a knife covered in peanut butter. "Don't try to understand. It's not one of those things to be understood. I don't understand it. I don't understand why I am the way I am. But I'm not going to blame my life on one tiny fucking moment. Sometimes, just, everything comes apart including you and there's nothing to stop it once it — that you don't have control over what you feel or —" I stopped talking and turned back to the bread because I was talking crazy and choking up again and I had an idea that if I started now it might be a couple years before I stopped. I sensed Scott behind me and I said, "Jesus, please! *Please* lay off me."

And Scott whispered, "Okay."

"Don't undo me now."

"Okay," he whispered.

"Okay?"

"Yeah," he said. "Okay." I turned on the sink faucet and watched the water pour out. I cupped my unbandaged hand underneath it and sipped the water from my hand. It was bad water. It tasted bad. I looked over at Scott for a second. He leaned against the counter but couldn't get comfortable. Fidgeting. "Ow. I need a sling or something."

"Use one of Debi's scarves," I said.

"Uh huh. I will." I went back to spreading peanut butter. He lit another joint and smoked it quickly to the nub. He

275

said, "You know if you're making me a sandwich, I want jelly. Lots of jelly."

We stood there in the kitchen eating the sandwiches. It was starting to get dark but neither of us made a move to turn on the lights. We ate leaning over the counter and didn't speak. And when we were done eating, we stood perfectly still in the gloom. Waiting.

After a while, Scott said, "I thought of something. What if you were really into the concept of reincarnation and you spent all this time trying to remember what you were in your past life. And after years of praying and meditation and hope, you figure out you were a bubble."

The phone rang. "Don't get it," I said.

"It might be Debi." Scott answered the phone, put it down again. "Hang-up. Probably a wrong number. Or Jan calling to talk to the kids. He hangs up if I answer. Icelandic prick. Want a beer?"

"No. Okay." He handed one to me.

"Open it over the sink. Cox shakes them up to piss me off." I popped the top over a stack of dirty dishes. Nothing happened.

"He should be back," I said. I moved to the living room and looked out one of the front windows. A porch light went on across the street. The TV was still blaring. I turned it down.

"Maybe we should watch the news," said Scott.

"I don't want to watch the news. I don't want to know. I don't want to see it." Scott flipped through the channels on the television. "Wait," I said, "go back." It was the John-O-Burger commercial. "Oh God," I said. I chuckled a little hysterically.

"What?" said Scott.

"I know that guy." I returned to the window. A figure was walking toward the house. Charles. I unlocked the door for him. He was breathing heavily.

"Ran out of gas about three blocks away. And it's all up-hill. Oh. You look better though." He was holding a paper bag. I let him in and locked the door behind him. He handed the bag to me. I turned on a light. Inside the bag was a book wrapped in teddy bear wrapping paper.

"How old is your nephew?" I asked.

"Aaah, it was the only paper I had." I unwrapped the book and opened it up, looking for the Grautzweller pages.

"That's it, right?"

"Yeah," I said. "That's it. Do you want six bucks for it?"

"Forget it. Just give me a store credit."

"I won't be back at the store," I said.

"Oh. That's true. I guess you wouldn't be. Well, you can owe me."

"I won't —"

"Never mind then. I'm going to get a glass of water. Then I'll move on out." Scott came over to look at the book.

"Let me see," he said. I handed it to him. "What are you going to do with it? Are you going to give it back?"

"I hate this book," I said.

"Maybe there's something hidden in it. Like dirty photos hidden in the binding. Do you want to cut it open?"

"No. If it's something else, I don't care." Scott gently flexed the back cover of the book. "Stop it," I said. "You'll hurt it." I slapped his hand lightly. Took the book away and put it back in the paper bag. I set the bag on the coffee table in front of me.

"Do you have any money?" I asked Scott.

"Ahem," said Charles. Scott and I looked over. Charles stood in the dining area with his hands in the air. One hand held an empty glass.

"We just have tap water," said Scott. Charles walked toward us and Seth emerged from the kitchen behind him. Holding a gun. He was all cleaned up. Wearing loose pants, a linen shirt, a Greek fisherman's cap turned backwards. Presumably to cover the bandages on his head. And a heavy work glove.

"Hi, again," he said to me. He took off his sunglasses and put them in his pocket.

"Huh?" said Scott. "Who's —Who's this guy?"

"Who?" said Seth. "I'm only her best fucking FRIEND."

"Oh Christ," I said. Seth took a few steps into the living room. He struck a casual pose but he looked wound up and wild and his gun hand jiggled gently, very gently.

"And she's mine. Since the position was recently vacated."

My throat dried up and I swallowed hard so I could speak. "These guys were just delivering some stuff," I said. "They don't even know me. Hey, why don't you guys get out of here." I jerked my head toward the front door. Scott and I were standing in front of the couch — halfway between the front door and Seth.

"Okay," said Scott.

"You think I'm some sort of retard?" said Seth. "A-*duh!*"

"No one followed me," said Charles. "I know that. He didn't get here by following me."

"Open your door," said Seth. He pointed the gun at Scott.

"Who?" said Scott. "I don't live here."

278

"Open your front door, Scott." Scott's eyebrows shot up at the sound of his name.

"I'll do it," said Scott. "But it's not my door. I'm just here delivering stuff."

"And you," said Seth to me. "Cross your arms in front of your chest. So you're holding your opposite shoulders."

"Not over my head?"

"That's the old way." He looked at Charles, who was standing by the television, slightly out of the line of fire, and said, "But you can stay right like that."

"Aahh!" said Scott. He had opened the door and Barry Knott, a.k.a. Joke Man, entered the house. Barry Knott ducked his head and removed his cap. I stepped back and almost fell onto the couch, waiting for some sort of showdown between Seth and Barry Knott. A quick exchange of gunfire. The sound of falling men. It didn't come.

"Hello," said Barry Knott. "It's nice to see so many familiar faces. Uh, Scott, you left your wallet at the house. . . ."

"Oh shit," said Scott. "My wallet. I forgot they took my wallet." Barry Knott closed the door and leaned against it.

"We thought we would return it in person. Make sure it made its way safely to the correct party." He flipped the wallet onto the coffee table. It landed next to the bag with the book.

"I don't understand," I said.

"My license," said Scott, "my address . . ."

"No, I get that." I looked at Barry Knott. "You two . . . what's going on? You're on the same side?"

"Well, after a series of negotiations —"

"He's working for my dad," said Seth. "For John. How 'bout that?"

"All along?" I said.

"No," said Barry Knott. "No. This is a rather recent event. A very nice offer, actually." He rubbed his hair with his hand. It stuck out at crazy angles. Like tendrils of a dead bush. He replaced his cap. "This house is really cute," he said. "I like it." He looked around. Bobbing his head and neck like a caterpillar at the end of a branch. "Bedrooms off that hall there?" he asked, pointing to a doorway on the side of the living room.

"Uh, yes," said Scott.

"Two?" Scott nodded, braced against the arm of the couch. "I bet the commute can be annoying. The driving. Still, it feels private, which I do like."

"You don't have to talk so much," said Seth.

"Excuse *me*," said Barry Knott. "I guess I haven't had a chance to read the training manual yet."

"I want to do this right," said Seth.

"I understand," said Barry Knott. "You had a bad experience in the recent past."

Seth slitted his eyes. The gun edged a couple degrees in Barry Knott's direction. "Fuck you," he said. They glared at each other for a moment. Then Barry Knott broke it by laughing.

"All right," he said. "Fuck me, kid. Let's get on with it." He turned to me. "Sweetums," he said, "where is that book?"

"It's just the dwarf working for the old lady now?" I didn't care anymore who the book really belonged to. Hell, I probably had as much right to it as anyone else in the game. I just wanted to figure out where I stood. I wanted a clean ending.

"Just Adam. Yes, that's right."

"So I give you the book and that's it? It's over?"

"That's right," said Barry Knott. "Nobody knows any-thing about anything."

"Well, I know plenty about a lot," I said. I was aching in so many places. Desperate to sit down.

"Oh, that's correct. But Mr. Malcome actually came up with a very good idea. We had a little powwow right before coming here, little strategy session. And you know, he has a lot of friends. Good friends. Even, you see, in the police de-partment. People will do anything for this guy. And a little birdie told me that you might be having some difficulties from them soon, the police. And when I told Mr. Malcome, he said he would be happy to use his influence. . . ."

"Uh huh," I said. "I get it. You already found out about that?"

"Oh sure."

"A trade-off of silence, is that it?"

"Exactly. Exactly."

"He can do that? He can make sure they don't — "

"What are you, kidding?" said Seth. "He's John Mal-come. Give me a fucking break."

"He can do it," said Barry Knott.

Scott, still gripping the couch, looked at me. "John Mal-come? The actor?" he said.

"Cross your arms over your chest," said Seth. "And stand right next to her." He waved his gun. Scott stood with me between the couch and the coffee table. He half-crossed his arms, grunting from the effort of moving the shot-up one. Seth said to Barry Knott, "You know, I don't like this gun you gave me. This gun sucks."

Barry Knott shrugged. "Short notice," he said.

"It's like some kind of discount gun." Then Seth asked me, "Where's that gun you had? I liked that gun. Yeah, I want that gun."

"I dumped it," I said.

"Aw," said Seth. He glared at the gun he was holding.

Charles said, "I'm going to set this glass down and do the same thing they're doing. My arms." He set the glass on top of the television and crossed his arms in front of him.

"I'm surprised you didn't throw the glass at his head," said Barry Knott. He pointed with one pinkie in Seth's direction.

"I thought about it and then I decided against it."

"You were smart," said Seth. "I would have shot you dead. Even with this piece-of-shit gun."

282   "If you were fast enough," said Barry Knott.

"What about these guys?" I said. Meaning Scott and Charles.

"I'm fast enough."

"Are these guys clear?" I asked Barry Knott.

"These don't strike me as the kind of men who want to live difficult lives. If they want to be clear, they're clear." Barry Knott addressed Scott and Charles. "Are you clear?"

"Clear," said Scott. "Totally."

The burn scar on Charles's neck caught the sweat as it dripped from his face. We were all sweating. "I'm good," he said.

"Clear?"

"Oh, quite clear."

"You see?" said Barry Knott. "They understand. Later on, they're not going to remember a thing. Hocus-pocus, they're getting sleepy, when they wake up it will all be gone."

He clapped his hands together suddenly and we all twitched like we'd been stung.

"If any of us dies suddenly," I said, "my lawyer's going to open a letter that tells the whole story." What the hell. I felt better throwing that in.

"Ha ha ha ha ha," said Barry Knott.

"I want a little cash," I said. "Whatever you've got on you."

Seth said, "Just hand over the book already, all right? Ya bitch."

"I think I have about eighty bucks," said Barry Knott.

"Okay," I said.

Barry Knott removed his wallet from his suit jacket and counted his cash onto the coffee table. "Seth-o?" he said. "Feel like adding to the kitty?"

Seth put his sunglasses back on.

"What's that, a 'no'?"

"That bitch killed my friend. She hurt my hand." He was just inside the doorway that led to the hall. Feet planted, gun pointing out from his hip.

"True, too true," said Barry Knott. "Your friend and your hand. And she whacked your cousin, don't forget. Whoowee." Barry Knott flipped his hand around like he had burned it. A slight smile on his face.

"Cousin? What do you mean, 'cousin'?" I said.

"Tim Harris," said Barry Knott. "You shot Tim Harris in the — " He rapped his hand against his head and whistled.

"What? No, Seth shot Timmy. Seth killed him. He's your — his — cousin?" I thought of Timmy's photo of Johnny Mathis. The other kid in the picture . . . of course, it was Seth.

"Everyone's related somehow in this business," said Barry Knott.

"I didn't kill him," said Seth. "You killed him."

"I'm probably related to you," said Barry Knott.

"You fucking killed him, you —"

"You fucking bitch!"

"— fucking bastard!" Timmy, Seth's cousin. It was like my mother said. No matter what you saw, there was always more.

"All right. All right, kiddos," said Barry Knott. "That's enough. It's all in the past. It's taken care of. It's water under the bridge. We're gonna take the book and live our separate lives. S'aright? S'aright."

Seth knew that killing Timmy was too much. That his dad would be pissed. So he was palming it off on me.

284

"Don't act like you're my boss or something, man," said Seth.

"I'm not. No no. I'm not. I'm just trying to keep some of the peace here. S'aright? S'aright."

What did it matter, anyway. I was already a two-time killer. Just throw another on the pile. I turned back to Barry Knott. "I want a guarantee that if I give you the book, these guys walk."

"You think we just kill people? Just like that? No no no. We don't do that. What a mess. No, we have a lovely little balance going on here. Have faith in the balance."

"I'm not good with faith," I said. I needed another drink. I felt the pain in my head pulsing up like a darkness. "It's in the bag on the table," I said. I made a move for the bag.

"No!" said Seth. "Don't let her touch it. Because there

could be a gun in the bag." To me he said, "You, cross your arms again."

"No," I said.

"I've got it," said Barry, soothingly. "I've got it." He picked up the bag and looked inside. Slowly, he removed the book and examined it. He took a pair of reading glasses from his breast pocket and put them on. "Now this is nice," he said. "It's nice when you get what you wanted." He read the inscription aloud. Peering down through his glasses like an old librarian. After he had read it, he said, " 'Francis.' Oh, so that was your grandfather? The kid actor."

"Yeah," said Seth. Then, "His middle name, I think."

"His middle name, ha ha," said Barry Knott. To me he said, "Adam stole one of this Francis's movie suits, ya get. Ha ha, a kid's suit." For a second, he ducked his head into his armpit. He was just wiping the sweat off his face.

"Check for the mixed-up pages," said Seth.

"They start on page ninety," I said. I wanted them gone.

"Thank you," said Barry Knott.

"Excuse me, but what is it?" said Scott. "It's kind of driving me crazy. Is there something hidden in it?"

"It's sentimental," said Seth. "For my dad."

"That's it? Sentimental? I took a bullet for sentimental?"

"That sounds like a song," said Barry Knott. "I took a bullet for sentimental bee bop badoom." I leaned against the couch as the world took its first step away. One of those moments I couldn't control. The wrong time for this to happen, of course. I crossed my arms again and pinched my flesh through the fabric of the suit. Stay a little while, I thought. A little while, please.

285

"Let's see the book," said Seth.

"To put you to rest, Scott," said Barry Knott, "I did not shoot you. That was the little man. Adam. He was worried about . . . well he screws up a lot. A kleptomaniac, et cetera. And he was heavily medicated."

"Let me see the book," said Seth.

"What book? Oh, I'm bad," said Barry Knott. "You look like you might eat me." He walked across the room to Seth, carrying the book like a waiter carrying a tray of desserts.

"Open it for me," said Seth. He kept his gun pointed at me.

"Put the gun down and take it. They're not going to do anything. This business is all concluded. If this were Russia, we'd be sharing a bottle of vodka now."

"Open it," said Seth. I gave all my weight to the couch and thought of my mother, asking me to please be strong. But I was sick of strong. Sick of my whole act.

"Now I may not be your boss, but you're not mine either, my friend. So stow your gat and take the book if you would like to look at it." Barry Knott manipulated the front cover of the book to make it seem like it was talking. "Look at me!" he said in a high, childlike voice. "Here I am! Take me! Take me!" Seth grabbed the book with his free gloved hand, ripping the book's jacket in the process.

"And that was an intelligent, well-thought-out move," said Barry Knott.

"And once again," said Seth, "fuck you." Using only the gloved hand, he awkwardly opened the book to the inscription page, then to the Grautzweller pages. He took the sun-

286

glasses off again. He would look for a second, then look back at me. Make sure I hadn't made a move.

"S'aright? S'aright. So let's be going." Barry Knott put a fatherly hand on Seth's shoulder. Seth squirmed away from it.

"She's coming, too," he said. I looked up.

"What?" said Barry Knott. "No. We just made an agreement with her that this concludes it. We have an oral understanding that that's that."

"I don't care about an agreement," said Seth. "I'm taking her."

Charles and Scott looked at me. With their arms crossed over their chests, they looked like a couple of wedding night virgins. Charles slid his eyes quickly at Seth and then back to me. I shook my head no.

"Do you want to make your dad angry? I don't think you want to do that," said Barry Knott.

"My dad's already pissed at me on account of her. He gets over it. He forgets fast. Let's go," he said to me. "Andalay."

I stood my ground. It was all so absurd. A kid's afterdark game where the rules keep changing. Not just this, but all of it. "I'm not going with you," I said. I sat on the arm of the couch and squeezed my knees.

Seth tipped his head at me. "Don't be cute now," he said.

"She gave you the book," said Scott. Seth shushed him. Hissed.

"Whatever you're going to do," I said, "you'll have to do it here. We're going to finish it."

"Nah," said Seth, "not here. You and I need some alone time."

"If I go with you, Seth," I said, "I'm going to kill you. And I actually don't want to." I felt the terrible implosion, the slow collapse. Worse than it had ever been.

"Kill me? I think you're going to fall in love with me. Now let's GO."

"NO!" I said. I stood up. It all felt so plastic and far away. Like I was stumbling drunk at a drive-in movie. I had to force myself to focus.

"Now wait," said Charles. "It really doesn't seem . . ." He faded off.

Seth cocked his gun and raised his arm so that the barrel pointed directly at my heart. "Let's go!" he said.

288 "NO!" I screamed. I couldn't go with him. I knew this was the time to end it. I walked toward him, out from behind the coffee table. Until he was only a couple feet away.

"NOW!" said Seth.

"MAKE ME! YOU NO-TALENT—" I heard the shots. I counted three of them. Bangbang and then bang. I sank to my knees thinking, It's true, you don't feel a thing. I said, "Oh, no," and suddenly I was sad, so sad. Because I was so stupid. Because it was not what I wanted. "Oh, shit," I said. I felt Scott next to me. Saying no no no. I looked down to see the blood. My own blood. But I couldn't find it. Another shot and then another. Still nothing happened. Seth was standing right over us now, firing the gun at my head. And nothing. Oh, I thought, a dream perhaps? So wily. Seth looked at his gun and something crossed his face. An understanding. Barry Knott, who was there, close, reached out to give Seth a fatherly pat. Put an arm around him.

"What's happening?" I said.

Barry Knott grasped Seth's shoulder tightly, as though they were posing for a picture. Seth was looking at the gun and then, "Hey . . ." and Barry Knott stepped to face him and curled his other arm around Seth's head and twisted violently. There was a loud and horrible cracking sound, louder, it seemed, than the gunshots, and then Seth's gun went off again. A reflex. Barry Knott held Seth in a bear hug. Patted his back. Walked him like a reluctant dance partner around me and Scott, over to the couch. Then slowly eased his body down onto it. Seth sat with his eyes open and his head turned as though someone behind him had just called out his name and he was looking to see who. He still held the book. But he was dead. And me? I was alive. That's the way it had gone down.

289

"I wasn't even a hundred percent sure I could do that," said Barry Knott. "It's been a long time."

"What . . ." I said. "What . . ." I bunched up the fabric around my heart. Felt my flesh through the layers.

"Blanks, cookie. A prop gun. Goofy gun. You think that kid could be trusted with the real mick?"

"I might puke," said Scott.

"It's all right," said Barry Knott. "Go use the bathroom. Do whatever you need to." Scott stood up and backed his way to the hall, then turned and ran for the bathroom. I heard him bolt the door.

"I would be dead," I said.

"Bad joke on you," said Barry Knott.

I rolled from my knees onto my back and looked at the ceiling. I made some wordless baby noises. Just a release of sound. Then a low scream. I brought my knees up to my chest and hugged them. Eyed the cottage cheese ceiling. Screamed at it and went limp again. Then I said, "Je*sus!* Jesus!" I said, "I'm lucky." A couple hot tears slid away from my eyes.

From the floor, I watched Barry Knott take the gun from Seth's hand and put it inside his coat. "I never saw it," he said, "but I heard once that rigor mortis can make a dead guy fire a gun. No bullets, but the sound might make us all piss a pant."

My nose itched, from the gun smoke or because I was crying, and I rubbed it on my sleeve. It was such a normal gesture it felt very good and I did it longer than I needed to.

Barry Knott flexed his back. "I need a better chiropractor," he said. "Someone with bigger hands. I'm not a chauvinist, but I don't think a woman can be a good chiropractor."

"What does this mean?" I said.

"Today ain't your day, Jolly Polly," said Barry Knott.

"But . . . don't you work for John Malcome? You killed Seth." I was still all over the floor like some dumped doll. Couldn't move quite yet.

"Yeah, I'm working for Mr. Malcome. This" — he gestured at Seth — "this was gonna happen regardless. It's just the timing is off a bit. Fact, I'm going to need to use the phone. Cancel something. Talk to some people. Is there a place I can talk privately?"

"Down the hall." I pointed. "Bedroom."

"You gonna stand up eventually?" asked Barry Knott.

"I'll stand up," I said.

As Barry Knott passed the bathroom door, he rapped lightly. "How's it going in there?" he asked.

"Just a minute!" Scott yelled.

290

I got to my feet slowly. Charles stood in a corner of the room with his hands touching the walls. Shaking his head. "I never wanted to see another dead guy," he said. "This shit is deep."

I went to the kitchen and took a long hit of whiskey. Shuffled around looking for a clean dishtowel, but I had used them all on Scott's arm and they lay in a bloody heap on the floor. I found one that wasn't so bad and I walked back to the living room and covered Seth's face with it. I moved very slowly and carefully, as though one false step could kill me.

"You think that's better?" asked Charles. He had edged toward Seth.

"You can't see his eyes," I said. The towel fell away. "I guess it doesn't matter." I let the towel stay on his chest like a lobster bib.

"It's a fine line," said Charles. He looked at Seth straight on. "It's a real fine line." And all I kept thinking was how I was still around and I was really very happy about it. "I froze," said Charles. "Man, I froze up."

"Don't worry," I said.

"You don't understand. I believe that we are ultimately judged by our actions. My action was nil. If those bullets had been genuine bullets —"

"No," I said. "It was a fluke you were here. Don't worry. Go back to the fatalist view. It was all mapped out."

He wiped the sweat from his face. "Yeah," he said. "I hear you."

Barry Knott came back into the living room. "We're all right. It's all set."

"What's set?"

"Hmm? Oh, nothing. I was mostly talking aloud." He took off his cap and rubbed his hair. Put his hands on his hips and looked at Seth like he was getting ready to lecture him.

"So this was his father?" I said. "His father wanted him dead?"

"Wait," said Charles, "he's that boy's father?"

"No," I said, "the guy he works for."

"I'm just not even sure I want all this to mull over." Charles sat down in an armchair and picked a magazine off the coffee table and put it on his lap but did not look at it.

"His father wanted him dead?" I asked again.

"Well, I think it would have more accuracy to say that he didn't want him around."

"His own son?"

292

"You know, that kid was an evil kid. A real bad case. And shallow. John just didn't like him. If they hadn't of been related, I don't think they ever would of been friends. He made a lot of trouble for his dad. Going way back. And now that the political thing is going to happen for John . . . well, you can only worry about so many things at once, you know? Kid would have destroyed it for him eventually. He had no morality, that kid. I mean NO morality." Barry Knott reached out and tousled Seth's hair.

Charles said, "Perhaps I should keep my mouth shut on this one, but it strikes me that you may not be the right person to comment on morality."

"Yeah, but I ain't anyone's son," said Barry Knott. "And in addition, I compromise my morality for personal gain and not for kicks."

"I guess he pays you pretty damn well," I said.

"It's not the money, sister. It's not the money."

Charles drove away in the station wagon. He drove to the Valley, parked it, and walked to a pay phone like we had agreed. Called the cops and told his story. The cops never pursued it. That was John Malcome at work. Hell, the guy has dinner with the president twice a year. The cop I shot is probably living in some beach spread now — semitoeless and happy.

After Charles left, Barry Knott pulled his car into the garage and loaded Seth into the trunk. He removed almost all the cash from Seth's wallet — a couple hundred bucks — and offered it to me. I took it. He made a quick tour of the living room to see if he was forgetting anything. Looking under furniture like he was a tourist checking out of a motel room. Then, right before he left, he handed me the London book.

"Here," he said, "John said you could have it."

"What?" I said. "What?"

"Yeah," he said. "Go ahead. He don't want it. When I talked to him before and I told him about the rip on the outside there, on the cover, he said forget it. It was no good." He held the book toward me. Pressed it into my belly. I stood still with my arms at my sides. "If you don't take it," he said, "I'm going to drop it."

"But it's sentimental," I said. "It doesn't matter if the jacket's ripped." Barry Knott let go of the book and it fell to the floor between us. Face down on bent pages.

"I told you," he said.

"This is crazy," I said. "What about sentimental?"

"Naah, forget sentimental," said Barry Knott. "He wanted to give it as a present to someone. But you don't want to give something that's messed up like that. It's unseemly. All right. It's for you now." I asked him why they wouldn't just give it back to the aunt and he said she didn't deserve it — that she didn't deserve air, never mind the book. And she wasn't exactly an aunt. After that, I stopped asking questions because I didn't want to know what was a lie and what was real. It made no difference. It was over. Then Barry Knott told me that I could work for John if I wanted. John liked me very much and Amy had just been hired by Disney to work in movie development. I said thanks but no thanks. He said John told him not to press, just put it out there.

294

"If you change your mind job-wise, I'll see you," he said. "If not . . ." He drove away slowly, as usual.

Three weeks later, I saw a story in *People* magazine. Seth and his friend, the John-O Burger boy, had died when their car went off the road on the way to Lake Arrowhead. They plummeted to their death, the story said. And Seth's father, actor/director John Malcome, was stricken with grief. They quoted him in the piece. "I feel like my whole world has fallen apart," the quote said. "I feel like I'm at sea."

The story on Timmy's death was a break-in at his house. Some stuff was stolen. Nobody heard the shot. Nobody saw a thing. I showed up for the service. It was big. I hung around in back along with the other shady-looking characters. Later, I went to check on his ducks. They were all right. They were at the place next to his, eating bread.

When Barry Knott was gone, I put the book in my backpack —
Cox's backpack — so Scott wouldn't see it. I put Debi's gun
back in her closet. Then I coaxed Scott out of the bathroom. I
spoke to him in a quiet, steady voice. I told him to tell Debi that
we had an accident on the bike. That he was okay except he
had landed on a spike. I was a little more messed up. I'd need
a better story when the bandages came off the question mark.
Or maybe I wouldn't. Scott told me he loved me. That he
would always be there for me. I said he was good, too. The best.
And we held on to each other for a little while. I kissed him on
the cheek and whispered some things into his ear. He nodded
slowly. Then I said I needed to borrow his truck.

He walked down with me to get the truck. He had a gallon of gas that Debi kept in the garage for these sorts of **295**
emergencies. He carried it with his good arm and waved
good-bye with that arm when I left.

I drove the truck to the veterinary clinic and claimed the
black dog. Though I didn't really want it. I took it across the
street to the bookstore and we sat there all night listening to
the radio. It was a pretty good night, and the next morning I
opened up early. The cat was the first one through the door.

I see that John Malcome is getting closer to fulfilling his political dreams. He's running for mayor of Los Angeles with
an exceptional show of support from the governor of California. I saw the governor interviewed on TV once. He
mentioned his passion for old books. "Who's your favorite
author?" the blond interviewer asked. I turned it off before
he answered. I already knew the answer.

I think about the ones who are dead. I have bad spells. But one day I confessed everything I know about myself to my veterinarian friend. He handled it very well and I believe it helped. Since then, Mike has confessed some things to him. Scott, too.

Last year, I went to see a John Malcome film. Not the flapper movie — a different one. The last film he made before focusing all his attention on politics. Barry Knott played the lead cop's best friend. He got good reviews and he was nominated for an Oscar as best supporting actor. But he didn't win.

296

I work on the Grautzweller puzzle almost every night. Trying to find the poem within the page numbers. It gives me something to do. Once, I spilled a glass of bourbon on the book. It didn't matter. It was already in bad shape.